KINGDOM OF CHAINS

TANYA BIRD

Trigger warning: Domestic violence
(not between hero and heroine)

CHAPTER 1

*I*sabel chased the eagle's shadow along the dewy lawn, arms outstretched like a pair of wings. 'You are in a lot of trouble, young lady!' she shouted up at the bird before coming to a stop, breathless and smiling. She raised one arm high in the air. Margery circled her a few times before swooping down and landing gracefully on her.

'It has been two days, and I have been sick to my stomach with worry. It is hardly fair that I am stuck here, alone, whenever you fly off on one of your little adventures.'

The eagle watched her closely as she delivered the lecture.

'And what if Lord Hodge had seen you? If he learns that I have been letting you out of your cage, then we will both be in trou—' Her eyebrows tugged together when she noticed a piece of fabric tied around the eagle's leg. She guided the bird to her shoulder so she could use both hands to retrieve it. Someone had tied it neatly and carefully—except that was impossible. Margery did not stand still long enough for people to tie things to her. Plus, there were only two people on the planet who could handle the golden eagle—and one of them was dead.

Ita. My sweet Ita.

Five years on, and grief still hit Isabel like a runaway wagon every time her friend came to mind.

'Is there something you wish to tell me?' she asked, kissing Margery's beak. 'I swear before God, if I find out you have a secret family outside these walls—'

'*Why* is that thing out of its cage?'

Isabel jumped at the sound of Lord Hodge's voice behind her, and Margery took flight. Oh, how Isabel wished she had wings.

Clearing her throat, she called to the eagle, 'Yes, off you go. Straight back to your cage. I shall be there to lock all windows and doors momentarily.' Forcing a smile, she turned to face the new Earl of Hereford. 'Good afternoon, my lord.'

Hodge glared up at the fleeing bird as he came to a stop in front of her, that shiny chin of his partially blinding her in the process.

'You know that thing is not permitted out of its cage.'

He refused to acknowledge her gender or name. It was always 'that thing'.

'We have the chickens to consider,' he added.

Margery had never even killed a chicken. She was nothing but a help around the place, keeping rats and mice at bay. Isabel suspected the real reason he insisted the eagle remain locked up was because she took time and attention away from him.

2

'Occasionally she needs to spread those large wings of hers and remember how to fly,' Isabel said. Then, noting his growing agitation, she added, 'Well, I best go and lock that cage. I may even add an additional lock, just to be extra sure she is secure.'

Hodge caught her arm when she went to step past him. 'Before you go, I would like to speak to you about the wedding.'

The dreaded wedding. His father was barely cold in the ground, and here he was charging ahead with his plans. She had hoped she had more time. 'Which wedding would that be?'

His face hardened. '*Our* wedding, of course. What other wedding would I be talking about?'

'I did hear rumours that one of the kitchen maids is soon to be wed.'

His brow creased with disapproval. 'It is safe to say that I did not come all the way out here to talk to you about the kitchen maid's impending nuptials.' He released her, running a hand through the coarse sandy hair that reached all the way to his jawline. 'Now, I have spoken to your mother, and we both agreed that the sooner the wedding takes place the better. It is the best way to ensure your family's place here at Hampstead Keep is secure.' He reached out to touch her arm. 'And we have waited so long for this day.'

She forced the muscles in her face to remain still. *He* had been waiting. *She* had been dreading. 'I assumed my family's place here at Hampstead was already secure.'

He gave her what was likely meant as a reassuring

smile that bordered more on patronising. 'Of course it is, my beloved. You will forever be secure at my side.'

There was always a catch—like the 'forever' part. 'I thought we could discuss the wedding after a suitable mourning period.'

He studied her a moment. 'What is there to discuss?'

'The timing, for one.'

He drew her closer until her face was a few inches from his and her heels lifted off the ground. 'Tell me you want this. Tell me you want to marry me, to be my wife until death.'

She could not help but do the math on that. If she lived until she was seventy, that would be fifty years. But since men generally died younger, she took that number down to forty. That seemed doable for the sake of her family. She opened her mouth to answer. 'I...' She willed the words stuck in her throat to move. 'Yes, of course.'

'You hesitated.'

'No, I did not.'

He might have behaved a little crazily at times, but he was no fool. 'Five years I have waited.' His grip on her was bruising now. 'Five years I have loved you and protected you like a brother, as my father wanted.'

A brother waiting for the day he could finally marry his sister. She suppressed the shudder threatening to pass through her. The relationship had been uncomfortable from day one—even before her mother had wed his father.

'You are hurting me,' she said when her fingers began to tingle from the lack of blood reaching them.

He held on to her a few moments longer, eyes moving

between hers, then let go. 'Forgive me. My love for you can be overbearing at times.'

Blood rushed back into her limbs. She stepped back from him—too fast. He hated it when she moved away from him like that. She expected him to grab hold of her again. When he did not, she said as gently as possible, 'I think we should wait a few months—out of respect to your father.'

'A few months?'

She had wanted to say a year. Two, maybe. Or as many as it took for him to find an alternative wife, someone who did not recoil inside every time he came close.

He opened his hands to her. 'I love you. I want the world to know it, to bear witness to it.' When she did not respond, he reached for her. She stepped backwards again, an instinct. His hands went into his hair, gripping and releasing while she stood awkwardly with her eyes averted. After a short silence, he cleared his throat and said firmly, 'I have a trip coming up. I shall be gone a few weeks. When I return, we will marry.'

He waited for her to look at him before continuing. Not wanting to aggravate the situation further, she obliged.

'That is one month from now,' he went on. 'I believe that is an appropriate amount of time for all of us to grieve the former Earl of Hereford. Do you not agree?'

She nodded. At least she hoped it was a nod.

His hands opened and closed a few times, as though he were deciding whether to attempt contact again. 'I promise you that, as my wife, you will want for nothing.

You will be Countess of Hereford in every sense of the word.'

Another nod. 'I know.'

He watched her a long moment, then bowed his head before striding away, chin high despite the gouging to his ego. She felt numb and cold all over as she watched him, picturing a lifetime of swallowing down her own discomfort.

'I don't trust him,' Ita had said of Hodge the day he arrived with Lord Tompkin and troops at Maddock House five years earlier.

Isabel had assumed her friend was jealous of the attention the then nineteen-year-old heir was showing a fifteen-year-old Isabel. But as usual, she had been right.

'Belle' came her brother's voice.

Isabel turned to find Everard jogging towards her. He was tall for fourteen, which meant his long legs reached her in a few easy strides.

'Mother is waiting for you in your bedchamber. She wants to speak with you.' He slung an arm around her and began dragging her off in the direction of the castle.

'Oh. Perfect' was Isabel's reply.

Everard drew back to look at her as they walked. 'Are you all right?'

What answer to give the young man who looked up to Lord Hodge, who lived safely inside the walls of Hampstead Keep, while those they left behind in Carmarthenshire were either dead or living in a camp? The young man who would eventually receive a title of his own if she played her hand right? 'Of course I am all right.'

'You look a bit pale. Do you need to see the physician?'

Isabel stepped out from beneath his arm and looped hers through it. 'Absolutely not. Now, tell me about your morning. What did you do?'

She listened as he spoke about his French lesson and the sparring match with Trahern, which he had apparently won. Trahern was one of Lord Hodge's longest serving guards and the man most often called upon to follow her about the castle when all she wanted was five minutes alone. That said, he was the least invasive of the guards and gave her as much space as he could while keeping her within sight. He was also the kind of man who would let Everard win a sparring match occasionally.

When they reached the door of her bedchamber, Isabel paused, keeping hold of her brother's arm as she worked up the energy for the conversation ahead.

Everard looked between her and the door. 'What is the matter? Are you in trouble or something? Did you let Margery out of her cage again?'

She looked at him. 'Yes. Yes I did. And I am certain a suitable lecture awaits me inside.'

He tutted. 'Serves you right. You know how His Lordship feels about Margery flying around the castle grounds.'

'Yes.' She reached up and smoothed the fine hairs back from his face, like she had done his whole life.

He immediately knocked her hand away, cheeks turning red. 'Stop. I am not a child anymore.'

That was so true and so heartbreaking. 'I know.' She gave him a weak smile, then drew a long breath. 'Wish me luck.'

He began backing away. 'Good luck.'

She crinkled her nose at him as she pushed the door open. Inside, the room was cold and the fireplace bare—just the way she liked it. The shaking of wings drew her attention to the large cage in the corner where Margery was now locked inside.

'There you are,' her mother said, rising from her chair. 'Did His Lordship find you?'

Isabel wandered over to the cage. 'He did.'

'And?'

'And we spoke.'

Lady Gwenore's face was pure impatience. 'About the wedding?'

The air left Isabel's lungs on a sigh. 'Yes, about the wedding. He has a trip planned. Perhaps we will marry after that.'

Gwenore stepped closer. 'What do you mean, *perhaps?*'

Less than a minute into the conversation and Isabel was already exhausted. 'There is no rush.'

'Is that what he said?'

'No.' She turned to face her mother. 'Are you sure this match is a good idea?'

Gwenore's face fell a little.

'I really do not care for him in that way,' Isabel added.

'The love comes *later*. Every woman knows that.'

'I have known the man for five years, and nothing has changed in that time.'

'It will be different when you are wed, when you have the opportunity to be... close.'

That image had Isabel looking away. She had no interest in being intimate with him—or any other man, for that matter.

Gwenore closed the distance between them, taking her daughter's left hand and holding it up between them. 'Look at the scars on your hand.'

Isabel dropped her gaze to the unsightly skin.

'It was Lord Hodge who dragged you from that burning house. The man has worshipped the ground you walk upon since you were fifteen years old.'

Isabel withdrew the unsightly hand and tucked it behind her back. 'It might be a different story if the burns had been on my face.'

Her mother made an exasperated noise. The problem was she assumed Hodge was like his father, Lord Tompkin. A *good* man, another *saviour* of the family. But the new Earl of Hereford was more of an unsettling kind of hero.

'Is all well between the two of you?' Gwenore asked, holding her breath as she braced for Isabel's reply.

What good would come of the truth? The family's circumstances were what they were. She forced a smile. 'All is well.'

Gwenore exhaled, then cupped her daughter's face. 'I know he is a very different sort of man, but we have built a life here at Hampstead. Your brother has such a bright future ahead of him. Inside these walls, you are the future Countess of Hereford. Outside these walls, you are nothing. We *have* nothing.'

'We could always go live with our uncle.'

Gwenore's hand fell away. 'And marry you off to some farmer while your brother toils in fields owned by families better off than us?'

Isabel rolled her eyes. 'Or we could return to Maddock House. The region is improving every day.'

'Not in the way your naive mind thinks.'

Isabel groaned audibly. 'Do you not ever miss home sometimes?'

Gwenore pinched the bridge of her nose. '*This* is our home. The place you are mourning no longer exists.' She looked up, exasperated. 'It is not the home you miss. It is Ita.'

Her name aloud was too much. 'It is both.' The confession came out all quiet.

Gwenore looked around the room, as though searching for an appropriate response, then said, 'Make sure Margery remains in her cage. You know how His Lordship feels about her.' She reached out and touched Isabel's arms briefly. 'I shall leave you to get ready for dinner.'

When she went to step past, Isabel said, 'Did you love him in the end? Lord Tompkin, I mean.'

Gwenore appeared taken aback by the question, then thought for a moment. 'Yes. Yes, in the end, I did. He was always kind to me and my children. What more could a widow from the wastelands hope for?'

The lord had been smitten with her mother from day one, while Gwenore had been so lost in her grief that she barely noticed. It made Isabel happy to hear that their love had been reciprocal by the end. 'I shall see you at dinner.'

Gwenore nodded once and made her way to the door.

Isabel's eyes met Margery's as it clicked shut. Silence filled the room. 'There is no escape for me,' Isabel whispered. She reached for the latch on the cage and opened it. 'But there is for you.' Stepping up to the window, she flung open the shutters.

The bird did not move from her perch.

Isabel returned to the cage and offered the eagle her arm. She climbed on. Kissing Margery's head multiple times, Isabel whispered, 'Best not to come back this time. Go be free for both of us.' Walking over to the open window, she thrust her arm through it, giving Margery no choice but to take flight.

She snapped the shutters closed, and pressed her forehead to the cool wood, swallowing repeatedly until the tears subsided.

CHAPTER 2

*R*yder Blackmane spat blood on the grass and wiped his mouth with the back of his hand. Looking down at Tatum, who was curled in a ball on the ground half laughing and half coughing, he said, 'That's the second time you've busted my lip this week.'

'You told me you wanted a challenge,' he croaked before coughing up a lung.

Blackmane kicked Tatum's sword out of reach, then offered his hand. 'That was supposed to be a dig at you, not an invitation to break my teeth.' He pulled the defender to his feet.

Tatum doubled over and held on to his knees, breathing deeply in and out. 'You're lucky my hours are done for the day or I'd make you pay for that unnecessarily aggressive disarming at the end there.'

Alveye wandered over, brushing grass from his freshly trimmed hair. 'Why do you two always finish training with bloody teeth and bruises the size of dinner plates?'

Blackmane frowned in his direction. 'Because we train properly. The better question is why don't *you* ever bleed?'

'He does when I train with him,' Tatum said, tugging his shirt up and wiping his face with it. 'Where's Hadewaye?'

Alveye gestured towards the armoury. 'He lost, so he packs everything up.'

Tatum held up a hand, stopping Blackmane before he had a chance to speak. 'Save your breath. It's not going to happen.'

The three defenders collected the weapons that were strewn about the place, then made their way off the training field, leaving behind the noise of clashing steel and fresh recruits emptying their stomachs. They stopped beneath the Chadorian flags that marked the boundary, their sweat-soaked bodies cooled by the icy wind blowing in from the sea.

'Ah. Here we go,' Tatum said, his voice low. 'Is it weird that I've been a defender for five years and I still get nervous when I see the warden approaching?'

The question prompted Blackmane and Alveye to look over their shoulders. There was Shapur Wright marching towards them, framed by the royal castle.

'Where's Hadewaye?' Shapur asked as he came to a stop before the three men.

Alveye straightened. 'Armoury, sir.'

They were either about to be reprimanded or given orders. Blackmane waited to see which one it was.

'I am sending the four of you to Carmarthenshire,' Shapur announced.

Orders were always preferable. So they were going to Carmarthenshire—again.

Tatum and Alveye exchanged a look of surprise.

Before the famine, Carmarthenshire had been a county in Wales. During the famine, the name became a blanket phrase used for all the land between England's border and the newly formed kingdom of Chadora. And when all the villages had been deserted, the forests stripped of food, and the region abandoned by their king, it became known simply as 'the wastelands'.

The return of the marcher lords along the border had been the first sign of renewed interest in the region. The dispatching of units was the second. The defenders had been keeping an eye on the situation for some time, watching from the safety of their walls as entire rebel groups were removed or extinguished.

'You will go to Hampstead Keep and meet with the new Earl of Hereford,' Shapur continued. 'Lord Hodge has offered to take you on a tour of the region and show you the advancements they have made. It seems progress has stalled. There are two groups proving to be problematic— St Clare and Emlyn.'

'Oh. The groups have names now,' Tatum said, pretending to be impressed.

Shapur gave him a disapproving look. 'General terms like 'wastelander' are not helpful in these types of situations. Better to identify what part of the region they are from in order to truly know what we are up against.'

Alveye nodded. 'Makes sense. Every county will have their own unique history.'

'And trauma response,' Tatum muttered.

Blackmane shifted his weight. 'What kind of problems are they having with these groups?'

Shapur crossed his arms. 'Lord Hodge claims they frequently attack the camps in the region. I suspect he is hoping for some assistance with this.'

Blackmane narrowed his brows. 'Why would these groups attack the camps? Food shortages are no longer an issue, and they can hunt and gather in the regions they still control.'

Shapur nodded. 'King Becket's thoughts exactly. That is why he is sending a small unit of defenders to see what is going on. He wants to fully understand what is happening before getting involved.'

'Exactly how small a unit, sir?' Alveye asked.

Shapur gestured between them. 'You are looking at it.'

Blackmane had been afraid of that.

'Plus Hadewaye,' Shapur added. He looked at Tatum. 'I am putting you in charge. Make sure everyone gets home safely.'

Tatum grew a little taller at that piece of news. 'You're making me commander?'

'For the purpose of this assignment,' the warden clarified. 'Someone has to take the lead. You all spent time in the region at the end of your training, and you appear to work well as a team—most of the time.' He paused. 'I need information and Lord Hodge alive at the end of that tour. It will not look good to our English friends if he dies in your company. Understand?'

'Yes, sir,' the defenders replied in unison.

'You leave at first light.' Shapur looked between them,

ensuring they understood, before turning and marching away.

The men watched him until he was well out of earshot. Then Tatum turned to face the others, looking very pleased with himself.

'You may address me as "Commander" from now on,' he announced.

Alveye's eyebrows shot up. 'With a straight face?'

Blackmane smirked at the ground.

Tatum flicked Alveye's ear. 'Yes, with a straight face.'

'Not to ruin your big moment,' Alveye said, rubbing his ear, 'but I really thought he would have put Blackmane in charge.'

Tatum laughed once. 'That's not ruining my moment. That's taking a giant shit on it.'

Hadewaye jogged up to the group, stopping next to Alveye. 'Was that the warden?' Then, reading everyone's expressions, he asked, 'What did I miss?'

'What did I miss, *Commander*,' Tatum said.

Hadewaye frowned at him. 'What?'

'We're going to the wastelands, and the warden put Tatum in charge,' Alveye explained.

Hadewaye appeared genuinely surprised. 'Really? Not Blackmane?'

Tatum threw his hands up. 'The absolute lack of respect from the lot of you.'

'I've no interest in commanding anyone,' Blackmane said. 'The warden made the right choice.'

Tatum waved a finger in his direction. 'Don't act like you don't care, like we barely matter to you. I know for a fact that you would take an arrow through the skull for any one of us.'

'Don't read too much into that,' Blackmane replied. 'It was beaten into us during training.'

Hadewaye tucked his hands under his arms, still looking confused. 'Why are we going to the wastelands?'

'To find a woman willing to sleep with Alveye,' Tatum replied.

Alveye gave him a tired look. 'Is that your attempt at winning my respect?'

'Is that your attempt at winning my respect, *Commander*?' Tatum corrected.

Blackmane clapped Tatum on the shoulder. 'I need a wash. I'll leave you to fill Hadewaye in on the details of our vague assignment and the size of the unit you'll be leading.'

Hadewaye perked up at that. 'How many men?'

Tatum cleared his throat. 'It's on the smaller side.' He looked over at Blackmane, who was now backing away from the group. 'Don't forget we're leaving at first light.'

The defender saluted him. 'Yes, *Commander*.'

*I*sabel woke during the night to tapping on the window shutters. Flinging back the blankets, she leapt off the bed and ran across the icy stone floor to the window, trying to stay on the balls of her feet. She peered through a crack and found Margery looking back at her.

'What are you doing here at this time of the night?' she whispered as she opened the window. 'You think simply because it is dark it is safe? All it takes is one guard mentioning that he saw you flying free and His Lordship will shoot you from the sky himself.' But as she was delivering her speech, she was also guiding the eagle onto her arm. 'Fine, you can stay, but you need to be gone before the sun rises.' She made a face as she added, 'His Lordship wants to take a walk in the morning.'

Isabel made her way back to the warm bed and climbed in. As she was lying down, she noticed something wound around Margery's leg. She slid the eagle across the linen until the bird was directly beneath the moonlight coming in through the open window. Isabel's breath caught when she saw it was a daisy chain, just like the ones she and Ita used to make when they were children.

'Where did you get this?' Isabel asked as she attempted to unwind it. Losing patience, she broke it apart and held it up to the light to study the handiwork. It was painfully, and impossibly, familiar. She held the ends together to see if it was the right size for a crown.

It was perfect.

'If she was alive, I would know long before now.' She laid the daisy chain on the table next to the bed. 'If she had made it out of the house, she would have run straight to me. Am I wrong?'

Margery blinked sleepily.

Isabel had screamed Ita's name over and over, pulling against Lord Hodge's iron grip to return inside the burning house for her friend.

'Stop,' her mother had cried.

'Do not go,' Everard had pleaded as he clung to her waist.

'It is too late,' Hodge had said moments before the roof collapsed, sending flames twenty feet into the air.

She could almost feel the heat from them. Her toes curled beneath the blankets at the memory of walking barefoot across a scalding floor. It had taken a month for the burns on the soles of her feet to heal.

She ran a finger over the rough skin on her left hand, a permanent reminder that she had tried to get into that room before Hodge had dragged her away through the thick smoke.

'It was locked,' Isabel whispered, stroking the eagle's back. 'That door was never locked.'

Margery turned her head, blinking at her.

'I suppose you are sick of hearing about it,' she said as she tucked her arms beneath the blankets to warm them. The eagle took that as her cue to sleep. The pair had slept together every night since Isabel's father had rescued the nestling—until they came to Hampstead Keep.

'Sweet girl,' she said when soft feathers brushed her forehead. 'I wish I could come with you.'

'Isabel!'

Isabel startled awake at the sound of Hodge's voice, then shot upright, looking around for Margery. The eagle was nowhere to be seen.

A fist pounded on the door. 'Are you in there?'

'One moment!' The sun was blaring through the open window, confirming that she had overslept. Pulling the sheet from the bed, she threw it over the cage to hide the fact that it was empty. She then yanked the first dress she reached from its hanger and wrestled it on.

'Are you all right?' Hodge called through the closed door.

She swished some vinegar and mint in her mouth and spat it into the basin. 'Just putting on my shoes!' After stepping into some boots, a few frantic moments of hair brushing ensued before she ran to open the door.

'Good morning, my lord,' she said breezily. Her chest

was rising and falling harder than it ought to. 'You are up bright and early.'

He frowned as he offered her his arm. 'I am up at the same time every day.' His gaze drifted past her. 'Why is the cage covered?'

She grabbed her cloak from the hook and swung it around her shoulders while pulling the door shut behind her. 'Margery is still sleeping.'

'Sign of a bird that is too well fed. If she were out in the wild, she would be up hunting at first light.'

It was as though he had forgotten that he was the reason she was locked up.

Isabel took his arm and led him away from the door. 'Did I hear that there are Chadorian defenders arriving this afternoon?' That was her attempt at changing the subject.

Hodge placed his hand over hers, then, feeling her scars, withdrew it again. 'Commander Tatum and his unit. Defenders are notorious for their tracking skills. Imagine the progress we could make with an army of men like that. They would weed out the ruffians in no time.'

It was a sore point for Hodge that two main groups remained at large.

'Is that why they are coming?' she asked.

'I suspect King Becket wants to get a handle on the situation first.' They headed down the steps at the end of the corridor that led outside. 'But do not worry. He will be most impressed with the progress we have made.'

They reached the gravel pathway that circled around the castle.

'Is it necessary to find these groups?' she asked. 'Are they causing problems?'

'Absolutely necessary.'

She drew her cloak tighter around her as the cold hit. 'Why? Are they stealing from the camps? Terrorising villages, perhaps?'

One corner of his mouth lifted. 'My beloved, there are no "villages" in the wastelands. There are only those living safely in the camps, contributing to our efforts, and those who evade us.'

She looked up at him. 'If that is true, then surely you can understand the reason for their evasion. You know, I think you will find that if you simply let them be, most would eventually return to their previous village or settle somewhere new.'

'The people of Carmarthenshire have proven them-selves dangerous, untrustworthy, and incapable of making good decisions.'

That stung. 'Perhaps you forget that I grew up in Llanelieu, in the heart of the region.'

'I forget nothing. You are lucky we got you out before King Edward withdrew his troops. That is when things got truly bad. Your family was one of the lucky few. If it were not for our generosity, you would all be either dead or living in a camp by now.'

She stared straight ahead, resisting the urge to with-draw her arm. Doing that would only start something, and if she played her cards right, their time together would soon be over. 'We are eternally grateful—as we have expressed many times.'

'God had big plans for us, my beloved.'

She rolled her eyes—inwardly, of course. 'So you will travel to the camps with the defenders? Show them around?'

'The eastern camp only. The western camp is yet to open. They have been experiencing a few difficulties.'

'What kind of difficulties?'

The muscles in Hodge's face twitched. 'Every time it is close to completion, rebels come along and burn it to the ground.'

That sent a strange spark of hope through Isabel that perhaps the spirit of Carmarthenshire was still alive. 'The Emlyn group?'

'That would be my guess.'

She let that piece of information settle. 'It sounds like the people have spoken, and they are not in support of this new arrangement.'

Hodge's mouth flattened into a thin line. 'Fools. They are only delaying peace and civility with their criminal acts.'

Isabel did not think camps were the answer but kept her mouth closed. To King Edward's credit, he had tried other methods first, sent armies in to restore order and bring much-needed supplies to families. But order could not be restored to a starving and desperate population, and the supplies brought in rarely made it to the intended families. The wagons fell into the hands of rebel groups known as wastelanders. Though Hodge preferred the term 'ruffians'. Eventually, the king had focused his efforts elsewhere.

The daisy chain popped into Isabel's mind. Moving

closer to Hodge, she leaned her head on his shoulder. 'I was thinking. May I come with you?'

'Come with me where?'

'To Carmarthenshire.'

Hodge drew back and gave her a confused look. 'Whatever for?'

'It was my home for fifteen years. I would quite like to see what has become of it.'

'You already know. It is a disaster, and I am working very hard to fix it.' His face creased with disapproval. 'Besides, you may have been born in the wastelands, but it is not your home. Your home is here at Hampstead Keep —with me.'

She fought to keep her expression neutral. 'That is very true. My home is wherever you are.'

He was visibly pleased by that response.

'I would be quite safe at your side,' she continued. 'Between you, your experienced guards, and the defenders travelling with us, I would be untouchable.'

'You want to travel with a bunch of men? Sleep in a tent?'

She had slept with Everard and Ita under the stars many times, wrapped in blankets next to a roaring fire— back when she had appreciated the heat of one instead of losing her ability to breathe around it.

'You shall remain safely within the walls of Hampstead Keep,' Hodge said. 'I shall be back at your side before you know it.'

He stopped walking and turned to her. One look at his face made her stomach fall.

Oh God. He is going to kiss me.

She braced, closing her eyes as he leaned in. The sensation was torturous enough without the visual. Cold, thin lips pressed against hers in a manner that he probably considered passionate.

'I cannot wait to have you in my bed.' He whispered the words against her mouth.

She swallowed down the nausea rising up her throat. 'I suppose I should let you get ready for your guests.' She was very careful to keep her tone cheerful.

He took her hand. 'I thank God every day that I got you out of that house.' He kissed her wrist, then offered her a smile. 'I shall let Trahern know that you are up and about.'

Not Trahern.

She watched the earl walk away, then pressed her eyes closed as she waited for her breathing to return to normal. Only then did she dare a glance up at the sky. Not a bird in sight. It was as empty as the feeling in her chest.

Tugging up the hood of her cloak, she headed for the wall.

CHAPTER 4

*T*he approach of horses had Tatum signalling to the others to take cover. The four defenders dispersed into the trees, making good use of the wide trunks and thick brush. Blackmane watched six English soldiers on horseback pass by, two men in irons trailing behind them. They were bloody-faced and looked ready to fall down.

'Keep them moving,' shouted the soldier at the front of the group. 'We don't have a lot of light left.'

The guards keeping hold of them gave the chains a sharp pull, and the already-struggling prisoners stumbled forwards.

Blackmane exchanged a look with Hadewaye, who was crouched nearby, a silent form of communication crafted over the years they had served together.

The defenders waited until the soldiers were out of sight and could no longer be heard before cautiously emerging from their hiding places.

'Why are we hiding from the English?' Alveye asked, brushing debris off his cloak. 'They invited us here.'

Tatum stared after the soldiers. 'I suppose you can differentiate between army horses and wastelander horses, can you?'

'Fair point.'

'I'm confused,' Hadewaye said.

'That's not unusual,' Alveye rebutted.

Hadewaye ignored him. 'These prisoners in irons who we keep passing, are they being brought in for criminal acts, or are they simply criminals by default?'

'Likely both,' Tatum replied, nudging his horse forwards. 'Let's keep moving. I suggest we go around our English friends if we still plan on reaching Hampstead Keep before dark.'

Hadewaye looked around before following him. 'This place still has the same feeling it did when we were last here.'

'You mean that feeling like you might die at any moment?' Alveye asked, riding up next to him.

'I mean empty—and sad.'

Tatum led the group off the road. 'Should we have Blackmane tell you a story to cheer you up?'

Blackmane had moved to the back of the group to keep watch since they were forced to ride single file. 'I'm busy making sure we don't die.'

'I thought we would pass *some* villages,' Hadewaye went on. 'Where are all the regular, non-violent, "just trying to get by with their one goat and a handful of chickens" people?'

'Probably killed for their goat and chickens,' Tatum said over his shoulder.

Alveye looked around. 'When we were last here, at the end of the famine, I'd have agreed with you. But there's plenty of game, nuts, and berries in the forests now. Wastelanders can hunt and gather until their heart's content. There's no need to steal from families.'

Hadewaye threw his hands up. 'What families? I haven't seen one child since we departed Chadora two days ago. Does no one else find that unsettling?'

Blackmane had to agree. A land stripped of its children was disconcerting.

'Save your questions for someone with answers,' Tatum said, moving into a trot.

The group fell silent.

It was nearing dusk when Hampstead Keep finally appeared before them. It was a simply designed, sturdy castle, secure with its high walls and generous moat. A handful of guards watched their approach from up high.

'Everyone happy to proceed?' Tatum asked.

They were riding side by side now. All it would take was one of them to say no or signal that something felt off, and they would abort.

'So far,' Alveye sang, watching their surroundings on the ground.

'Wall,' Hadewaye said. 'Western turret.'

Blackmane's gaze shifted to the location specified, eyes narrowing on a woman standing on one of the embrasures. 'What in Belenus's name...?'

'Do you think she means to jump?' Hadewaye asked, concern lacing his voice.

Her eyes were skyward, arms outstretched like a bird, hair blowing forwards over her face, and dress billowing in the wind. She looked like she was about to take flight. It was a miracle she had not fallen to her death already. Then her arms fell to her sides suddenly, and she looked down at the ground—straight at him.

'Problem?' Tatum asked.

Blackmane's eyes went to the commander, who was now many paces in front of him. That was when he realised that his horse had stopped—or he had stopped it. He nudged the mare forwards as the gate lowered before them, focusing his attention ahead.

They crossed the drawbridge and entered the outer bailey, looking around at the small houses and healthy livestock grazing nearby. The gate to the inner bailey sat open, and standing in the middle of the path up ahead was a tall and proud-looking nobleman—presumably the new Earl of Hereford.

As they passed beneath the inner wall, Blackmane took mental notes of the arrow loops on either side of them, the number of guards in the vicinity, and the weapons they carried.

'Welcome,' the man called to them. 'I suppose I should not be surprised that you arrived here safely.'

Blackmane glanced sideways at Tatum to gauge his thoughts on the new earl. The set of his mouth confirmed their first impressions aligned.

Tatum stopped his horse and dismounted. 'Lord Hodge, I presume.' He handed the reins to the eager groom, then made his way over to their host.

'You must be Commander Tatum,' Hodge said, sizing

him up. 'I welcome you and your men to Hampstead Keep.'

Tatum bowed his head. 'Thank you.'

A young boy jogged up to them, glancing nervously in the direction of the defenders as he caught his breath. 'Apologies, my lord, but I have looked everywhere and cannot find her.'

Hodge gave a curt nod. 'Keep looking. She cannot have gone far.' Turning back to Tatum, he said, 'I was hoping Lady Isabel would be here to welcome you also. She can be a difficult young lady to track down at times.' He clapped his hands together. 'However, you can meet the future Countess of Hereford at dinner this evening.'

Blackmane resisted the urge to look over his shoulder. It was unlikely that the future countess would be suspended atop a wall, but possible.

'There will be four of us at dinner,' Tatum said. 'If you don't mind.'

The earl looked past him to the three defenders who were now handing their horses over to the groom—sans weapons. 'Very well. I shall have someone show you to your sleeping quarters.' Turning on his heel, he strode off with his luxurious green cloak blowing in the breeze.

The men followed him to the castle, where a servant greeted them and then took them to their sleeping quarters on the ground level. They washed and rested until the same servant returned to escort them to the hall for dinner.

It was an intimate affair with only one table set for the occasion. Hodge was seated at the head of it.

'Ah, there they are,' he called out when they entered.

'Our allies from the west.' He rose from his seat, and the other guests did the same.

The woman to the left of the earl looked suspiciously like the one from the wall, though her rich honey hair had been tamed into a low bun, and her lips were painted a soft red. But the second their eyes met, he knew it was her.

Lord Hodge reached for her hand, gesturing to her with the other as though presenting a prized rooster. 'Commander Tatum, allow me to introduce you to the future Countess of Hereford, Lady Isabel.'

Dimples appeared on both her cheeks. She had the kind of smile that men paid attention to—bright and warm.

'Welcome to Hampstead Keep, Commander,' she said. 'Your arrival has caused much excitement around the castle.'

And the voice definitely matched the smile.

'May I introduce my comrades, Blackmane, Alveye, and Hadewaye,' Tatum said.

The three defenders bowed their heads.

Lord Hodge gestured to the people on the other side of Isabel. 'This is my father's widow, Lady Gwenore, and her son, Everard.'

Lady Gwenore was like an older version of her daughter, bright-eyed with a youthful face. She nodded in their direction. 'Defenders.'

Everard was grinning ear to ear as he stared at the men standing opposite him. 'Is it true that defenders are thrown over a cliff during their training to see who survives the turbulent seas below?'

Blackmane was always amused by some of the myths that circulated outside Chadora's walls.

'First they cut you,' Alveye said, 'to attract sharks.'

Isabel suppressed a smile and looked down at her feet.

'And I heard a training session ends when a defender empties his stomach and not a minute before,' the boy went on.

'Everard,' Gwenore said, tapping her son's arm. 'That is not appropriate dinner conversation.'

Hadewaye leaned forwards and said with a wink, 'That one's mostly true.'

Hodge gestured for everyone to take their seats. Tatum sat closest to the earl, then Blackmane, Alveye, and Hadewaye.

The food arrived on silver trays. Meat and poultry, roasted vegetables, hard-boiled eggs, cheese, and crusty bread. Everyone filled their plates while polite conversation carried back and forth across the table.

As Isabel was serving herself, Blackmane noticed that her left hand was heavily scarred. Burned, perhaps. She happened to glance in his direction at the same time he was looking. She held his gaze a moment before averting her eyes.

'Dig in,' Hodge said.

Everyone began to eat, though Blackmane noticed Isabel spent more time pushing food back and forth than actually eating it. Hodge noticed too.

'Eat up, my beloved,' the earl said, pushing her plate towards her like one did a child. 'The cook informed me that you skipped lunch earlier.'

Gwenore looked up at that. 'Where were you this

afternoon? The servants tore the castle up looking for you.'

Blackmane waited to see what response she would come up with.

'I was reading in the garden,' she said, eyes on her plate.

Everard swallowed his food. 'Impossible. I checked the garden several times.'

'I moved indoors due to the wind.'

'You should have been indoors to begin with,' Hodge said.

Isabel placed her fork down and looked up.

'What sort of books do you read, my lady?' Hadewaye asked. He was an expert at dissipating tension.

Hodge sawed through a piece of chicken. 'I recently gave her the Psalms.'

'Which I plan on reading very soon,' Isabel said.

Gwenore tutted. 'I have heard that before.'

Isabel ignored her. 'Have you read *Secreta Secretorum*, defender?'

Hadewaye shook his head. 'Afraid not. Blackmane likely has. He's the reader of the group.'

So far Blackmane had managed to stay out of the conversation entirely—which was his preference.

'You like to read, defender?' she asked him directly.

He reluctantly met her gaze, noticing the blue flecks in her eyes amid swirls of grey. 'I may have flicked through the French translation a long time ago.'

She appeared impressed by that. 'Jofroi's translation has been highly praised.'

Hodge snorted. 'Pagan philosophy.'

Isabel looked down again.

Blackmane leaned back in his chair. 'I thought someone in your position would find the parts about the ethical dilemmas facing rulers useful.'

Tatum cleared his throat, which translated to 'Shut up.'

'My ethics are guided only by God,' Hodge replied.

It was official. Blackmane did not like him.

'Don't read too much into anything that comes out of Blackmane's mouth, my lord,' Alveye said. 'He's this way with everyone.'

Tatum nodded in agreement. 'The best fighters usually come with some quirks.'

Isabel pushed her plate away and looked at Blackmane. 'Best? That is high praise from your commander. Do you agree with that assessment?'

He just wanted to finish his food and leave. 'Every defender has their strengths.'

'But no weaknesses,' Everard said. 'Those are trained out of them.'

Isabel's eyes creased at the corners.

'Blackmane frequently loses sparring matches, but he has exceptional instincts,' Tatum said, clapping the defender on the back—hard.

Lord Hodge regarded him across the table. 'Is that right? Well, I look forward to witnessing these exceptional instincts first-hand in the coming days.'

Blackmane did not reply.

A lute player wandered in, taking a seat on the stool at the far end of the room.

'Perhaps you will do me the honour of a dance after

we finish eating,' Hodge said to Isabel when the music started.

Blackmane could have sworn she rolled her eyes.

'Normally I would love to. However, I am afraid I am rather tired this evening.'

'Do defenders dance?' Lady Gwenore asked no one in particular.

Hadewaye paused eating to reply. 'On the rare occasion we get the opportunity—but not Blackmane.'

And once again, he was being dragged back into the conversation.

That seemed to pique Isabel's curiosity. 'Why do you not dance, defender?'

'We think he's allergic to fun,' Alveye said.

Blackmane laid down his knife and fork. 'Like I said, we all have our strengths. Dancing isn't one of mine.' He did not hate dancing so much as the memories of home that surfaced every time he witnessed other people partaking. Memories of his parents laughing and spinning in circles to familiar tunes. Memories of his sister dancing with the man she was supposed to marry in the summer. Memories of their pox-covered corpses mere weeks after celebrating the news.

Smallpox was not always a death sentence, but it was in Ireland back when the whole country had been emaciated. They had been halfway to dead before the disease hit their shores.

'Take Tolly and go,' his mother had pleaded, eyes red and lips pale. 'While you still can.' Her final words before her chest sank and the light left her eyes.

He had not had it in him to tell her on her deathbed

that her youngest son had boarded a ship to Carmarthen-shire two weeks earlier—a ship that had been set alight before any passenger could disembark due to an outbreak on board.

'Take care of your brother.' His father's last words.

His sister had passed soon after, and then the man she would never get to marry.

Alveye waved a hand in front of Blackmane's face. 'I think we've lost him.'

Blinking away the dark memories, the defender pushed Alveye's hand out of his face and slid his plate away before rising. 'Thanks for the meal. It's time for me to retire.'

'Will you not sample some of the wine, defender?' Hodge said. 'It came from Italy by ship.'

'I don't drink on duty.'

Hodge's eyebrows lifted. 'But you are not on duty, defender. You are a guest in my home.'

A defender was never off duty outside of Chadora's walls. 'Maybe another time. Excuse me.' He made a point of not looking at Isabel as he turned to leave, but he felt her eyes on him all the way to the door.

CHAPTER 5

'Could you have run away from dinner any faster?' Tatum said upon entering their sleeping quarters.

Blackmane reached for his boots and tugged them on. 'I don't trust him.'

'Who? And where are you going?'

'Lord Hodge. Perimeter check.'

Tatum watched him get to his feet. 'I know he's a little arrogant, but show me a wealthy man who isn't.'

'It's not that.'

Tatum leaned against the doorframe, blocking his exit. 'You don't need to do perimeter checks in someone else's home.'

'But I can *choose* to.'

Tatum did not move. 'I'll let you pass if you answer one question.'

He let out a tired breath. 'What question's that?'

'Is it possible that you resent Lord Hodge a little more

than your average lord because he's engaged to Lady Isabel?'

He was not expecting that one. 'What in Belenus's name are you talking about?'

'You could barely look at her during dinner.'

'I barely look at anyone.'

'Then you bit Hodge's head off when he insulted her choice of reading.' A smile spread across his face. 'I think you've taken a shine to the young lady.'

'A *shine*? Are you drunk?'

He poked Blackmane's chest with his finger. 'That was her atop the wall when we arrived, wasn't it?'

Blackmane released a tired sigh. 'So?'

'So she made you *pause*, and you never pause for anyone.'

Blackmane shoved him aside. 'I thought she was about to jump.'

Tatum caught hold of the frame to stop from falling. 'Don't worry. Your secret's safe with me.'

Alveye and Hadewaye appeared, blocking the only exit.

'What secret?' Hadewaye asked.

Tatum swung theatrically around the edge of the doorframe. 'Blackmane has taken a fancy to Lady Isabel.'

'Fairly sure that's *not* how keeping secrets works,' Alveye pointed out.

'Get your drunk arse into bed,' Blackmane said as he pushed between the two defenders still in his way.

'Where are you going?' Hadewaye called to his back.

'Perimeter check.'

'What?' Alveye's voice followed him out into the open corridor. 'I'm confident they have that covered.'

Blackmane kept walking without responding.

The air was crisp and sharp outside, and every inhale woke him up a little more. He headed down the path that led to the outer wall, then climbed the icy steps to the top. Two men on patrol stopped talking when they spotted him. They looked down at his uniform, then watched him with a wary expression as he passed them. He did not care if his presence made anyone uncomfortable, because going to sleep without knowing the castle was secure made *him* uncomfortable. He was not at Hampstead Keep in search of new friends.

His boots landed quietly as he took in his surroundings, listening for anything unusual. He passed four more guards on the north wall, nodding in place of a greeting, then entered the turret at the end. They appeared to have a decent number of weapons, which was something.

As he stepped onto the west wall, he felt someone's presence. Stopping, he looked around, finding only shadows. But he was definitely not alone. His eyes narrowed on the darkest corner. 'I suggest you show yourself *before* I draw my sword.'

Nothing.

He drew his weapon. A beat later, a cloaked figure stepped into the flickering light cast by a nearby torch.

'How did you know I was there?' came Lady Isabel's voice. She pulled down the hood of her cloak and waited for his response.

'It's a defender thing.' He sheathed his sword. 'What

are you doing out here on the wall at this time of the night?' He looked past her. 'Are you alone?'

'Now I am.' She looked over her shoulder. 'Margery had to go.'

It was an odd time and place to meet a friend. 'You should have left with her.'

That made her smile. 'Oh, I wanted to.' She closed the distance between them. 'But I would need wings for that.'

'I'm going to assume from your response that Margery is either an angel or a bird.'

'She is both.' Her face turned serious. 'But please do not mention the meeting to His Lordship. She is not supposed to leave her cage, and he is rather strict with that rule.'

He blinked. 'I will try my hardest to refrain from discussing your *pet bird* with the lord of the house.'

She angled her head. 'I appreciate that, defender.'

'And might I suggest you return to the castle now.'

'You know, you are a little high-handed given that this is not your home.' She regarded him a moment. 'What are you even doing up here?'

He looked around the wall walk. 'Perimeter check.'

Her eyes shone with amusement. 'Right. Well, do not let the guards overhear you. They might take that as criticism of their work.'

Before he could respond, a flash of light caught his attention behind her. He stepped up to the embrasure and peered down at the ground below. There were several fires burning approximately fifty yards away. 'Is this normal?'

She came up next to him, eyebrows drawing together. 'What on earth—'

A burning arrow passed over their heads before she could finish that sentence. Shouting along the wall ensued.

'Archers to the wall! We're under attack!'

That was not good.

'Time to go,' Blackmane said.

When he went to head back into the turret, she did not follow. She was pressed up against the wall—not moving.

He clicked his fingers in front of her face. 'There are people shooting fire at us.'

She turned her head in his direction, moving as though the action took enormous effort. 'Will the castle burn?'

There was genuine terror in her voice. His gaze fell to her scarred hand. 'No. The grounds are too wet.'

'You are sure?'

He was mostly sure. He offered his hand. 'Come on. I'll get you to the castle.'

She stared at the open hand for the longest time before finally reaching for it. But as she did, a burning arrow smacked the wall walk a few feet from them and skated across the stone to the other side. Isabel dropped into a crouch, arms going over her head.

Blackmane cursed, then walked over to the arrow, stomping the flame out with his boot. Returning, he pulled her to her feet and dragged her into the turret. 'You focus on walking and let me worry about the rest, all right?'

She nodded.

Guards swarmed the wall now, running back and forth while putting out small fires.

'Down you go,' he said when they reached the narrow steps. 'I'll be right behind you.'

Smoke drifted up the stairwell, and she immediately backed up when she saw it, breathing hard and fast. He took her hand again and led the way, keeping her close behind him. The farther down they got, the darker it became and the thicker the smoke was. He could hear her sharp intakes of breath every time she misjudged a step, while his own feet moved swiftly and instinctively down the stairwell.

When they reached the bottom of the turret, Black-mane saw through the door that a nearby garden bed was on fire, most likely laid with straw. Two stable boys were attempting to contain it. Isabel froze the second she spotted the flames. When he tried to pull her towards it, she anchored her feet.

'I cannot breathe,' she said, now hyperventilating.

'It'll be better outside. Keep moving.'

She shook her head.

Normally he would instruct a person paralysed by fear to take a few deep breaths, but the turret was full of smoke. So he did the only thing he could. He picked her up and carried her out, almost colliding with Tatum in the process. The commander looked down at the woman clinging to him, her face buried in his uniform.

'I see the perimeter check was eventful,' he said.

Blackmane was never going to hear the end of this.

They moved away from the fire, and then Blackmane

set Isabel down on the ground. He kept hold of her while she drew greedy breaths.

Tatum nodded towards Isabel. 'Our generous host is tearing the castle apart looking for her. I suggest you take her straight inside.'

Blackmane nodded. 'I'll meet you on the wall.'

Tatum took off at a jog, disappearing into the smoke-filled turret.

Another arrow landed on the ground nearby, sending Isabel scampering sideways. Luckily, Blackmane still had hold of her.

'Close your eyes.' It was better if she did not see the fireballs raining down on them.

Isabel pressed her eyes shut and held tightly to his hand as they ran along the path towards the castle. At least her legs were working again.

'Almost there,' he said, guiding her up the front steps.

A moment later they were through the door. He slammed it shut behind them. The only sound inside was Isabel's fast breaths.

'You all right?' he asked.

She looked around before focusing on him. 'Yes.'

'I need you to slow your breathing for me.' He gave her a moment.

'I am sorry,' she said. 'I am not usually that useless in a crisis.'

He nodded. 'Fear can be a fickle beast.'

'Isabel!'

She jumped at the sound of her name thundering down the corridor. Blackmane stepped back from her right before Hodge entered the hall.

'I am here,' she said, her voice barely carrying.

Lord Hodge jogged over to her, his face distraught. 'Praise God. Where were you?'

She looked past him. 'Where are Mother and Everard?'

'Safely in their quarters, no doubt worried sick about you.' He took hold of both her arms, looking her up and down. 'You are unharmed?'

She shook her head. 'Yes.'

Hodge turned to Blackmane. 'Where did you find her?'

There was something in his demeanour that made him uneasy. 'Hiding from the arrows' was all he said. She could craft the rest of the story however she needed to. His gaze flicked to Isabel, who was kneading the skirt of her dress between her fingers. 'I need to return to the wall.'

Hodge looked back at Isabel. 'Are you going to thank the defender for returning you safely?'

Isabel let go of her skirt and looked between them. 'Of course. Thank you for escorting me, defender. It was fortunate that you came across me during my walk.'

Hodge sniffed. 'Very fortunate—especially given you had both retired for the evening.' He paused. 'We are both grateful.'

Blackmane nodded once, then exited the hall without a backwards glance.

CHAPTER 6

*I*sabel's tongue moved in her mouth, tasting smoke. She lay on her back, still in yesterday's clothes, staring up at the ceiling, while five-year-old memories pummelled her.

'Ita! Wake up! Get up and open the door!'

She could still feel the unbearable heat coming from the flames licking the bottom of the door, heating the handle to skin-melting temperatures. She winced at the memory of taking hold of it, the creak and groan of the roof above her. Then Hodge had arrived, throwing a woollen blanket over her head and pulling her away from the door and out of the house.

Ita.

Isabel sat up and moved to the edge of the bed, pouring herself some water. She eyed the wilted daisy chain as she drank. Hope crept in every time she looked at those flowers. As she placed the cup down, she noticed fresh bruises on her wrists. Hodge had held her in an iron grip as he scolded her about leaving her quarters after

45

dark. Endless ramblings about trust and how much she meant to him and how his life would be over if anything happened to her. He said all this while her wrists turned to powder in his hands.

The fact that he had found her alone with Blackmane had made it so much worse.

Rising, she grabbed the woollen blanket from the chair and drew it around her as she stepped into a pair of boots, not bothering to tie the laces. She exited her quarters and made her way outside. All was still and quiet now.

She climbed to the top of the wall, stepping onto it just as the sun reached the horizon, painting the castle in golden light and chasing away the shadows. She had a bird's-eye view of the damage from up there and was surprised by how little there was. Blackmane had been right. Aside from some singeing of the lawn and gardens and soot covering the wall walk, everything was still standing. It had been too damp for any real harm to be done.

Her eyes went to the sky, wondering if Margery was close by and what she would have made of all the chaos.

'I thought you would have learned to stay off the wall by now.'

Blackmane's impatient tone had her looking over her shoulder. She took in his filthy face and the dark circles enclosing his eyes. 'Have you not slept yet?'

He came to a stop several feet from her. 'While the castle was under attack? No.'

She chose to ignore the sarcasm. 'Was anyone injured?'

He shook his head. 'It was a lot of running around putting fires out and shooting blindly in the dark.'

'I do recall a little of that.' She adjusted the blanket around her, and the sleeve of her dress slid up her wrist. Blackmane's eyes narrowed on it, prompting her to tuck it beneath the blanket. But he continued to stare at the spot as though he could see through the wool.

'What happened to your arm?' he asked.

There was a short silence as she tried to come up with an answer that would not fill her with shame. 'Margery.'

He lifted his gaze to hers. 'Your *pet bird* left those marks?'

She nodded and looked away.

'The aversion of your gaze, lack of words, and noncongruent gestures suggest you're lying.'

She felt hot suddenly—seen. 'Is that another defender trick?' When he did not answer her, she said, 'His Lordship can get a little... enthusiastic when communicating his point.'

'Perhaps you mean aggressive.'

She bit down on her lip and went for a change of subject before things got even more uncomfortable. 'When do you leave for your tour?'

He let out a short breath, eyes never leaving her. 'Tomorrow.'

She was grateful that he let the subject go. 'What was it like? Riding through the region, I mean?'

'Empty.'

She had been expecting that answer, but it still made her chest ache. 'It was such a vibrant place once upon a time. I adored growing up there.'

'Where did you live?'

'Llanelieu.'

He nodded. 'Not much there now.'

She studied him. 'These camps. Will they help?'

'Apparently.' His tone suggested otherwise.

'I had hoped to come along, maybe visit my old home —or what is left of it. But His Lordship was not keen on that idea.'

'As much as it pains me to agree with that man, he's right.'

She studied him a moment. 'I gather you are not a fan of my future husband, defender?'

Nothing changed on his face. 'I think he's fan enough for all of us.'

Isabel did not smile, but she wanted to.

A bullfinch landed on an embrasure a few feet away, drawing their attention.

'Is this Margery?' Blackmane asked.

Isabel suppressed a smile as she looked back at him. 'No. Margery is a tad bigger.' She pinched her fingers together.

Commander Tatum stepped out of the turret behind Blackmane, looking between them before saying, 'Lord Hodge wants to see us.'

Blackmane gave him a casual salute before turning his attention back to Isabel. 'I strongly suggest you go back inside.'

'People have been strongly suggesting that for the past five years. What makes you think I will start listening now?'

They watched each other for the longest time.

'Stay off the embrasures,' he said before turning away.

She watched him until he disappeared into the turret, then turned her attention to the sky.

'I really do not feel like socialising, Mother. Can you not tell His Lordship that I am unwell?' The thought of sitting at Hodge's side for the evening had her imagining all kinds of symptoms.

Gwenore held up a pastel blue dress with drop sleeves, studying it like one did a painting before laying it on the bed. 'His Lordship is leaving tomorrow. He will want to spend as much time with you as possible before he departs. Is it too much to ask that you eat dinner with the man so he can remember your lovely face while he is away?'

Isabel rolled her eyes.

'I saw that.' Her mother stepped up to unbutton her dress, then tugged it down to Isabel's waist. Gwenore stilled when she saw the bruises enclosing her daughter's wrists.

Isabel's first instinct was to move her hands behind her back, but a part of her wanted her mother to see the marks, to ask her about them. At the very least acknowledge them. Instead, Gwenore averted her eyes and went to fetch the gown from the bed.

Isabel's chest pinched.

What else had she expected? Questions would lead to answers, and answers would force her mother to admit that Hodge was not the man everyone needed him to be. On went the dress, buttoned to the neck. Her lips were painted, hair pinned back, and jewellery selected according to Lord Hodge's tastes.

'His Lordship always compliments you when you wear the sapphire earrings,' Gwenore said, stepping back to admire her work.

'Because they were a gift from him.' He complimented her so she was forced to express her gratitude over and over again. She glanced at the window to gauge the time. 'Where is Everard?'

'Likely with His Lordship.'

She resented how much time they spent together. Every ride, every sparring match, every game of chess, every conversation they shared while shooting at the butts felt like another claw in her.

'Shall we?' Gwenore asked, heading for the door.

Isabel had no choice but to follow her.

It was a far more social affair than the evening prior. Many noble families used Hampstead Keep as a safe stopover when travelling through the region. Isabel's gaze swept over the rows of people seated at the long tables, searching.

But searching for whom?

Her eyes paused on Blackmane, who was standing at the back of the room talking to Hadewaye. His muscled arms were crossed, his stance wide. Inky hair fell forwards in a tousled mess. His dark eyes and black leather uniform only added to his lethal appeal—if there was such a thing.

'Are we entering, or are we simply going to stand at the door all night?' Gwenore asked.

Isabel's cheeks flushed. She had forgotten her mother

was beside her, and she knew how ridiculous she must have looked standing there gaping at the defenders. Not *all* the defenders, however.

Stepping into the room, she snuck another glance at Blackmane, who appeared oblivious to her presence. Probably a good thing. It was better to focus on the man she would soon marry. He was definitely looking at her, eyes raking her up and down—making her want to turn around and leave.

She kept her focus on him from that point. The last thing she needed was him catching her looking at another man. Lord Hodge settled for nothing less than her undivided attention. He needed a lot of it, all the time, and for whatever reason, he had chosen her for the role. So she would either need to find it within her or fake it convincingly for the rest of her life. The problem was, the more he demanded, the further out of reach it felt.

Hodge rose from his seat when she approached, and she made an effort to smile. He waited for the women to take their seats—*so chivalric*—then dragged his chair closer to Isabel's so he could hold her hand.

'Those earrings look absolutely beautiful on you.'

He was so predictable.

'You have exquisite taste, my lord.' She gave her mother a look, but she pretended not to see it.

The room grew louder as the evening progressed. And when the music began, it got louder still.

'Will you come dance with me, sister?' Everard asked, offering his hand.

Anything to free herself from Hodge. Of course, she needed his permission before leaving his side.

He nodded his consent, and Isabel fled the table, making her way into the middle of the room where other guests were already dancing. If anyone else had asked her, his hand would have tightened around hers, and she would have smiled and said to them, 'That is such a kind offer, my lord, but I am afraid I am rather tired.' And only when that person was far away would Hodge's grip ease. Then after, she would return to her quarters, open the windows wide, and watch the sky, imagining all the sights Margery was seeing while flying free outside the walls.

Everard and Isabel were both terrible dancers. They only ever did it when they needed a laugh or a means to blow off steam. They were always a fraction out of time and forever stomping on each other's toes, but it felt good to forget about everything else for a few minutes.

'Ready for the fast part?' Everard asked her when the music changed.

She was barely keeping up as it was. 'Do not let me fall.'

'I make no guarantees.'

Around and around they spun until they were out of breath and flushed from laughter. When the music stopped, she curtsied before him, almost falling in the process as the room continued to spin.

'I feel like you have gotten worse,' Everard shouted over the applause.

That made her laugh again.

As she caught her breath, Isabel's gaze drifted to the defenders' table. There was Blackmane, watching her. His stare was so penetrating that it halted her laughter.

'May I have the next dance?' Hodge asked, seemingly appearing from nowhere.

She flinched and quickly looked away. 'Yes, of course.' Saying no was not an option. Rejecting him in private was one thing. Rejecting him publicly was quite another.

Everard bowed to his sister before returning to their table. Hodge took hold of Isabel's hand and brought it to his mouth, kissing it for an uncomfortable length of time. She could feel heat rushing to her cheeks, but not in a good way.

'I was thinking,' Hodge said when the music started and they stepped together, 'that perhaps you *should* accompany me to Carmarthenshire.'

Her eyebrows rose. She had not been expecting that. 'Really?'

'Hampstead Keep is not exactly a safe haven right now, and I would prefer not to be separated for a long period. You are quite right in your thinking that you are safest at my side.'

She never felt safe at his side—far from it. She was usually on edge, bracing for the moment his love warped into something he would be forced to apologise for later. But she did want to go to Carmarthenshire. Home was calling to her.

'Can you take me to see Maddock House?'

He laughed. 'To see a pile of rubble?'

'Yes.'

He gave her a pitiful look. 'Leave it with me.'

The song came to an end, and they stepped apart, applauding.

'I suppose I should tell the defenders that you will be

joining us,' Hodge said. 'I discovered earlier today that they are very fond of details.'

They had finished eating and were preparing to leave. Hodge took her by the hand and led her over to their table. 'Commander Tatum.'

All four defenders looked in his direction, as though that name applied to all of them.

'Yes?' Tatum asked.

'Might I have a word outside?'

The four men exchanged a look before heading for the exit. Isabel noticed that Blackmane appeared annoyed by the conversation before it had even begun.

'I wanted to let you know that Lady Isabel will be joining us on the tour,' Hodge announced when they were far enough from the door to hear.

The muscles in Blackmane's face tightened. 'No.'

Tatum raised a hand to silence him. 'With respect, I don't think that's a very good idea.'

Hodge gave Blackmane a cold stare before responding. 'I was not asking for your opinion on the subject, Commander. I was telling you the plan.'

The heat of Blackmane's glare had Isabel looking down at the ground.

The earl straightened. 'She will be quite safe with me.'

'What she'll be is easy prey' came Blackmane's reply.

'If I want your input, defender, I will ask for it,' Hodge snapped. 'Hampstead Keep will be at its most vulnerable during the next few weeks, as a portion of the guards will be with me.'

'Then take fewer guards,' Blackmane said.

Tatum gave him a look that made it clear that he was not to speak again.

'Better she remains behind guarded walls than out in the open in rebel territory,' Alveye said.

Hodge blinked. 'Perhaps you meant to say England's territory.'

Isabel looked down at her hand, which was turning white beneath his grip. When she looked up again, she saw that Blackmane had also noticed. His expression darkened even more, if that were possible.

'Our orders are to keep *you* safe,' Tatum said. 'Bringing Lady Isabel will divide our attention.'

Hodge waved a hand. 'I have an army of men to keep us both safe.'

Nausea rolled over Isabel as the bones in her hand ground together.

'Let go of her,' Blackmane said, the words a growl from his lips.

Everyone looked at him.

'You're hurting her.' He gestured to their joined hands. '*Let go.*'

Isabel held her breath, unsure how Hodge would react to another man coming to her aid while simultaneously bringing attention to the ill treatment.

The two men stared daggers at each other, the tension palpable. Surprisingly, Hodge loosened his grip but did not let go.

'I suggest you keep your men focused on the task at hand,' Hodge said to Tatum.

Alveye cleared his throat. 'Last night's attack suggests rebel numbers might not be as low as you think. And clearly they know we're here and aren't happy about the fact.'

Tatum rubbed his forehead. 'However, you're free to bring whomever you like. Our protection extends to everyone travelling with us.'

That had Blackmane turning and walking away without another word. Hadewaye and Alveye mumbled some form of pleasantry before following him.

Tatum looked at Isabel. 'It won't be a comfortable journey.'

She offered him a weak smile. 'I assure you there will be no complaints from me, Commander.'

He nodded. 'Then I shall see you both bright and early.' With that, he turned and followed the others.

Once alone, Hodge's grip tightened on Isabel again. She winced and looked up at him questioningly.

He turned to face her. 'Why is Blackmane telling me to let go of your hand?'

She could see the jealous glaze visible in his eyes despite the poor light. There was no right response to that question. 'I do not know.'

Hodge wet his lips and looked in the direction of the castle. 'We will discuss this later in private.'

Dread filled her. 'There is really nothing to discuss—'

'Let us go. We have guests.' He then proceeded to drag her back in the direction of the castle.

She wanted to tell him to let go, that he was hurting her—but he already knew. That was the point. The new bruise would serve as another reminder that the only person who could protect her from him was *him*.

'Smile,' he told her as they neared the entrance to the

hall. 'Light up the room, as you always do.' He finally released his hold on her.

She cradled her hand briefly before letting it fall to her side. Then, raising her chin, she stepped into the room with a smile.

CHAPTER 7

'What's the matter with you?' Tatum asked, pausing mid-saddling of his horse and looking over at Blackmane.

'Nothing.' He was becoming increasingly frustrated with the strap of his saddle bag.

Tatum walked over to him. 'So you're *not* still angry about the fact that Lady Isabel is coming on the tour?'

Of course he was angry. It was reckless and dangerous —and Hodge was an idiot for agreeing to it. 'It's not only dangerous for her but for everyone. Her presence will distract the guards.'

Tatum's lips twitched. 'Oh, the *guards* are going to be distracted. All the other men and definitely not you.'

'And when she's killed, we'll be blamed.'

Hadewaye mounted his gelding. 'I don't think His Lordship will let an arrow or weapon anywhere near her. He's rather protective.'

'Perhaps a more accurate term is *over*protective,' Alveye said, joining the conversation. 'He holds on to her like she might flee at any moment. Have you noticed that?'

Oh, Blackmane had noticed all right.

'People in love are weird—period,' Tatum said. 'The way they behave generally is unsettling.'

Alveye laughed. 'And that's why you'll die alone.'

'I don't think his feelings are reciprocated,' Hadewaye said. 'Lady Isabel is simply doing what she must to keep her family safe. And he holds on to her that way because she probably *is* tempted to flee. I certainly would be.'

Blackmane checked the girth of his saddle before gathering the reins. 'Doesn't matter why they're together or how they feel about each other. It only matters that the death toll during this assignment is kept to a minimum.' He landed softly in the saddle. 'That said, if Hodge did love her, he wouldn't be bringing her into a war zone.'

Alveye wagged a finger in his direction. 'Now *you* will make a great husband one day.'

Tatum frowned. 'So I'm to die alone while Blackheart here, who hates the entire world and everyone in it, is destined to be a great husband? That's your assessment of things?'

Hadewaye's eyes returned to him. 'How come you get away with calling him Blackheart, but when one of *us* says it, we get shoved off our horse?'

Tatum returned to his mare. 'Because I'm his commander, and the respect runs deep.'

'Or maybe I'm just waiting for you to get on your horse,' Blackmane said.

The others laughed, then fell silent when Hodge approached on horseback.

'Good morning,' the earl called to the group. 'Are we all ready for day one?'

Blackmane busied himself with the saddlebag once more, leaving the others to respond. His gaze drifted to Isabel, who was at the far end of the mounting yard with her mother and brother. Her hair was half up, her face scrubbed clean. She wore a simple green dress beneath a heavy cloak and riding boots. At least she was dressed sensibly for the journey. He watched as she hugged them farewell before walking over to her waiting horse.

'Trahern has been my trusted guard for many years,' Hodge was saying to Tatum. 'He will protect Lady Isabel with his life.'

That got Blackmane's attention. His eyes went to the seasoned guard Hodge was referring to, a greying man whose reaction time would likely leave a lot to be desired.

'What about you?' Tatum asked the earl. 'Who will be riding at your side?'

Abrupt laughter erupted from Hodge. 'I am quite capable with a weapon, defender. You do not need to fret about me. We also have a unit of twenty men.'

Numbers like that meant nothing without the necessary skills.

'I'll ride at your side, just to be safe,' Tatum said.

'As you wish. You can entertain me with heroic tales of your time in Carmarthenshire—before the return of the marcher lords.'

Blackmane really wanted to smack the fool off his horse.

'Ready, my beloved?' Hodge called to Isabel.

She looked in his direction. 'Ready.' But instead of joining him, she rode straight over to Trahern.

'Come ride beside me,' Hodge called to her, waiting.

She released a rather heavy breath before doing as she was told. 'Good morning, defenders,' she said as she passed them.

'My lady,' said Hadewaye, Alveye, and Tatum. Blackmane simply nodded.

Tatum signalled for everyone to move out, and they made their way to the outer wall.

The gate lowered before them, forming a bridge across the moat. Thick fog and frosted grass awaited them on the other side.

'Want me to ride up front?' Blackmane asked Tatum.

One corner of the commander's mouth lifted. 'Knock yourself out.'

Blackmane trotted off until he was at the front of the unit, needing to be as far away from Hodge and Isabel as possible so his mind was entirely on the job.

That tactic worked for the entirety of the morning. It was around noon when they reached a fork in the road and Blackmane heard arguing behind him. He turned his horse around and backtracked past the soldiers to see what was going on.

'That is why I wanted to come. You know this,' Isabel was saying, her horse stirring beneath her.

Hodge took hold of the horse's bridle, attempting to still it. 'Is it? Is that really the reason?'

'Let go of my horse.'

He did not let go. 'What about all the other reasons? Like to be at my side and witness first-hand how hard my family has worked to restore *your* homeland to something resembling civilisation.'

'I am always at your side, and on the rare occasions I am not, you have me followed.'

Blackmane nudged his horse forwards until he was next to Tatum. 'What the hell is going on?'

'Hodge wants to go straight to the camp.' Tatum talked out of the side of his mouth, voice low. 'She thought we were going to Llanelieu.' He gave Blackmane a warning glance. 'And we're going to stay out of it.'

That was easier said than done with Isabel growing more upset. Then Lord Lunatic reached for her, catching hold of her wrist. But before Blackmane even had a chance to intercept, a large golden eagle swooped down, its talons slicing Hodge's face. A collective drawing of swords followed, drowning out the roar of pain.

'I didn't see that coming,' Hadewaye said, looking thoroughly confused by the scene unfolding.

Blackmane went straight for his bow. He had it loaded and pointed at the bird a beat later.

'Do not hurt her!' Isabel shouted. 'Margery, stop!'

Alveye lowered his weapon. 'Who the hell is Margery?'

Isabel had failed to mention that her pet bird was also a lethal predator capable of killing large mammals.

Hodge reached back for his own bow, but by the time he had it loaded, the eagle was twenty feet above them. 'What in God's name is that thing doing here?'

Isabel's eyes were wide with panic. 'She must have escaped her cage. I am sorry.' She moved her horse closer to Hodge's. 'You are bleeding.'

'You let it out.' His tone was shrill with accusation.

'After I explicitly told you not to, that if I ever caught it outside I would—'

'Shoot her from the sky. Yes, I know. I am sorry. I take full responsibility. Please, put the bow away.'

Hodge did no such thing. Instead, he took aim at the eagle.

'No!' Isabel screamed, reaching for him. But he was too far away.

Hodge released the arrow, but it never reached the bird because Blackmane's arrow intercepted it, knocking it out of the sky. Margery disappeared into the trees.

All eyes went to the defender.

'Shit,' Tatum muttered.

For a moment, Hodge simply stared at Blackmane with a look of shock. That level of accuracy was probably unheard of outside of Chadora. But then the embarrassment and anger kicked in.

'What the hell was that, defender?' he yelled, wiping blood from his eye. 'How dare you interfere?'

Blackmane glanced at Tatum, whose expression made it clear he had overstepped. 'Apologies. I was aiming for the eagle and missed.'

'You *missed?*' Hodge laughed abruptly. 'Are you trying to tell me a highly trained *defender* missed a bird with a seven-foot wingspan that was positioned directly overhead?'

'To be fair, the sun's at a bit of an awkward angle,' Alveye said, looking up and blinking dramatically.

Hadewaye nodded in agreement. 'We all have our bad days.'

Hodge looked at Tatum and shouted, 'Is there no discipline within your unit, Commander?'

'For missing?' Tatum asked, feigning ignorance.

Isabel was looking from tree to tree, likely worried that the eagle would return. When she did not spot it, she turned her attention back to Hodge. 'I am so sorry. I did not think she would follow.'

He lurched for her again, seizing her arm and proceeding to rub her hand all over his bloodied face. 'Look at what she did. Look!' He held her hand in front of her face, forcing her to see.

Blackmane instinctively reached for the knife strapped to his leg, but a single glance from Tatum made him pause.

Isabel's eyes welled up. 'I am sorry.'

'I have told you time after time that an eagle is not an appropriate pet for a woman of your status,' Hodge ranted.

Blackmane, on the other hand, now thought it the perfect pet.

'I do not want that thing near you ever again,' Hodge went on. 'Do you understand?'

She blinked, and a few tears escaped. 'I cannot simply—'

He squeezed her hand. 'Promise me, or God help me, I will hunt that thing to the ends of the earth.'

'I understand,' she whispered, reaching for his face in an attempt to soothe him. 'I understand. I am sorry.'

She was trembling now, as was Blackmane, but for a different reason.

Hodge brought her hand to his mouth, lips pressing so

hard that Blackmane was sure his teeth would leave an imprint. 'I love you,' he whispered. 'I love you. I love you.'

The man was insane, and Blackmane was beginning to realise just how trapped she really was. The English guards had all averted their gaze at this point. Alveye and Hadewaye looked on with bewildered expressions. Tatum appeared utterly confused by the whole scene.

'I suggest we get moving,' Blackmane said at a volume that only his commander would hear, 'before I summon the bird for another go at him.'

Tatum nodded. 'We should keep moving.' His voice cut through the awkward silence.

Finally, Lord Hodge released Isabel's hand and looked around like he had forgotten he had an audience. 'One moment.' He reached for his waterskin. 'Hold out your hand, beloved. Let us get you cleaned up.'

She held out a shaking hand and let him wash the blood from it. He then used some of the water to clean his face.

'All right,' he said when they were ready to leave. 'Let us go.'

Slowly, Isabel gathered up the reins and followed him without lifting her gaze to anyone.

Blackmane rode behind the pair for the next part of the journey, and Tatum did him the favour of not bringing attention to the fact. Time passed in silence. Thankfully, there were no more incidents, and the eagle was smart enough to stay away.

When it was time to make camp, the party found a clearing next to a creek a mile off the main road and set up a guarded perimeter. Two tents were erected for

Hodge and Isabel while the rest of them slept around fires out in the open, ready to take their turn keeping watch.

Isabel retreated to her tent the moment it was ready and did not emerge until Hodge had retired for the evening. Blackmane had just finished eating when he noticed her standing outside, hugging herself against the cold. He rose and walked over to her.

'Need something?'

She looked around with a worried expression. 'Will someone be keeping an eye on the fires overnight?'

He noted the colour rising in her cheeks after asking the question. 'There will be plenty of men keeping watch over everything. Go get some sleep.'

She met his gaze. 'And what about you? Will you be getting some sleep? Surely even defenders must surrender to their mortal needs occasionally.'

He nodded.

Still she did not return inside. 'Thank you for earlier. You saved her life.'

He looked away. 'Birds of prey keep the pests under control. They're important.'

'Of course. So, you saved her to keep the pests at bay?'

'Yes.' He had to lie, because admitting he did it for her would raise other questions.

'What is your name?' she asked, crossing her arms.

'You know my name.'

She tilted her head. 'I mean your given name.'

No one used his given name. It had all but died with his family. He hesitated before saying, 'Ryder.'

'Ryder,' she repeated, testing it out. 'My family and friends call me Belle. You can call me that if you like.'

'Because we're friends now?'

'You saved Margery's life. That may even qualify you as family.'

She gave him a tired smile, one he drank up.

'Goodnight, Lady Isabel,' he said, making it clear that he was neither friend nor family.

Her smile faded, and he was the reason.

'Goodnight, defender,' she said quietly before disappearing inside the tent.

Blackmane headed down to the creek for a wash, splashing handfuls of cold water over his face. She was getting to him, and that was dangerous for everyone.

When he returned from the creek, he saw that one of her tent flaps was snagged on something, which meant she was visible to anyone passing by. Releasing a heavy breath, he walked up the gentle slope to the tent, trying very hard not to peer inside—and failing. He was a few feet away when he glimpsed her seated on a roll-out bed in her nightdress. She had a blanket draped around her shoulders and long hair spilling down one shoulder. She was staring at the candle at the far end of the tent, a hairbrush idle in her hand. He should have quickly pulled the tent closed and walked away, but he did not do that.

The hem of her nightdress sat mid-calf. Her slender ankles were crossed, the soles of her feet visible. Both had angry red scars from toe to heel. His chest tightened as he wondered what form of hell this girl had walked through to end up betrothed to the devil himself.

As though sensing him there, her gaze snapped to the gap in the tent, and a soft gasp escaped her. She tugged her nightdress down over her legs and feet. He should have walked away. But then her face and shoulders relaxed, and she released the hem of her nightdress. It slid back up her legs, her scars on display once again. It felt like an invitation, a baring of her soul. Neither of them moved or spoke. Then his eyes fell to her feet again, her toes curling as his gaze landed. It was an honest moment, and he was utterly captivated by it.

Captivated by *her*.

It took all his effort to reach up, take hold of the canvas, and drag it closed. Darkness fell over his face once again. He was painfully aware of the change in his heart rate as he let go of the fabric and retreated to the campfire.

CHAPTER 8

*a*larm might have been Isabel's first reaction when she spotted Blackmane's face through the gap in the tent, but it had been short-lived. Something in his expression had put her at ease. His dark eyes had looked a golden brown beneath the soft light spilling from the tent. There had been tenderness in that gaze as it moved over her scarred feet. He wanted to see, and she wanted to be seen. It had been so long since someone had wanted to see the *real* her.

And she had felt things too. Like blood roaring through her veins and heat gathering in her belly. She had felt both desire and desired, despite all the ugly parts being on display. It was entirely comfortable. And while she probably should have felt guilty, she felt only relief. For five years everyone around her had been saying she must feel this and she must feel that. She had started wondering if there was something wrong with her, something broken. But she was not broken.

Her heart sped up as she emerged from her tent the

next morning. She looked over at the now-abandoned campfire where Blackmane and his comrades had slept.

'Morning, my lady,' Trahern said, approaching. 'Your horse is ready.'

'Thank you.' She looked around for Blackmane, finding him by his horse, speaking with Commander Tatum. He glanced in her direction, and heat rose in her cheeks at the simple act of eye contact. He nodded once before turning his attention back to Tatum. The exchange was so casual, his demeanour so different from the night prior, that she worried she may have dreamt the whole thing up.

'Good morning, beloved,' Hodge called as he stepped outside his tent.

All the heat inside her dissipated at the sound of his voice. She looked in the earl's direction. 'Good morning, my lord.'

'Sleep well?'

No, she had not. She had lain awake thinking about another man's eyes on her. 'Yes, thank you.'

Hodge walked over to her, taking hold of her face. Oh, how she wanted to push his hands away.

'I feel dreadful about yesterday. You know I cannot bear it when we argue.'

The fact that he referred to such incidents as arguments spoke volumes. 'All is well now.' She gently guided his hands away from her face, making sure to smile as she did so.

'We are about thirty-five miles from the camp, which means I will have you safely behind walls by mid-afternoon.'

He loved to put her behind walls.

A guard approached. 'Your horse is ready, my lord.'

'Very good,' Hodge replied.

Their belongings were now being carried out of the tents and pegs torn from the ground. Hodge offered her his arm, and she reluctantly took it.

'I think you will be most impressed with the camp when you see it,' he said as he led her away.

It grated on her that he spoke about the camp as a point of pride rather than with disappointment that it had come to this.

'Prepare for departure,' Hodge shouted at the men who were already scrambling about doing just that. He walked her to her horse and turned to help her mount.

'Thank you, my lord, but I need no assistance.'

'Nonsense,' he replied, taking hold of her waist.

She gently pushed his hands away. 'I am quite capable of getting on a horse.'

He reached for her again. 'I am standing right here.'

She stepped out of his grasp this time. 'I can do it myself.' The words came out far more abrasive than intended, taking them both by surprise. 'I... I apologise. It seems I did not get enough sleep after all.'

He pulled her to him, taking hold of her face once more and kissing her forehead. 'You must let me love and care for you as I see fit.'

Must I? Really? She pressed her eyes shut, waiting for him to release her. When he did, she turned back to her horse, and he helped her onto it. But because he was not the strongest of men, she ended up doing most of the work herself anyway.

Her eyes met Blackmane's as she landed in the saddle. The look in his eyes was confirmation that she had not dreamt their shared moment after all.

When everything was packed up and loaded onto the horses, the group continued east, Isabel tucked between Trahern and Hodge with Blackmane at the very front, the farthest from her that he could be. Likely not a coincidence. He never looked back at her—not once. He was focused entirely on his job. Though she noticed all the defenders wore the same serious expressions. Perhaps that was part of their training too.

Four hours into their journey, Blackmane emitted a high-pitched whistle and raised a fist in the air. Everyone stopped. The defenders reached for their bows while the English guards looked around, confused.

'What is going on?' Hodge asked Tatum, who was now watching the trees down his arrow. 'Why have we stopped?'

'Quiet.'

Hodge scowled but did as he was told.

The guards followed the defenders' cue and drew their swords. Realising he was the only person without a weapon in his hand besides Isabel, Hodge followed suit.

Isabel looked up, studying the branches above. It was as though the breeze had stilled suddenly. Trahern flinched beside her, and she whipped her head around to look at him. She sucked in a breath when she realised there was an arrow protruding from his chest.

Hodge looked past her to the wide-eyed bodyguard, who was now falling sideways. 'We are under attack!'

The defenders were already shooting at things Isabel

could not see while Hodge's men turned in circles with their useless swords. More arrows came at them, flashing in and out of sight. One hit the horse in front, and it backed into hers. The gelding's front legs lifted off the ground.

'Easy, boy.'

Blackmane appeared out of nowhere, filling the space where Trahern had been, his muscled frame shielding her from the trees on that side of the road. Her former body-guard was now on the ground, bloody-mouthed and wheezing.

Isabel went to dismount to help him.

'Leave him,' Blackmane instructed, as though he had eyes in the back of his head. 'He'll be dead before your feet touch the ground.'

When Isabel looked back at Trahern, he was still.

Hodge continued to bark orders at the men around them while the defenders worked calmly and meticulously under a veil of silence.

It will be over soon, she thought. There were only so many arrows someone could shoot.

That number was higher than she expected, however. It was quickly becoming one of the longest moments of Isabel's life—excluding the night Maddock House burned down.

Blood roared in her ears, and she had no idea what to do or where to look. Then men began to drop from the trees around them, armed with axes, short swords, and shields. And some with nothing at all, because they were already dead.

Blackmane dropped his bow to the pommel of his

saddle and drew his sword while reaching for Isabel with his spare hand. 'Jump.'

Without hesitating, she kicked the stirrups off her feet and drew her legs up. But then Hodge's horse slammed into hers before she had a chance to leap, knocking her forwards. Blackmane caught her arm on the way down and swung her under his horse.

'Don't move from that spot,' he barked.

The defenders' horses were clearly far better conditioned to the sounds and sights of battle. Blackmane's mare barely moved a hoof as people fell and weapons screeched, the smell of blood taking over the air. Isabel pressed her eyes shut and clapped her hands over her ears. Then she hummed loudly so it was all she could hear.

Seconds ticked by.

Minutes.

Then someone tapped her arm, and the humming stopped. Slowly, she peeled her eyes open, terrified of what she would see. A bloody-faced Blackmane was crouched beside her, saying things she could not hear. Maybe her hearing was damaged from the noise.

Blackmane pointed to his ears, bringing attention to the fact that she was still covering hers. She cautiously lowered her hands.

'Are you injured?' he asked.

His voice was surprisingly calm and oddly soothing. She leaned into it. 'I do not think so.' Her eyes moved over his face, arms, and uniform. 'Are you?'

'No.' He reached out his hand to her, signalling it was safe to come out.

'For the love of all that is holy' came Hodge's voice behind her. 'What on earth are you doing down there? You could have been trampled.'

She was still reaching for Blackmane as Hodge dragged her out from under the horse and away from the defender.

He began checking her for injuries. 'Let me have a look at you. I cannot tell if any of this blood is yours.'

Blood? She wiped her face with her hand, then stared down at the red smeared across it. It was someone else's blood. She looked around at the injured and dead. Wastelanders, soldiers, horses. She walked unsteadily over to Trahern, bending to press his eyes closed. He had a wife, five children, and eight grandchildren waiting for him at home.

Hodge followed her over, hands going to his hips. 'Such a shame. My father thought the world of him.'

No outpouring of grief for the man he, too, had known since boyhood.

Tatum strode over to where they stood, gaze dropping to the corpse at their feet. 'Alveye and Hadewaye are doing a check of the area. Eight of your men are dead and three more injured. Is there a medic at the camp who can treat them?'

Hodge nodded. 'Yes.'

'Good. We'll dress the wounds in the meantime.'

Isabel looked up at that. 'I will help you.'

'Leave it to the soldiers,' Hodge said. 'You are far too sensitive for such things.'

She wondered if that was true or if Hodge said these things to remind her that she was basically helpless. 'I will wash, you bandage,' she told Tatum, refusing to believe that about herself.

A few feet away, she saw Blackmane drive a sword through the head of an injured horse, and her stomach rolled. He looked in her direction as he stepped back from the animal. He was the reason she got through unscathed. He kept stepping in and helping her, and she could not figure out what she had done to deserve his protection.

Her eyes went to the injured men propped up against tree trunks. Two had deep lacerations and the third an arrow protruding from his leg. She had not seen these kinds of injuries up close before.

'Normally we'd push the arrow through,' Tatum explained, 'but this one's too close to the artery. We don't want him bleeding out.'

Isabel used the cloth Tatum gave her and the remainder of her own water to help clean the guards up as best she could. 'Are you well enough to ride?' she asked the man with the arrow in his leg.

He was trying very hard not to look down at it. 'We'll soon find out.'

'Area's secure, Commander,' Alveye called as his horse cantered by.

Tatum nodded. 'Good. Let's get out of here.'

The injured were lifted into saddles and the dead guards wrapped in blankets and loaded onto horses.

'What about the others?' Isabel asked Hadewaye, who had returned to help.

He glanced around at the corpses. 'You mean the wastelanders?'

She nodded.

'I imagine they'll be picked apart by crows over the coming days.' Then, seeing her fallen expression, he added, 'Try not to look at their faces. It's the hardest part to forget.' He handed her his waterskin. 'Here. Go clean yourself up.'

'Thank you.' She moved to the side of the road and washed her hands and face as best she could beneath a few drizzles of water.

Blackmane walked her horse over to her. 'We're leaving.'

She turned to him and looked over at Hodge to ensure he was not listening. 'At some point you will find yourself in need of help. I want you to know that you can count on me when the time comes.'

His eyes shone with amusement. '*You're* going to help me?'

'Yes.' Colour filled her cheeks.

He nodded slowly. 'All right.' He watched her a moment, then said, 'You getting on?'

She gathered the reins and mounted without any help from him. Someone had paid attention earlier.

Blackmane let go of the bridle and returned to his own horse, saying to Tatum as he passed, 'The lady rides with me.'

Lord Hodge looked up at that. 'Lady Isabel is to remain at my side at all times.'

Blackmane looked tiredly in his direction. 'We're in the heart of enemy territory, and one third of your unit is dead or injured. You have no idea where the rest of the wastelanders are located, how many there are, or how far they're willing to go to see you dead. Do you want Lady

Isabel at your side, or do you want her safe? You don't get both.'

A tense silence followed. Hodge's face went all blotchy before he finally said, 'If anything happens to her, I will have your head, defender.'

Alveye and Hadewaye exchanged a look that translated to 'Good luck with that' while Blackmane swung himself into the saddle. He glanced at Isabel with an annoyed expression. 'Let's go.'

She followed him without hesitation, feeling the safest she had in years despite everything that had just occurred. Her eyes went skyward, where she glimpsed an eagle circling far above them. One corner of her mouth lifted before she looked back at the road.

CHAPTER 9

*B*lackmane kept Isabel at the back of the group, not only because it was the safest place for her, but because he did not like the thought of Hodge's eyes burning holes in their backs all afternoon. She seemed to breathe easier away from him. Blackmane also noticed that she kept her horse right beside his, and for once, he did not mind—for safety reasons.

An hour into their silent ride, she leaned in and whispered, 'I know you are angry that I came, but I hope you understand why I did.'

Blackmane glanced at Hodge to see if he had heard, but the collective thud of horse hooves drowned out the conversation. 'I get it. You wanted to visit your old house.'

Her eyes went to him. 'I wanted to go *home*.'

He met her gaze. 'How long did you live in Llanelieu?'

'Fifteen years. I was born in Maddock House, lived there right up until my mother married Lord Tompkin.'

He caught the bitterness in her tone when she said that last part. 'How did that match come about?'

Hodge glanced over his shoulder, looking between them, then faced forwards again.

Isabel let a few moments pass before moving her horse closer to Blackmane's—if that were possible. 'Right place, right time. Or wrong place, wrong time. That depends on who you ask.'

'I'm asking you.'

'Then the latter.'

He kept his eyes ahead.

'It was a little over five years ago. The marcher lords' final campaign,' she continued. 'Their last attempt to salvage what civility remained in Carmarthenshire in hope of remaining in their own homes.' She paused. 'Maddock House was one of the few households in the region still functioning. After my father died, Lord Tompkin took it upon himself to use it as an army base.' Her eyes went to Hodge's back. 'My father defended that house until he drew his last breath. Then it was only the three of us and a handful of workers who were like family.'

It was well known that the majority of workers in the region had laid down their tools when the food had run out, joining various groups believing they would be better fed. Sadly, that was not the case. Those groups then had to find ways to survive. Laws became irrelevant, as did the borders. Carmarthenshire was no longer a county but a word used to describe the mess of land between England and the newly formed kingdom of Chadora.

'So the earl asked your widowed mother to return to Hampstead Keep with him as his wife?' Blackmane asked.

'Yes.'

'And you want to know what became of Maddock House?'

She shook her head. 'I already know what became of it. It burned down the night before we left for Hampstead Keep.'

Blackmane blinked slowly as that piece of the puzzle fell into place. 'I gather that was a factor in your mother's decision.'

'The fact that she was homeless in a dangerous region with two dependent children and a rich lord was offering her a safe home? Yes, that was a factor.'

Blackmane was silent for a minute. 'How did the house burn down?'

Isabel edged her horse closer, her leg brushing his. 'Lord Hodge was at his father's side throughout that campaign. He was staying at the house and woke to horses. Most likely rebels. They rode away when he went outside to investigate, and when he returned indoors, the kitchen was ablaze. It spread so quickly.' She reached up and touched her throat, as though she were breathing the smoke in once more.

He normally avoided these conversations because the risk of empathy was too high. The only reason he was able to function and perform at such an elite level was because he had done away with every emotion except loyalty. But the question came out anyway. 'Did everyone make it out?'

She shook her head, and he felt the weight of the silence that followed.

'Lord Tompkin withdrew his men shortly after,' she said when she could speak again.

Blackmane nodded slowly. 'And the wastelands were born.'

'And the wastelands were born.'

He edged his horse away from hers. Their knees brushing every second stride was proving distracting, which was never a good thing when travelling through rebel territory.

Hodge looked over his shoulder. 'Beloved, come see the crops.'

Isabel looked to Blackmane, as though seeking his permission.

'Fairly sure he's talking to you,' the defender said. 'Go ahead. I'll ride behind you.'

She made her way over to Hodge, and he followed.

'All these crops you see before you are ours.' Hodge made a sweeping gesture with his arm. 'Wheat, barley, cabbages, carrots, turnips. You name it, we planted it.'

Isabel looked around. 'When you say ours—'

'I mean England's, of course. This project benefits everyone.'

Blackmane was immediately suspicious when he said that. Food should benefit the region in which it was grown. He looked out at the fields, eyeing the uniformed guards patrolling the fence line. There were a lot of them given the size of the area. He glanced at Tatum, who looked equally as perplexed.

Alveye rode up beside him. 'What the hell is this?' He kept his voice low. 'The farmers look ready to fall down.'

Blackmane returned his attention to the fields, spotting workers in the distance. These were not your typical farmers. They moved with stooped heads and rounded backs. These were people weighed down by exhaustion, fatigue, and... He narrowed his eyes.

Chains.

Each worker wore a shackle around one ankle, a chain running between them.

Isabel stopped her horse and lifted a hand to her brow. 'What is that around the farmers' ankles? Are they... are they chains?'

Hodge pulled up his horse, and the rest of the group stopped also. 'We had a few teething issues in the beginning, people disappearing. The chains simply ensure the same number of people who go out to work in the fields at the beginning of the day return at the end of it.'

All eyes went to him.

'Why would they want to leave?' Blackmane asked. 'Why would anyone flee a camp offering food and safety?'

'I have wondered that many times' was Hodge's reply. 'You would think they would be grateful.' He pushed his horse into a walk. 'Though flight risk is less of a problem *inside* the camp. The majority work without need of weights. Or, as I like to call them, the *grateful* majority.'

Blackmane and Alveye exchanged a glance.

'You look tired,' Hodge said, eyeing Isabel. 'We are about a mile from the camp now. Let us continue so you may rest.'

They forged ahead in total silence, eventually reaching a ten-foot stone wall with drawn wire atop it, confirming what Blackmane already knew.

This was not a camp. This was a prison.

The gate opened as they approached, a guard standing on each side of it. Their attention was focused inside, ensuring no one escaped in the few minutes it sat open. The defenders shifted in their saddles when the gate closed behind them. Blackmane looked around, taking note of every detail, from the condition of the roads to the number of guards watching them. When he glanced at Isabel, she looked appalled. It seemed Hodge had kept some of the finer camp details from her up until this point.

They dismounted, handing their exhausted horses over to the young men who came to take them. The surviving guards took the injured to be treated, leaving the defenders alone with Hodge and Isabel.

'Shall we get straight into the tour?' Hodge asked the group.

The defenders looked at the injured being carried off, then at each other.

Tatum answered on their behalf. 'Why not?'

Hodge clapped his hands together. 'Very good. Let us start with the kitchen area. The heart of the camp.'

Blackmane detected no pulse in the vicinity.

'This way,' Hodge said, striding off.

Isabel glanced solemnly at Blackmane before following him.

'On the right, you will find the kitchen area, where all the food is prepared,' Hodge said, beginning the tour. 'Every worker receives a parcel of items each week and one hot meal per day.'

Isabel looked at him. 'Did you say *one?*'

'Every day. No one goes hungry around here.'

Women moved back and forth between large pots that hung over open flames. The air smelled of salt and boiled bones. Those cooking stopped to watch them pass, their faces drawn and bleak. Either the pots were missing some vital ingredients or the women were working too hard for what they were receiving. The hate and resentment coming from these people was stifling.

Blackmane paused when he noticed Isabel stopped a few paces back, her clasped fingers turning white as she stared at something. He followed her line of sight to an older woman with weathered skin, staring back at her with the same intensity.

'Isabel,' Hodge said, turning to look at her. 'Are you all right?'

She whipped her head in his direction on a sharp inhale. 'Yes. I... I was simply enjoying the smell.' She hurried to catch up to him. 'Please continue.'

Hodge reached for her hand before walking on. 'We need to get you some food when we are done. You have not eaten all day.'

The sight of the man's hand wrapped around Isabel's evoked the same feelings in Blackmane as the shackles enclosing the workers' ankles. It made his blood boil and his hands itch.

'Now, on the left you will find the sleeping quarters,' Hodge continued, pulling Isabel along with him.

Her face fell the second his focus was elsewhere.

Blackmane looked over his shoulder at the woman now staring after Isabel, despite everyone else returning to their work. She immediately looked away when she realised he was watching her. He committed her face to memory before moving on.

'The sleeping quarters were designed to be space efficient,' Hodge said, gesturing to the poorly built houses casting long shadows over the road. 'Each house is designed to sleep five hundred people. We currently have three of them with space to add another.'

Blackmane frowned. 'Did you say five *hundred* people in each house?'

'Correct,' Hodge replied proudly. 'As I said, they were purpose built.'

Tatum shifted his weight. 'You have fifteen hundred people living in a camp this size?'

Hodge kept a firm hold on Isabel. 'Actually, it is a little over sixteen hundred at present, but only until the western camp is built.'

'You mean *rebuilt*?' Isabel pointed out.

Hodge's mouth flattened into a thin line. 'Correct.'

'What happened to the western camp?' Hadewaye asked.

Alveye muttered, 'I could hazard a guess.'

'Ruffians,' Hodge said simply. 'Ruffians standing in the way of progress.'

'Hard to imagine,' Tatum said, gaze flicking to Blackmane's.

The sarcasm was lost on Hodge. 'All going well, the second camp should be open by the end of the month.'

Blackmane looked back at the buildings. 'So where do the excess people sleep?'

'Inside, of course. We cannot have people sleeping out in the cold. We pack them into the lower bunks.'

Silence followed that statement.

Hodge began walking again, and the others followed. Blackmane's jaw tightened in unison with the earl's grip on Isabel.

'Careful,' Tatum said quietly, stepping past him. 'You'll break a tooth.'

Blackmane feigned ignorance as he forced his focus to the fenced area up ahead, presumably for livestock.

Hodge stopped in front of the fence and finally let go of Isabel's hand. He turned to face them. 'A children's section was my idea.'

There was a collective exchange of confused looks.

Blackmane peered through the drawn wire fence, freezing when he saw them. Children. Not running or playing like they should be but seated in groups, some with infants on their laps. Still and silent, watching them through the fence.

'What the hell is this?' Hadewaye asked, not holding back with his tone.

Hodge waved a hand. 'This is where the children are kept when their parents are working.'

Isabel walked over to the fence, pressing a finger to a sharp piece of wire—just like the wire used to keep cattle in. She turned to Hodge, eyes blazing. 'Why are they locked up like this?'

The earl appeared perplexed by the question. 'We cannot very well have them wandering about the camp unsupervised. That is hardly safe.'

Isabel blinked. 'Where are their mothers? Fathers? Aunts?'

'Working, obviously.'

More looks were exchanged between the defenders, an entire conversation taking place without a single word being spoken.

Isabel brought a hand to her temple. 'Are you telling me that you separate children from their mothers and fathers and lock them in a pen, like pigs?'

An annoyed expression settled on Hodge's face. 'We cannot have children getting underfoot. Containing them in one central area is the most sensible approach.'

Isabel covered her face with her hands. 'Oh my goodness.'

'My beloved, this is a unique situation of which you cannot possibly understand the complexities,' Hodge said in his most patronising tone.

Her hands fell to her sides, and she stared at him for a few beats before saying, 'You are right. I do not understand.' She cleared her throat. 'I would like to go to my tent, please.'

'But you have not seen the holding cells yet' came his reply.

She winced.

Tatum squinted in the earl's direction. 'You have holding cells inside the camp?'

Hodge straightened. 'Of course we do. Do you think troublemakers outside of the camp are suddenly going to be on their best behaviour when brought inside?'

The man had built a prison inside a prison and failed to see the irony in that.

'I really need to lie down,' Isabel said. 'Is there a tent? Or shall I find room in one of the overcrowded houses?'

'Touché,' Alveye said under his breath.

A few tense seconds passed before Hodge said, 'I shall come with you.'

'No.' Her response was a fraction too firm and far too quick. 'What I mean is I am tired and need a quiet moment.'

Blackmane was ready to tackle Hodge to the ground if he did not give her a few minutes' reprieve. Thankfully, it did not come to that.

Hodge gestured to a passing guard. 'Webb, take Lady Isabel to her quarters. She is in need of rest.' His eyes never left her. 'And stand guard outside until I get there.'

Normally, Blackmane would agree with such precautions, but this felt a lot like she had just become one of the prisoners.

'This way,' Webb said, gesturing back in the other direction.

She glanced a final time at the children, then walked ahead of him.

'Shall we continue with the tour?' Hodge asked.

Alveye, Hadewaye, and Blackmane all looked in the direction of the children. Tatum was forced to answer on their behalf.

'Yes. Let's see the infamous holding cells.'

Hodge turned and marched off.

'Relax. She's quite safe in here,' Tatum said as he fell into step with Blackmane. He spoke in a low voice so Hodge would not hear.

Blackmane scraped his teeth over his lower lip, eyes

boring into Hodge's back. 'You're wrong about that. Her biggest threat is nearby at all times.'

Tatum glanced sideways at him. 'Just remember our orders. We're here to observe, not interfere.'

Blackmane nodded, then fought the urge to look over his shoulder at Isabel's retreating back.

CHAPTER 10

*I*t was definitely her. A ghost from Isabel's past. Yvaine. Beautiful Yvaine. The best cook in Carmarthenshire in Isabel's opinion.

And Ita's mother.

She was alive. And if she was alive, that meant there was a chance Ita was alive too. But Isabel had to be careful how she proceeded, because it was clear Hodge had no idea who she was, and there was a reason Yvaine had not identified herself to him despite there being a hundred reasons why she should.

The guard escorted her along the muddy road, beneath an overcast sky that made it impossible to gauge how late in the day it was. When the kitchen area came into sight, she searched for Yvaine among the women. They were hard to tell apart in their drab clothing with their hoods pulled up to protect them against the cold December winds.

'I am going to need something to eat,' Isabel told the guard.

Webb gave her a tired look. 'Do I look like a lady's maid?'

'I am not asking you to cook it for me. I am quite capable of organising my own food.' She stopped at the kitchen area, glancing around.

The women paused their work and looked in her direction, giving her a chance to see their faces again.

'I was instructed to take you to your tent,' Webb said, sounding irritated.

She looked up at him. 'Shall I tell His Lordship that my request for a simple bowl of soup was denied?'

The guard exhaled and gestured for her to go ahead.

She walked into the kitchen area, eyes darting left and right. Her vision snagged on a familiar pair of brown boots with pointed toes, boots her mother had given Yvaine as a gift many years ago. She lifted her gaze, her heart squeezing as she met warm hazel eyes—eyes that always seemed to smile. A few moments passed, and then Yvaine noticed Webb standing there and straightened.

'Can I help you with something?' she asked, her tone lacking its usual warmth.

Isabel closed some of the distance between them. 'I was wondering if I might trouble you for some soup. It has been a long day of travel.'

Yvaine nodded. 'I'll bring a tray to your tent.'

Isabel swallowed. Soon she would have the opportunity to look at her properly, to touch her and confirm she was real. 'Thank you.' Turning, she headed back to the waiting guard.

The pair continued along the road that ran through the middle of the camp, passing the stables and barracks as they headed towards the large tents at the back. Each was big enough to stand up in.

'That one's yours,' Webb said, gesturing to the one on the far left.

Isabel stepped inside and looked around. There was a cot with linen and blankets, plus a small table and stool. The bag containing her belongings had been brought in and sat on the end of the bed.

'I'll be outside,' the guard told her. It came out more like a warning than a reassuring sentiment.

Isabel watched the canvas fall back into place, then paced the two strides of space between the table and the cot until the flap opened again and Yvaine finally appeared. She said nothing as she set the wooden tray down on the table, but her hands shook a little. Realising Webb was standing there waiting for the woman to exit, Isabel asked, 'Could you help me unbutton my dress before you leave?'

'Yes, my lady.'

Isabel looked back at Webb. 'Are you planning on standing there and watching?'

He gave her another scowl before releasing the canvas.

Isabel went to check it was fully closed before rushing over to Yvaine and wrapping her arms around her. The woman held her as she had done so many times through her childhood, rubbing gentle circles on her back. Only when Isabel was sure she had control of her tears did she let go to look at her properly.

Yvaine smiled softly at her and whispered, 'You are even more beautiful than I remember.'

'And you are *alive*.' Isabel's eyes welled up.

Yvaine glanced nervously at the exit. 'Lord Hodge has no idea who I am. He cannot know.'

Isabel had so many questions about that but so little time. 'And Ita?'

A part of her already knew the answer. Who else would attach a daisy crown to the leg of the eagle they raised together? But it still felt like a flock of birds had taken flight in her chest when she heard it confirmed aloud.

'Yes.'

Isabel pressed the back of her hand to her mouth to stop from making any noise. Her shoulders shook for a few moments as all the grief, pain, and relief came to the surface.

Yvaine took hold of her hand. 'They came when we were doing laundry at the river. She got away.'

Isabel searched her eyes. 'They took you while you were doing laundry?'

A nod.

'How long have you been in here?'

'A little over a year.'

A year. 'Where is she? Where is Ita?'

Yvaine gestured for her to turn around and began unbuttoning her dress, speaking into her ear. 'She lives with the St Clare group.'

It was not too much of a surprise that her dearest friend was part of one of the largest rebel groups in Carmarthenshire. 'How do I find her?'

'You cannot find her. They find you.'

Isabel turned back around. 'Then how do I make that happen?'

Yvaine's eyes filled with uncertainty. 'He cannot know she is alive.'

Isabel's chest pinched as she realised she was missing vital pieces to this story. 'I will go alone. He will not know.'

Yvaine looked torn, then gave a resigned nod. 'Head southeast for fifteen miles, sticking close to the creek. When they come for you, raise your hands immediately and tell them you are unarmed. You have a very short window of time to convince them you are no threat. They will shoot you without hesitation if they are at all suspicious.'

Isabel's bravery was diminishing, but her need to lay eyes on a living and breathing Ita had her nodding. 'All right. I understand.'

The tent opened suddenly, and Hodge stepped inside. Yvaine turned her face from him and walked over to the tray, fiddling unnecessarily with the cutlery.

Hodge looked from Yvaine to Isabel's open dress. 'Oh. You are changing. I shall wait outside.'

Isabel closed the front of her dress. 'I will be out in a moment.'

Thankfully, he left without another word. The second he was gone, she rushed over to Yvaine. 'I will figure out a way to get you out.'

Yvaine reached up and touched her cheek. 'I am too old to run from soldiers. I will wait for the day they open the gates and walk out of here free—alongside everyone else.'

Isabel brought Yvaine's hand to her mouth and kissed it, praying that day would come. Her friend went to fetch a clean dress from Isabel's bag, and as she was helping her into it, she whispered, 'Do not trust that man.' She tugged the hood of her cloak up and fled before Isabel had a chance to respond.

Isabel stared after her, taking a moment to compose herself before going outside to face Hodge.

When she exited, he turned, looking her up and down, no doubt assessing her dress choice, which she had paid no attention to at all.

'I am pleased you got some food,' he said.

It was not really surprising that he had forgotten Yvaine's face. He was not the kind of man who paid attention to the help. 'One of the women in the kitchen brought me some soup and was kind enough to help me change.'

'Good. How are you feeling?'

Isabel glanced at Webb, who was pretending he was not listening to every word. 'Is it really necessary to post a guard outside my tent?'

He took hold of both her hands. 'You know how protective I am of you. What if something should happen when I am not around?'

She would need to lose Webb if she stood any chance of getting out—or at the very least make it clear to him that she was in charge. 'You are so caring.'

'I love you. You know this.'

She placed a hand on his chest. 'So Webb is here for my protection only?'

'Yes.'

'And I am free to come and go as I please?'

He placed a hand over hers, moving it to her wrist

when he felt her scar. 'Of course. My beloved, you are my guest, not my prisoner. Let there be no confusion about that.'

She smiled sweetly at him. 'And when it comes time for me to leave, he will remain here inside the camp—like a good soldier.'

'Of course.'

She looked over at the guard, who was barely holding back a glare. 'And Webb will open the gate and wish me a safe journey home.'

Hodge touched the tip of her nose with his finger, like one did a child. 'It is always a safe journey when I am at your side.'

How her smile remained intact she had no idea. 'I should eat my soup before it goes cold. Then I shall get some much-needed sleep.' She stepped back from him.

'I think more rest is a good idea. I can see your mood is much improved already.'

She bit her lip to stop her tongue.

'Perhaps tomorrow you will come see the holding cells,' he said, preparing to leave. 'The gallows out front are worth your time also.'

She crinkled her nose. 'Something to look forward to.' Her eyes went to the four defenders outside the tent at the far end. Blackmane was crouched, making a fire, those beautiful hands of his meticulously stacking bark and twigs. He glanced in her direction, and she could tell by his expression that he had seen the cute little display she just put on.

When Hodge looked over his shoulder to see what she was looking at, Blackmane returned his attention to the fire. 'I think the defenders were impressed with the camp, though it can be difficult to get a read on them sometimes.' He sighed. 'I suppose I should go make sure they have everything they need. We want glowing reports back to King Becket, do we not?'

She found her smile again. 'We do.'

'I shall see you in the morning.' Hodge kissed her firmly on the forehead before marching away, each stride exuding confidence that he drew from goodness knew where.

The defenders tensed up as he approached—except Blackmane. He remained focused on the fire, ignoring Hodge entirely. She waited for Blackmane to look up again, somehow knowing he would. And sure enough, those dark eyes flashed in her direction once more.

I am sorry. He was going to be very unhappy with her in the morning.

He rose to his feet with a questioning look, like he was reading her mind. Fearing he could, she retreated to her tent, saying to the cranky guard, 'Goodnight, Webb. I do hope it does not get too cold out here overnight.'

His reply came in the form of a grunt.

She ate the half-cold soup while standing, then cleaned her bowl with a chunk of brown bread—not because she was hungry but because she needed to keep her strength up.

That night she forced herself to sleep, but it was restless as she was afraid of oversleeping. It was a few hours before dawn when she peered out of her tent, relieved to find Webb asleep sitting up, his arms crossed and chin resting on his chest. She crept past him, eyes going to the defenders' tent. Hadewaye was awake and keeping warm by the fire. There was always someone keeping watch. She was glad it was not Blackmane or she would not have gotten far. He seemed to sense her presence.

She made it all the way to the stables before she encountered her first hurdle.

'What do you want a horse for?' asked the marshal, suitably suspicious of the early morning request.

She raised her eyebrows. 'I do not owe you an explanation.'

He looked past her. 'Does His Lordship know you're here?'

'I am his guest, free to come and go as I please. Now, are you going to fetch me a horse, or will I be forced to wake His Lordship at this hour because you are being difficult?'

He appeared annoyed by the ultimatum. 'Stay here.'

She was a bundle of nerves as she waited, and she had to make a conscious effort not to snatch the reins from his hands and run when he returned with a horse.

'Thank you,' she said as casually as she could manage.

He watched her mount. 'I'm not going to get into trouble, am I?'

'For assisting the future Countess of Hereford with a simple request? Is that not your job as marshal?' She rode away before he changed his mind.

As tempting as it was to gallop to the gate screaming, 'Open up,' she walked the gelding calmly and prayed someone would let her out when she got there. Her stomach fell when she spotted Webb waiting for her at the gate, arms crossed in a very different way now.

'Where in God's name do you think you're going at this time of the morning?' he asked.

She was terrified that his voice would carry to the camp where Hodge and the defenders were sleeping. 'Out for a ride.'

He turned to the guard at the gate, grinning. '"Out for a ride," she says.' He looked back at her. 'Have you lost your mind?'

She tilted her head. 'Not to my knowledge. Is there a problem?'

'You can't just ride off into enemy territory.'

She adjusted her grip on the reins. 'The thing is, they may be England's enemy but not mine. I was born and raised in Llanelieu.'

His smile faded. 'Lord Hodge will have my head if I let you leave.'

She laughed at that. 'Nonsense. You were right there when he said, "You are my guest, not my prisoner. Let there be no confusion about that." So all that's left for you to do is open the gate and wish me a safe journey.'

He opened his mouth, then closed it again. 'You can't leave.'

'You are mistaken. Step aside, please.' She looked to the other guard. 'Open the gate.'

The man looked from her to Webb and back to her. 'I don't think I'm allowed.'

She released an impatient breath. 'Webb, did His Lordship not say that I was free to come and go as I please?'

Webb looked utterly confused now. 'Well, yes, but—'

'But nothing. Step aside and open the gate, or I shall go

wake him and tell him that I am being harassed for simply wanting to enjoy an early morning ride.'

'Early morning?' the guard said. 'It's the middle of the night.'

'Hampstead Keep is farther east,' she explained. 'The sun rises earlier there.'

Webb frowned. 'A few minutes earlier at most—'

'Open. The. Gate.' The words came out like a queen commanding her subjects.

He shook his head as he wrestled with the decision, then finally turned to the gate guard. 'Open it.'

The man looked far from confident as he made his way over to the drawbar.

'I'll be speaking with His Lordship the moment he wakes,' Webb said when she rode by him.

She glanced in his direction. 'I do not doubt it.'

Her heart sped up as the gate closed behind her, the drawbar sliding into place. She had done it. She was out of there and on her way to see Ita—or to be killed by wastelanders trying.

Feathers flashed overhead, and a smile spread across Isabel's face. Extending an arm into the air, she watched as Margery swept down and gracefully landed on her.

'Hello, sweet girl.'

Margery eyed her in the dark.

Guiding the eagle to her shoulder, she said, 'You are going to want to hold on. It is time to pick up the pace.'

CHAPTER 11

Blackmane's eyes opened as the first light of morning pushed through the gap in the tent. Rising, he glanced over at Alveye and Tatum as he stepped into his boots. They were still asleep. He grabbed his cloak from the end of his bed and swung it around his shoulders as he exited the tent. Hadewaye was seated by the fire, cleaning his sword. He looked up when Blackmane stepped out.

'Morning,' he said.

Blackmane nodded, then looked over at Isabel's tent. He immediately noticed that her guard was not at his post. 'Where's Webb?'

'The guard?' He glanced in that direction. 'Likely getting a few hours' sleep.'

'Where's Lady Isabel?'

Hadewaye frowned. 'If Webb's missing, then she's likely with His Lordship.'

Every muscle in Blackmane's body tightened at that response. 'Did you see her go into his tent?'

'The sun's barely up. I'm struggling to see that far with light.' Hadewaye sheathed his sword, sighing. 'Don't torture yourself hanging about outside.'

'You don't know what you're talking about, so shut your mouth.'

The remark appeared to blow right past the defender. 'Why don't you head to the kitchen and get something to eat? It smells fairly palatable for prison food.'

Blackmane was still reconciling the notion of Isabel and Hodge in bed together. It was not uncommon for a couple about to be wed to get ahead of themselves, but he had hoped she would refrain until after. Not after they exchanged vows but after he went home.

'Watching his tent isn't going to make her appear any sooner,' Hadewaye said.

Blackmane had not even realised he was staring. He looked away and cleared his throat. 'The food does smell edible.'

Hadewaye released a long exhale. 'A couple more days and this will all be over for you.'

'Do me a favour and stop talking.' His tone was sharper than he intended.

Hadewaye raised his hands, saying nothing further.

Blackmane walked away then, knowing he would not be able to contain his jealousy when the pair finally emerged from Hodge's tent.

There was a handful of women wandering about the kitchen area when he arrived, having hushed conversations while adding vegetables to pots. Blackmane spotted the woman Isabel had reacted to the day prior. Curious as to who she was, he headed towards her. She appeared uncomfortable when she saw him walking her way, but he did not read too much into that. That was most people's reaction.

'Morning,' he said.

She offered a strained smile. 'Defender. Are you after some food?'

He nodded.

'We only have soup. No bread yet.'

'That's fine.'

She went to fetch a clean bowl, then began ladling beefy liquid into it. Blackmane watched her, recalling the way she had looked to Isabel. 'How do you know Lady Isabel?'

She flinched ever so slightly when the name left his mouth, then held the bowl out to him. 'I met her yesterday. She requested some food.'

The distinct lack of eye contact suggested otherwise.

He took the bowl. 'Did you live at Maddock House too?'

She froze for half a second, then feigned confusion. 'Maddock House?'

'In Llanelieu.'

She shook her head. 'I have to get back to my work. We have a lot of people to feed, as you know.'

'She's trapped,' Blackmane said. 'With him.'

The woman finally met his eyes, studying him for a long moment. 'You have been paying attention.'

He stared back at her. 'Why the big secret? I would have thought a connection to the future Countess of Hereford would work in your favour.'

'Perhaps you have not been paying close enough attention or you would know His Lordship decides who the lady befriends.' She hung the ladle on the hook dangling from the pot. 'I really must get back to work.'

He did not want to get her into any trouble. 'Thanks for the soup,' he said, then left.

He was thirty yards from the tents when he heard Hodge shouting at someone. Concerned the someone was Isabel, he dropped the bowl of soup and broke into a jog, slowing when he spotted the earl standing face to face with Webb. Alveye, Tatum, and Hadewaye now stood outside their tent, watching. Blackmane looked around for Isabel, but she was nowhere in sight. A bad feeling enclosed him as he headed for the other defenders.

'I will have your head for this,' Hodge was saying. 'Then I will display it on a pike in the middle of the camp so that every crow in a twenty-mile radius can feast upon your eyes.'

'What happened?' Blackmane asked Tatum when he reached him.

'Lady Isabel left.'

Blackmane lowered his brows. 'What do you mean "left"?'

'The camp,' Alveye said.

Hadewaye leaned in, voice low. 'Webb let her go for a ride, and she hasn't come back.'

If Hodge did not kill Webb, then Blackmane likely would. 'How long ago?'

'A couple hours,' Tatum said.

'He let her leave in the middle of the night?'

'Clearly he's paying for it now.'

'If anything happens to her, I am holding you personally responsible,' Hodge was saying. 'Now get out there and find her. I want as many men searching as we can spare.'

Blackmane looked back in the direction of the kitchen, then took off at a run.

'Where are you going?' Alveye called to his back.

He ignored the question and headed straight for the woman who had given him the soup, approaching so fast she scurried back from him.

'Where did she go?' The question came out as a growl.

'Who?'

'You know exactly who. She's gone, and I want to know where.'

She swallowed. 'She left the camp?'

He leaned in, prompting her to back up even more. 'I'm not playing this game with you. Tell me where she is right now, or I'll drag you before Hodge and you can tell *him* instead.'

She pressed a hand to her chest. 'You do not understand what you are threatening. He cannot know we are alive.'

'We?'

She hesitated. 'I have a daughter. Ita. She is the same age as Isabel.'

Blackmane searched her eyes. 'Has she gone to your daughter?'

Silence.

'Has she?'

'Yes.'

'Where?' When he was met with silence again, he brought his face close to hers. '*Where is she?*'

'I cannot tell you.'

'You cannot, or you will not?'

Her eyes pleaded with him. 'Isabel *wanted* to go. She knew the risks.'

He took hold of her arms. 'Every second I waste on this conversation is a second I could be looking for her.'

She began to tremble. 'I... I told her to head southeast, to follow the creek. If she is there, they will find her.'

'They?'

She swallowed—twice. 'The St Clare group.'

She had sent Isabel into a lion's den. He released her. 'You better pray she's still alive.' He marched away, dark thoughts screaming inside his head.

When he arrived at the tents, there were soldiers and horses rushing about in all directions.

'I know that face,' Tatum said, handing him the reins of his horse. 'You know something.'

Blackmane looked around to ensure no one else was listening. 'I think I know where she went. I'm going to track her.'

Tatum turned to him. 'Great, because I told Lord Hodge we'd help with the search.'

'He can't come where I'm going,' Blackmane replied.

Tatum frowned. 'Why not?'

'Because she's on her way to the St Clare group.'

Alveye, who was strapping his weapons on, looked over at that. 'Hoping I misheard that.'

'She has some connection with the group,' Blackmane said. 'A friend.'

Hadewaye frowned. 'Do the St Clare people know that? They're likely to shoot first and ask questions later.'

That was Blackmane's fear also. Gathering the reins, he mounted. 'Then I need to get to her before she reaches them.'

Tatum grabbed for his horse. 'If I tell Hodge where she's headed, it'll become a genocide mission.'

'So we don't tell him,' Alveye said.

Tatum rubbed his forehead, then looked up at Blackmane. 'Take Hadewaye with you. I want the extraction done as quietly as possible. In and out with minimal damage. Alveye and I will try to keep Hodge busy in the meantime.'

Blackmane nodded and gestured to Hadewaye to move out.

'Blackmane,' Tatum called.

He looked back, waiting.

'I want you both back here in one piece.'

Blackmane saluted. 'Yes, Commander.'

CHAPTER 12

How does one measure distance in the dark? She could have been thirty-five miles from the camp or ten. A good sense of direction was not on her list of strengths. There was a chance she was travelling southeast as instructed, but there was also a chance she was heading too far south or too far east. Or possibly west. She looked up, searching for the moon. Had someone once told her it moved east to west like the sun? What was the point of being fluent in French if she could not survive a few hours alone in the dark?

She turned her head to Margery. 'What do you think? Should we continue straight or wait for the sun to rise to get our bearings?'

The eagle was looking tired despite being a passenger for the last hour.

'Where is Ita?' Isabel said on a sigh. 'Do you know where she is? Can you show me?'

Margery spread her wings and took flight.

'I should have thought of that sooner.' She nudged her

horse into a trot. 'Do not get too far ahead. I can barely see five feet in front of my face.'

As though understanding the request, Margery circled back every few seconds.

Around thirty minutes later, Isabel heard running water. It was the creek Yvaine had been referring to.

'Clever girl,' Isabel told the eagle when she returned. She dismounted, taking hold of the reins and leading the gelding down to the water for a drink. She rested there for a few minutes, noting the slight lightening of the sky, but it was too cold to sit still for long. Her hands ached, and her face was numb.

'Let us keep moving,' Isabel told the horse, who was now tearing large mouthfuls of leaves off a nearby bush. In an attempt to warm herself, she walked for a while, leading the horse along the creek's edge.

The sun rose in the exact spot she hoped it would, painting the frosty grass in pink light as it kissed the horizon. She stopped to admire the sight, enjoying the open space and distinct lack of walls. Then, looking to the trees ahead of her, she said aloud, 'Where are you, Ita?'

Margery hovered overhead, causing the horse to lift its head and sidestep.

'Easy,' Isabel told the gelding, stroking his neck. 'You are quite safe being the size you are.' She looked up as Margery flew off towards the trees. 'I think you hurt her feelings.'

Isabel mounted the horse and continued along the creek at a steady walk. She was soon swallowed up by tall oaks and glistening beech trees. Weaving quietly between the thick trunks, she navigated the bulging roots rising from the ground.

She was just beginning to warm up when an uneasy feeling took hold of her. Isabel looked around for Margery, but the eagle was nowhere to be seen. There was nothing to do except continue forwards. The goal was always to be found, so to fear that part seemed senseless. But she was afraid anyway. Afraid she would be shot in the back and left to rot in the woods, but more afraid of dying without ever finding Ita.

The uneasy feeling grew until she could barely draw breath. Stopping her horse, she looked around in all directions. Nothing. Her heart was thudding so loudly now that she could no longer hear the running water from the creek. Someone was near—watching her.

Letting go of the reins, she raised both hands in the air and shouted, 'I am unarmed. Please do not shoot me.' She wished she could pull her hood back and show her face, but she was too scared to reach for it.

Silence... until she heard the creak of a bow.

'I am searching for a friend and pose no threat.' The words came out shaky.

The trees stirred to her left, and a man emerged on foot with a loaded bow aimed at her. She kept her eyes ahead, too afraid to look directly at him.

'Dismount and get on your knees,' he instructed.

Hands shaking, Isabel climbed off her horse and got down on her knees. 'I am looking for Ita Chapman.'

'I want your eyes on the ground and hands on your head.' His tone was far more aggressive this time.

Her breaths came faster, her vision blurring. 'Please. I am alone, and I have no weapons.'

'The reason I stand here alive and free is because our kind know your kind are all fucking liars.'

She pressed her eyes closed. 'I swear to you.'

He took a few steps fowards. 'If there's a God you would like to pray to, now's the time.'

Isabel held her breath when she heard the bow creak again, the sound cut off by a familiar beating of wings. Her eyes snapped open, and she saw the eagle dive at him in warning. Fearing for the bird, she shouted, 'Margery, leave!'

The eagle took off again, flying up and away.

Out of the corner of her eye, Isabel saw the man lower his bow. She dared a glance in his direction. He was probably only a few years older than her, but his hardened features and the silver scar crossing one eye were evidence of a tough few years.

'What did you say?' he asked, his voice quieter now.

Isabel shook her head. 'Nothing.'

He took a step in her direction, and she tensed.

'You spoke to the eagle.'

Her mind scrambled to try and remember what she had said. 'I... I didn't want her to get hurt.'

He continued to stare at her. 'You know the bird's name.'

As did he, it seemed. And there was only one way he could have found it out. 'You know Ita?'

Nothing changed on his face.

'Where is she?'

He looked over his shoulder as a cloaked figure

stepped out from behind one of the trees, face partially covered by the hood of their cloak. Isabel did not need to see her face to recognise her. She would recognise Ita anywhere. Via form, height, posture. Via heart waves.

Margery appeared overhead, gliding down to land on Ita's shoulder, in case she needed further confirmation. Isabel's hands slid from her head, falling uselessly at her sides.

Ita reached up and dragged the hood of her cloak back. And there was her beautiful round face and pale green eyes, wide with shock. The visual was too much for Isabel. She covered her face with her hands as tears fought their way out, then sank down to the ground until the backs of her hands pressed against the dirt. She heard Margery take flight, her work there done. Then feet padded towards her, and Ita pulled her up until Isabel was seated on her heels, drawing her hands away from her face.

Isabel had no choice but to look at her.

They sat there crouched in the dirt, eye to eye, staring at each other. Then Ita turned to the man behind her and said, 'I've no idea who this is. You can go ahead and shoot her.'

Isabel's face fell. 'Wait. What?'

Ita turned back to her, laughing. 'I knew you would come back.' She took Isabel by the hand and pulled her to her feet before wrapping her arms around her.

The tears started again, but this time Isabel did not cover her face. She hugged Ita back, breathing in her buttery scent. She always smelled like the ingredients her mother used to cook with. She smelled of home.

'I thought you were dead,' Isabel said.

'It was safer that way.' She drew back, tucking Isabel's hair behind her ears. 'Nobody hunts the dead.' She searched Isabel's eyes. 'Why on earth are you out here by yourself? Rabbit almost shot you through the neck.'

Isabel looked past Ita to the scowling man. 'That is his name?'

'We don't use real names,' Ita explained. 'It protects others if you're caught and questioned.' She looked back at him again. 'The name came about from the fact that he can survive on very little food. He seems to grow stronger while the rest of us wilt.'

Isabel glanced briefly in his direction. 'And what do they call you?'

'Twitch. It started when I was learning to hunt—and unfortunately the name stuck.'

Rabbit shifted his weight. 'Are we in the clear here or what?'

Ita rolled her eyes at Isabel. 'He takes safety very seriously.' She turned to him once more. 'Yes, all clear.'

Rabbit whistled, and two more people stepped out from their nearby hiding places, coming to stand on either side of him.

'Seal and Walnut,' Ita said, pointing. 'Walnut because she's quite palatable once you're through the tough exterior. I won't tell you the story behind Seal, because it requires a rather strong stomach.'

The others ventured closer but not too close.

'How did you know where to find us?' Walnut asked.

Isabel glanced back at Ita. 'I saw your mother. At the camp.'

'You were at the camp?' Rabbit asked.

Walnut looked Isabel up and down. 'As an invited guest, not a prisoner. This is Lady Isabel, the future Countess of Hereford. Hodge's muse.'

Isabel's eyebrows lifted. 'I see the St Clare group is up to date with news from Hampstead Keep.'

'How is she?' Ita asked. 'How's my mother?'

Isabel thought carefully about her answer. 'She seemed well.'

There was a beat of silence, and then Ita released Isabel's hand. 'And what did you think of the camp?'

'I could barely believe what I was seeing. They have children locked in pens, men chained together in the fields. Hundreds of people packed into sleeping quarters.'

The St Clare group all exchanged a look, one Isabel could not interpret.

Ita crossed her arms. 'It doesn't end there. The man you're to marry is capable of more than you know.'

Isabel shifted her weight. 'I know him well enough by now.'

'I doubt that' was Ita's reply. 'Tell me why you came here.'

'You know why. To find you.' Isabel raised her chin. 'Tell me why you let me believe you were dead all these years.'

'Because I couldn't reach you without him knowing.'

'Why can he not know?'

'I already told you why.' Ita's voice was laced with agitation. 'I'm safer dead.'

They watched each other through a veil of tension before Ita uncrossed her arms. 'Well, you found me. Now what?'

The question was a good one. Isabel's circumstances had changed because of this meeting. Her mother and brother were still waiting for her at Hampstead Keep, dependent on her sticking to the plan. 'I would like to visit Maddock House.'

Ita frowned. 'Why?'

No sensible reason came to mind. Her shoulders rose an inch. 'Because I want to visit my home.'

Ita's face filled with pity. 'Oh, Belle. There's nothing left of it.'

She knew that—she had watched it burn—but her throat closed all the same. 'I need to go home.'

Ita studied her for a long moment. 'Does Hodge know you're here?'

'No, and he will likely be looking for me by now.'

'Perfect,' Rabbit replied, head shaking.

Ita released a breath. 'Fine. I'll take you there.'

'No you won't,' Rabbit said quickly. 'Hodge will have soldiers tearing the forest apart searching for her.'

Isabel nodded in agreement. 'That is true. The last thing I want is to put any of you in danger. I shall make my own way there.'

Laughter burst from Ita. 'Alone? You'll never find it. You have the worst sense of direction of any person I've ever known.'

'Not true. I found *you*.'

Rabbit snorted. 'Right.'

All the laughter in Ita's eyes faded. 'Hodge will find you eventually.'

Isabel nodded. 'I know.'

Ita dropped her gaze and turned to the others. 'I'll take her by myself. The risk will be mine alone.'

The other three exchanged a look, and then Rabbit said, 'We'll all go, but no loitering. If Hodge knows of this house, then that'll be the first place he goes looking for her. And we travel in silence, like normal. The two of you will save the chitchat for a safer time and location. Understood?'

Ita turned back to Isabel with a smirk. 'He can be a little broody, but he really knows how to keep a lady alive.' Her eyes went to the trees. 'I'll get the horses.'

A few minutes later, the five of them were on their way to Maddock House.

They travelled without ever setting foot on a main road. The St Clare people seemed to read the forest the same way the defenders did, as if they shared a secret language with the trees and received warnings mere humans like Isabel were not privy to.

It took seven hours to get to Llanelieu. Seven hours of silence, afraid Hodge would find them before they reached Maddock House.

Isabel soaked up the vibrant scenery and familiar land-marks. The closer they got to Llanelieu, the more her soul awakened. She was thrilled to discover lush green surroundings, a contrast to the bleak, muddy landscape she had left behind five years earlier. She drew greedy lungfuls of air, savouring the smell of pine and honeysuckle.

'Welcome home,' Ita said quietly.

These were the only two words spoken throughout that time.

They were around a mile from the house when Walnut said, 'Wait here.' She and Seal rode ahead to ensure it was safe before they continued as a group.

All the good feelings Isabel had built up during the journey dissipated when she finally laid eyes on the crumbling remains of Maddock House. The stone walls were covered by moss and weeds. The stone path that led to the house was completely overgrown and no longer visible. The picket fence was gone, likely ripped out and used for firewood. The garden beds at the front now blended with the lawn. There was not a vegetable or flower in sight. Her mother's rosebushes were now thorny sticks poking from the ground. No hounds bounded out to greet them. There was no sign of life of any kind.

Isabel swallowed.

'It's hard to look at, isn't it?' Ita said.

Isabel could not speak, only stare.

'You have five minutes,' Rabbit told them. 'Then we need to set up camp before dark—as far from here as possible.'

The women dismounted and wandered over to the house, pushing debris around with their feet as if there was some chance they might salvage something from the past, but there was nothing. Anything of value was either now ash or had been taken by scavengers long ago. They stood in what was once the kitchen, remembering things.

'Yvaine was always yelling at us to either make ourselves useful or get out from under her feet,' Isabel said.

Ita smiled. 'Rarely did we make ourselves useful.'

'We would flee to the stables and annoy your father

instead.' Ita's father had died defending the home the same night Isabel's father was killed. Grief had hung over the household like a permanent grey cloud in the days that followed.

A whistle sounded behind them. They turned to look, and Seal gestured towards the trees. Ita grabbed Isabel's hand and began dragging her back towards the horses.

'We have to go.'

Panic reared up inside Isabel. It was one thing if she was found but quite another if Ita and her friends were caught.

The others loaded their bows and aimed them at the tree line along the south boundary. Isabel and Ita were a few feet from the horses when two men burst into view from the east shouting, 'Weapons on the ground—now!'

Rabbit and Walnut swung their bows around and took aim, but before they had a chance to shoot, arrows sliced through the strings of their bows, rendering them useless. Isabel's feet stopped. There were only a handful of people she knew with that level of accuracy.

Her eyes landed on Blackmane.

'I said weapons on the ground!' he shouted as he ran towards them, fury radiating from him.

Hadewaye took aim at Seal. 'I assure you no one will be asking a third time.'

Isabel raised her hands. 'Do not hurt them.'

Blackmane's dark eyes flashed at her. 'I'll deal with you in a minute.'

Rabbit reached for the dagger strapped to his leg.

'I *really* wouldn't do that,' Hadewaye said, stopping a safe distance from the group.

'Defenders,' Rabbit said through gritted teeth. 'She set us up.'

'No,' Isabel said.

Ita looked from Blackmane to Isabel. 'Are they here for you?'

Isabel swallowed. 'That is a very strong possibility.' She positioned herself in front of Ita. 'Everyone stay calm. Please. Let me handle this.'

Blackmane's eyes landed on her, as black as the charred ruins of Maddock House. Someone was clearly not happy about her little excursion.

Head high, she braced for impact.

CHAPTER 13

*A*ny other time, Blackmane would have shot every rebel dead, put Isabel on his horse, and ridden off before anyone else had a chance to join the fight. But he could tell by the way she stood in front of that woman, her expression determined, that this was Ita, the friend she had been searching for.

'You can't expect them to put their weapons down when you have yours pointed directly at them,' Isabel told Blackmane. She looked around at the others. 'What if we all agree not to kill each other for a moment while we sort this out?'

The St Clare group looked between themselves, a non-verbal conversation. Then Ita said, 'Let's see the defender put his away first.'

Blackmane signalled to Hadewaye, and they lowered their bows at the same time. Then his eyes returned to Isabel. 'What the hell were you thinking leaving the camp by yourself?'

Scowling, she walked over to him. 'I am not a prisoner, you know. I am free to come and go as I please.'

He pointed to the others. 'Do you even know all these people?'

She looked over her shoulder. 'A good percentage of them, yes.'

'Twenty-five percent of them?'

She swallowed. 'If Ita trusts them, then I trust them.'

Her naivety was sending him mad. 'So you're safe in their company, then? These people are going to protect you from Hodge's mood? Return you to the camp later when you're done reminiscing?'

It was clear by her expression that she had no real plan.

'You know,' she began, crossing her arms, 'you have the most unusual way of expressing concern for my safety.'

'So you *are* safe?'

She hesitated. 'Yes.'

He nodded slowly. 'Great. Then I'll leave you to it.' He looked past her to the others. 'There are guards swarming the area. You might want to fix your bows before they get here.' Then he gestured to Hadewaye. 'We're leaving.' With that, he turned his back to Isabel and walked away.

She ran after him, catching hold of his arm. 'Wait.'

He stopped. 'What?'

'Are you angry at me?'

He brought his face close to hers. 'Am I *angry*? My rage is barely contained right now. So I suggest you get your hands off me and go back to your friends.'

She let go of him, eyes never leaving his. He should

have walked away at that point, but her wounded expression held him in place.

'I only learned yesterday that she was alive,' Isabel said. 'I knew this was my only chance to see her. You know as well as I do that it will be a long time before Hodge ever lets me leave Hampstead Keep again.'

The muscles in his face relaxed. 'You need to go somewhere else. Hodge will most certainly come here looking for you.'

Ignoring his earlier warning, she reached for his arm again. 'Come with us. Your horses must be exhausted, and soon you will lose light. We can make camp somewhere.' She hesitated before continuing. 'And in the morning, I will return with you and explain to Hodge that I foolishly went for a ride and got myself lost.'

His eyes moved between hers. 'So you plan to return to him?'

She lifted her shoulders in a resigned shrug. 'My family remains at Hampstead Keep. My circumstances have not changed.'

He really only had two choices at that point: stay and ensure she got safely back to the camp, or go ahead without her and hope Ita was up to the task. He looked over at Hadewaye, who was watching them with a slightly amused expression. 'Fetch the horses.'

'Is Lady Isabel coming with us?' the defender asked.

Blackmane's gaze returned to her. 'She'll return with us in the morning. We need to find somewhere safe to make camp tonight.'

Isabel smiled up at him victoriously while Hadewaye went to fetch the horses.

'Do you mean all together?' Ita asked.

The man with the scar on his face shook his head. 'I'm not sleeping next to defenders.'

The woman on the horse next to his frowned. 'I don't think he meant side by side.'

'Safety in numbers' was Isabel's reply.

The St Clare people looked suitably wary.

'We're going to need to hunt,' Blackmane said. 'Or go hungry.'

'Oh, you can leave that to me,' Isabel said, raising an arm into the air and looking around.

Blackmane blinked, confused. 'What are you doing?'

'Waiting for Margery. She is far more efficient at hunting than any of us.'

He looked to Ita to gauge if she was serious. 'The *eagle's* going to hunt for us?'

'Assuming she is... ah, there she is.' Margery appeared overhead, circling a few times before coming to land on Isabel. 'How do you feel about catching us a couple hares? Go hunt.'

As though comprehending the request, the eagle took flight.

'Dinner is on its way, defender.'

Ita and the others were talking in a hushed voice and looking in his direction.

Hadewaye returned with their horses, handing the reins of his mare to Blackmane. 'You sure about this?'

'No' was his reply. 'Let's go.'

The group travelled around four miles to a dense section of forest, then lit two separate campfires. Margery returned with not one but two hares, dropping the corpses at Isabel's feet like a dog. Hadewaye and Black-mane went to skin and clean the hares while the two women got reacquainted.

'How often have you seen Margery over the years?' Isabel asked after the eagle had gotten her fill of attention and flown off. She sat well back from the fire with her cloak pulled tightly around her.

'Sometimes I would go months without seeing her at all. Then she would find me, and I'd be so happy, because I knew each time she was coming from you.' Ita took a drink from her waterskin and handed it to Isabel. 'But then she started staying with me for longer periods, and I began to worry about you.'

'So you tied things to her legs to see if I was still alive?'

'Oh, I knew you were alive. I just had no idea what state you were in.'

Hadewaye took his hare over to the other group. The one they called Rabbit took it, muttering some form of thank you, and then the two groups cooked their food at their own fire.

Blackmane went to fetch his blanket, tossing it to Isabel. 'Here. I'm cold just looking at you.'

Ita studied him. 'How incredibly kind of you, defender. Do I get a blanket too?'

He glanced in her direction, noting her half smirk. 'I only have one, and you're near the fire.'

Hadewaye passed his blanket to Ita. 'You can use mine. I'm on first watch.'

Ita looked genuinely taken aback. As the defender rose, she said, 'I actually have one. I was just—'

'Making trouble,' Blackmane finished. He looked up at Hadewaye. 'We'll save you some food.'

'The guards rarely move around at night,' Ita told them.

Blackmane poked at the meat. 'Forgive us if we don't take our safety advice straight from the enemy.'

'It's difficult to comprehend why people hate defenders so much,' Ita said to Isabel. 'I assume they're not all this bad?'

Isabel stifled a yawn. 'He is actually a big softie underneath all that leather.'

Ita's eyes shone with mischievousness. 'So you've seen underneath the uniform, then?'

Ignoring her, Blackmane took the meat off the flames and set it aside to cool for a moment.

'What's the reason for all that hostility, defender?' Ita asked. 'Something must have happened that has you wearing this attitude like another form of armour. Usually it's a tragic story.'

Isabel looked at him. 'Is there a tragic story?'

'No,' he replied.

'Ah, yes,' Hadewaye called from somewhere nearby.

Blackmane rolled his eyes in the defender's general direction. 'Stop eavesdropping and concentrate on keeping us alive.'

'He lost his entire family before coming to Chadora,' Hadewaye replied as if he had not heard.

Blackmane picked up the meat and began tearing pieces off.

'That'll do it,' Ita said.

He could feel Isabel watching him in the dark.

'How did they die?' she asked.

'Smallpox.' He rose and walked over to her, handing her some of the meat without making eye contact.

'Dreadful disease,' Ita said, shaking her head sadly.

He went to give her a portion also. 'Never mind all that. I want you to tell me about the camp.'

She waited for him to sit down again. 'You mean to tell me that you came all this way and didn't get the full tour?'

'Hodge was a little sketchy on some of the details, like where all the food's going.'

Ita began picking through her meat. 'The food doesn't stay in Carmarthenshire, that's for sure. Most is transported west and loaded onto ships.'

He wondered if King Edward was aware of that.

'Word from inside the camp is that the marcher lords are running quite the lucrative business,' Ita added.

Isabel leaned forwards. 'Did you say word from *inside* the camp?'

'Yes, those who make it out are often armed with more information than Hodge is comfortable with.'

'And how does one make it out?' Blackmane asked.

Ita swallowed her mouthful of meat before answering. 'There are only two ways out of that place—as a corpse on the back of a wagon or escaping over the fence.'

Blackmane's eyebrows came together. 'The fence is heavily guarded. They would be caught before they'd even secured a rope.'

Ita nodded in agreement. 'Oh, there's no time for rope. The only way out is via the woodpile against the fence at the back of the kitchen. If you get a run up, you can use it as a step to reach the top. Of course, the wood needs to be stacked correctly or it can result in spectacular failure.' She threw bones on the fire. 'But it's not for the faint of heart or the unfit. Any prisoner caught outside the fence line without permission is publicly executed. They never waste an opportunity to teach those inside a lesson— comply or die.'

Isabel looked down at her lap. 'But how do they know who is from the camp and who is not?'

'You've been gone too long, my darling friend.' Ita tucked her legs in beside her. 'There are only two kinds of people left in the wastelands: criminals who have been caught and criminals yet to be caught. They don't care which one you are. Both are enslaved or killed in the end.'

Blackmane picked up a stick to move one of the burning logs, and immediately Isabel moved back from the fire. He put the stick down. 'What form of execution do they use?' He wanted to better understand their mind-set.

Ita closed her eyes for a moment. 'At first it was a simple hanging, but when the message didn't get through, they became graphic events. It's not uncommon for people to be drawn and quartered, disembowelled, or burned alive.'

Isabel stared off into the dark. 'Now I understand why your mother did not want to leave with me. Leaving is not freedom.'

Ita watched the flames. 'You should know better than anyone that no one is free anymore. There are just different forms of prisons outside the camp. It's understandable why most choose the safety of shackles.'

Isabel shuffled forwards slightly until Ita looked at her. 'I need to know what happened the night of the fire.'

The tension in the air was instant. Blackmane wondered if he should leave, but Isabel's eyes were already shiny with tears, so he stayed.

'I think it's too soon for this conversation,' Ita said, looking back at the fire.

'You have had five years to think about what you would say to me if we crossed paths.' There was a long pause. 'I tried to get to you, and the door was locked. That door had never been locked in the fifteen years I lived in the house.'

Ita's gaze fell to Isabel's scarred hand. 'We crawled out the small window at the top.'

Isabel looked thoroughly confused. '*Why?* Did you not hear me pounding on the door? If Hodge had not dragged me from the house, then I would have been buried in it while waiting for you to appear.' Her voice broke. 'I have spent the past five years wishing you were alive, going over every detail of that night in my head, wondering if I could have gotten you out if I had stayed a little longer, fought a little harder. And now I find out that you were not even behind the door I tried so hard to open.' She scratched at her scarred hand, breaths coming faster. 'Why did you lock the door?'

Ita's face looked pale despite the orange light from the fire. 'We didn't lock it. It was locked from the outside.'

Isabel blinked and fell silent for a moment. 'What?'

Blackmane stared at the flames, having already figured out the end of the story.

'He wanted us dead,' Ita said. 'So we climbed out, and we ran. We couldn't risk being seen.'

'Who wanted you dead?' Isabel demanded, her voice raised and choked.

Ita reached out and stilled Isabel's hands. 'Hodge locked the door.' She swallowed. 'He locked the door, and he lit the fire.' There was a brief pause. 'The only reason we're still alive is because he thinks we're dead.'

*I*t took Isabel a moment to piece the threads together, to accept what Ita was actually telling her. It took longer than it should have because her mind was repelling the facts. 'No. No. I know he has his faults, but he would never…'

He would, though. He was very good at removing obstacles.

'I woke up to noise in the kitchen,' Ita said. 'I peered through the keyhole to see who it was and saw Hodge fiddling with the stove. I had no idea what he was doing, so I kept watching, curious. Suddenly the kitchen went up in flames. And not small flames but instant fire, climbing all the way to the ceiling. Hodge fled and screamed at my mother to wake up. When I went to open the door, it was locked.'

Isabel pulled her hand from Ita's. 'Maybe it was an accident.' Her throat closed. 'The man would have no idea how to use a stove.'

Ita tilted her head, face filling with pity. 'Seven days it

took that man to fall in love with you. You were barely fifteen. Marriage was the last thing on your mind, and he knew that.' She smiled. '*I* was the love of your life at that age. *I* was the person who made you laugh, who walked with you arm in arm. We used to laugh at how ridiculous he was, do you remember?'

Isabel nodded. 'I remember.'

'I was in the way,' Ita said. 'And the fact that you already had a home, one you and your mother wished to remain in, was problematic. Gwenore wasn't scared off by the rebel groups moving through Carmarthenshire at the time.'

'My husband died defending this home,' her mother had told Lord Tompkin the first time he asked for her hand.

He had been respectful of that because *he* was a good person. When the house was gone, she had been left with no choice but to accept his hand.

'Hodge knew exactly what he was doing,' Ita finished.

Pressing her palms to her eyes, Isabel drew a shaky breath. The air felt stifling suddenly, despite being quite far from the fire. 'I need a minute.' She rose and walked twenty yards or so, leaning against a tree for balance.

'You can't just wander off' came Blackmane's voice in the dark.

She startled and spun around.

'Sorry,' he said.

She hugged herself against the cold. 'I cannot breathe that close to flames.'

He stopped a few feet from her. 'You all right?'

'I cannot marry that man. I did not want to marry him

to begin with, but now…' She shook her head. 'I pray this new information will finally convince my mother that he is bad news for the whole family.'

He watched her in the dark. 'You're going to have to be smart about this. Hodge has the power to raise you up like a queen and tear you down just as fast.'

'I do not care about that. If it were not for my family, I would have scaled the walls of Hampstead Keep long ago. Or jumped from them,' she added quietly.

He dropped his gaze.

'This is so much bigger than me and my family. You saw the people in that camp.'

'I did.'

'We can help them.'

'We?' he asked, looking up.

'All of us. We can work together to get them out.'

'You going to join forces with your new St Clare friends? Whose numbers have dwindled so low they've resorted to hiding?'

She stepped up to him, reaching for his weapon, but he caught her hand. His grip was firm enough to hold her in place without hurting her. She did not have the same urge to pull away that she had with Hodge.

'What are you doing?' he asked.

'I want to feel how heavy your sword is.'

'You going to learn how to fight too?'

'That depends on the weight.'

His gaze fell to her mouth. 'That's not a good idea.'

The heat in his stare made her step back, and he let go of her the second she did. 'My father would not let me near weapons of any kind. He wanted me to be a proper lady, like my mother. I do regularly watch my brother spar, however. I have often wondered if I have it in me to kill a man.'

'And what did you decide?'

'The right man, perhaps.' She saw him smile at the ground. *Smile*. 'Will you help me?'

He looked up. 'Kill a man? That depends on the who and why.'

'I meant help me get them out.'

'I know what you meant.' He exhaled. 'Not unless I'm ordered to.'

'But you are a defender. You protect people.'

'A defender who follows orders, and I've been instructed to observe and ensure Hodge gets safely back to Hampstead Keep.'

'Well, that is terribly inconvenient.'

He watched her with an amused expression.

'What if I decide to get my revenge on Hodge?'

'I'd suggest you do that in private to avoid my inter-ference.'

Her eyes widened with realisation. 'Does that make us enemies? Will we meet on the battlefield, swords in hand and bloody-faced, eyes locking on each other mere moments before our fate is decided?'

He bit back another smile. 'I think you're getting your-self confused with Isabel of Conches.'

'Now *she* could handle a sword.'

'She could, yes.'

Isabel fell silent for a few seconds. 'Would you struggle to kill me if ordered to?'

'Yes.'

The speed of his reply made her chest feel light. 'That might be the nicest thing you have ever said to me.'

They watched each other for a moment.

'What am I supposed to do now?' she asked, her voice barely above a whisper.

'That depends on the outcome you're chasing. The safest path is to return to Hodge and forget everything you just learned. Let Ita remain dead, and avoid her mother when you reach the camp.'

'What if I chose to be dead too?'

His brow creased with concern. 'That's not as easy as you think. If the woman I loved went missing, I wouldn't stop searching until I had a corpse to confirm it.'

'So, you want me to marry him?'

'I want you *safe*.'

There was that feeling in her chest again. 'I stand corrected. *That* was the nicest thing you have ever said to me.'

He immediately looked away. 'Why don't you get some sleep? You'll think more clearly in the morning.'

She nodded. 'All right.'

He gestured for her to go ahead of him, and they made their way back to the camp. When they arrived, Ita stood and walked over to Isabel, hugging her tightly.

'I'm sorry,' she whispered.

Isabel pressed her eyes closed. 'It is not your fault. You did what you had to.'

Ita released her and dabbed the corner of her eye. 'I'm going to take first watch.'

'Hadewaye's on watch,' Blackmane said.

She looked directly at him. 'Forgive me, defender, if I

don't entrust the safety of my group to the enemy.' Smirking, she disappeared into the dark.

Blackmane went to add another log to the fire but, after seeing Isabel's face, changed his mind.

'Have you ever slept outdoors before?' he asked.

'In the summer, when we were children.'

'The temperature will continue to drop. You're going to want to sleep close to the fire.'

She looked around. 'What if one of the logs does that popping thing and embers land on the blanket?'

'It's wool. It won't burn.'

'Or lands in my hair? That happened to a cousin of mine once.'

Exhaling, he dragged his bedroll a good distance away and gestured to it. 'You go ahead.'

'I cannot take your bed.'

'I have a fire to keep me warm, remember?'

They lay on their backs, him beside the fire wrapped in his cloak and Isabel four feet back from it huddled beneath the blanket. The St Clare people, clearly used to sleeping in these conditions, were already asleep.

As the temperature dropped, cold air seeped through the blanket, and Isabel's teeth began to chatter.

'You're too far away from the fire,' Blackmane said quietly.

'I will be fine once I fall asleep.'

He turned on his side and looked at her. 'How do you expect to fall asleep with your teeth clanging away in your mouth?'

It felt like he was closer when he was facing her like

that. She had a strange urge to reach for him. 'Will you lie next to me for a minute? Until I am warm?'

He blinked at her in the dark. 'I don't think that's a good idea.'

She opened the blanket to him. When he did not move, she held it open, waiting, her shivers growing as the small amount of warmth she had generated was carried away by the breeze.

With a resigned breath, he crawled to her, covering them both. The warmth from him was instant and better than any fire. He was so rigid at first, but when her legs found his beneath the blanket, he began to relax.

'I am so sorry about what happened to your family,' Isabel said.

'Don't be. You didn't kill them.'

'But to lose everyone...' His face was mere inches from hers, his warm breath hitting her skin every time he spoke. 'What were their names?'

There was a spell of silence. 'My parents were Kinnat and Domangard, but people in our village called him Dom.'

'What about your siblings?'

He was tensing up again. 'Morna and Tolly.'

'Older or younger?'

'Morna was older, Tolly younger.' He swallowed. 'Now go to sleep.'

She studied his face. 'You do not like to talk about them.'

'My dead family? No.'

'Why?'

'Because they're dead.'

She noted his clipped tone. 'And now you're angry.'

'Because you're supposed to be going to sleep, and instead we're having this conversation.'

She waited a moment before asking, 'What was your sister like?'

He was quiet for such a long time that she thought he was not going to answer. 'Morna was always the loudest person in the room.'

Isabel smiled at that. 'And were you always the quietest?'

He nodded. 'My mother always said it was because I did not stand a chance against her in social settings.'

'What about your brother, Tolly?'

He went silent again as he remembered. 'He was a lot like me, actually.'

'Mean-spirited and always in a mood?'

His lips twitched. 'He had my adventurous spirit, loved to read and learn, but he also had a big heart and a joke always ready. He was funny. People liked that about him.'

A few minutes passed.

'Who was with you at the end,' she asked.

'Tolly—until I sent him away.' Blackmane swallowed. 'He would be twenty-one this year.'

She could hear the pain lacing his words.

'He didn't want to board. Fought me the whole way to the port. I had to drag him up the gangplank, then wait on the dock to make sure he didn't jump overboard and swim back to shore.'

Isabel's throat thickened. 'Was he healthy then?'

A nod. 'My sister was also alive then—barely. I needed

to stay and take care of her, to bury her. I planned to meet him in Wales.'

Isabel's hand went to his chest. 'Did he catch it on the ship?'

'Maybe. Or maybe he brought it to the ship.' He paused. 'It doesn't matter now. They wouldn't let anyone ashore before setting it alight.'

Oh God. Her hand moved to his cheek. 'And now you feel guilty because you lived and they did not. You blame yourself for Tolly's death and wonder if he would be alive if he had stayed with you.'

His hand went over hers, heavy and calloused.

'Now I understand why you take your job so seriously,' she said. 'Failing those under your protection feels like failing him all over again.'

Blackmane searched her eyes for a long moment, then removed her hand from his face. 'I think you're warm enough now.' Pulling back the blanket, he climbed out, tucking it around her before returning to the fire.

CHAPTER 15

Blackmane relieved Hadewaye from his post a little after midnight. He sat in the dark twenty yards from the fire, alternating between watching his surroundings and watching Isabel sleep. She was hard to look away from. The man they called Seal studied the trees opposite. The two men made a point of staying out of each other's way.

Hadewaye woke a little before sunrise and came to find him. 'Everything quiet?'

Blackmane nodded.

'So what's the plan?'

Blackmane looked over to where she was sleeping. 'I don't see she has much choice but to go back to him.'

'I feel for her, knowing what he did.'

Blackmane was trying not to think about it, because every time he did, his jaw tightened and his hands curled into fists. 'We should do a proper check of the area and separate from the St Clare people as soon as possible.'

Hadewaye nodded. 'I'll go. You wake Lady Isabel and make a plan.'

It was a conversation Blackmane was dreading. Even if she agreed with him and returned to the camp, he could not predict the outcome of her reunion with Hodge. But running was not an option, not from that man. He would lose his mind, and it would be the wastelanders who paid the price for her disappearance.

Hadewaye mounted his horse and cantered away. Seal had now returned to the other campfire and was dousing it with water, likely thinking along the same lines as them.

Drawing a breath, Blackmane headed for Isabel. He was halfway there when he felt the small hairs on the back of his neck stand up. He whipped his head around, listening. Nothing. Yet the hairs remained erect.

Changing course, he went straight over to Ita, who was now sitting upright, watching him.

'What's wrong?' she asked.

'Don't know yet.' He glanced at Rabbit, who was now tugging on his boots. 'But I think you should all get as far away from us as possible.'

Ita stood up and looked over at Isabel. 'Is she going back to him?'

'Do you see another way?'

Her throat bobbed, and she shook her head. 'Will you take care of her?'

'While I can.'

Her expression bordered on heartbroken as she went to join the others, who had already gathered their belongings and were preparing to mount. They had done this dance before—likely many times.

Blackmane went to retrieve his bow and quiver, eyes going to the trees around them. All was still.

'Isabel,' he said. 'It's time to go.' He snatched up his waterskin and threw the contents over the fire. It hissed, sending swirls of smoke into the air.

Isabel blinked her eyes open and sat up, looking over at Ita, who was now on her horse preparing to leave. 'What's going on?'

A flash of movement in the trees caught Blackmane's eye. Turning, he gestured for the other group to move out. Something told him if they did not leave now, they would not be leaving at all.

Isabel scrambled to her feet and went to run after Ita, but Blackmane caught her around the waist and brought his mouth to her ear. 'Do you want her to live?'

She went limp against him.

The sound of hooves prompted Blackmane to swing Isabel behind him and load his bow.

Hadeweye rode into sight. 'Get out of here—now.'

Margery appeared overhead, swooping down over them with a shrill chirp.

'It is too late,' Isabel said. 'They are already here.'

Hiss.

Blackmane heard the arrow before it hit its target. Seal roared as an arrow struck his chest, toppling backwards off his horse. Walnut dismounted and ran to him while Ita and Rabbit released arrow after arrow into the trees.

Hiss, hiss.

An arrow pierced Rabbit's leg, and another flew past Blackmane's head. They were all going to die if he did not do something. Since shooting at English guards was not an option for him, he did the only thing he could.

'Cease fire!' he shouted. 'I have Lady Isabel with me.'

The shooting stopped, and the trees went still around them. A full minute passed before a handful of guards emerged, weapons ready. Hadewaye had his bow loaded and aimed at them, but the weapon was as useless as Blackmane's in that moment.

Hodge and Tatum appeared next, and Blackmane heard Isabel suck in a breath behind him. Tatum's gaze shifted left and right, and he appeared visibly confused by the scene before him.

'Someone better start talking,' he said.

Blackmane looked over to where Seal was gasping for air while coughing up blood. 'There was no need for that.'

Hodge stopped his horse, looking from Blackmane to Isabel, who was still hiding behind him. 'Bring her to me —right now.'

Blackmane could not bring himself to lower his bow.

'Weapon down, defender,' Tatum said.

That was when he realised his bow was pointed at Hodge.

'I suggest you listen to your commander and get out of my way,' the earl said.

It took all his effort to lower his weapon and step aside.

'Beloved,' Hodge said, extending a hand. 'Come. You are safe now.'

Isabel made no move towards him.

Confused by the response, Hodge looked over at the St

Clare people. Recognition settled on his face when his eyes landed on Ita. 'You.'

She lifted her chin. 'Me.'

A flash of panic passed over his face before he regained his composure. 'Where did you come from?'

'The brink of death,' Ita replied. 'Right where you left me.'

Tatum looked to Blackmane for clues as to what was going on, but it was not a conversation that could be had without words.

'Tell your men to put their weapons away,' Ita said, 'or my final living act will be releasing this arrow into your face.'

Hodge laughed abruptly. 'You always were a rather unstable sort of girl. Whomever thought it was a good idea to hand you a weapon clearly does not know you as I do.'

Her bow creaked, and every guard around them shifted nervously in their saddles. Tatum also had an arrow trained on her, but Blackmane knew instinctively that he would not be the one to shoot her.

'I should have known you had something to do with her disappearance.' He seemed unafraid of the arrow aimed at his face. 'Tell me, what lies have you told my beloved that have her in such a state?'

'There is only one liar among us, my lord.'

Hodge exhaled sharply through his nose. 'It is clear that you have gotten away with this behaviour for too long.' He looked to the guard on his left. 'Kill her.'

The defenders raised their bows, a reflex. What happened next should have been part of an elaborate plan but was simply a result of serving closely with someone for five years and being able to predict their actions. Blackmane took aim at the guard's bow, sending it jolting sideways so it missed Ita entirely. Simultaneously, Tatum struck the arrow headed for Hodge mid-air, splitting it in two.

Miraculously, no one was injured.

Isabel ran forwards. 'Stop. I will come with you. Just stop.'

Hodge raised a hand, pausing the onslaught that was about to unfold. He had that unhinged look in his eyes that Blackmane had come to recognise.

'Do you know how worried I was?' he asked Isabel. 'I lay awake all night imagining the things that might be happening to you.'

'I am sorry.' Her voice was shaky. 'I want to return to the camp with you. Please.'

Slowly, the muscles in his neck began to relax. But there was more he wanted to say on the subject. 'And to come here and find you liaising with our *enemy*.' His eyes went to Ita. 'Did you honestly think you could simply show up after five years and be welcomed back into her life?'

Ita glared back at him, saying nothing.

Rabbit and Walnut had managed to reload their bows, but they were grossly outnumbered. Seal was no longer gasping. He was completely still.

'Let them all go,' Isabel said to Hodge, 'and we will leave together, right now.'

He gave her a pitiful look. 'You are smarter than that. You know how this ends. Now, let my men do their job.'

'Then I refuse to return to the camp with you,' Isabel replied, her voice raised.

The corners of his mouth lifted. 'And where will you be going instead? To live among the trees, in the mud, with these ruffians? Will you tell your mother, or shall I?'

Isabel looked defeated. 'Please. She is my dearest friend.'

'She is trouble is what she is.'

Blackmane was watching the drama unfold down a fresh arrow. So were the guards. There were arrows pointing in all directions as everyone held their breath, waiting to see what Hodge would say next.

Before he had a chance, Walnut shot one of the guards through the stomach. Three arrows hit her half a second later. Rabbit released his straight into the face of one of the men. Blackmane was about to draw his sword when Tatum's horse appeared in front of him.

'If you cross this line, we'll be forced to cross with you.'

He was right. Once they started, it would not end until every guard was dead. And then what? They would be forced to kill Hodge, too, breaking a direct order.

In his peripheral vision, Blackmane saw Isabel run for Ita, flinging herself at her friend and wrapping her like a human shield.

'Cease fire!' Hodge shouted.

Blackmane stepped around Tatum's horse at the same time Isabel pulled an arrow from the quiver on Ita's back. She pressed the tip of it to her neck before turning to Hodge.

'If she dies, I die,' she said through gritted teeth.

All the colour left Hodge's face. 'Put that down before you hurt yourself.'

'Not unless you agree to let them both walk away, unharmed,' she said, ice in her tone. 'Promise me that, and I will come with you now. If one more arrow reaches them, I will drive this through my neck.' She blinked back tears. 'Do you hear me?'

Ita dropped to her knees beside Walnut, staring down at her dead friend.

Hodge raised his hands in a calming gesture. 'All right.'

'Swear it,' Isabel demanded. Her hand was shaking now, the tip of the arrow drawing blood.

This was one of those rare moments where Blackmane felt completely helpless. He had no control over the situation, and the fact that Hodge did made it so much worse.

The earl swallowed. 'All right. I swear it.'

Hodge rode over to Isabel, holding out his hand for the arrow.

She looked at Ita. 'I am so sorry.'

Ita was too grief-stricken to even look up.

Slowly, Isabel removed the arrow from her neck, handing it to Hodge. The earl took it from her before gesturing to one of the guards to fetch her mare. When Isabel was safely on her horse, he looked at Tatum. 'The tour ends here, Commander. I think you have seen all there is to see.' His gaze slid to Blackmane. 'It is time for you and your men to go home.'

Blackmane went to take a step towards him, but Tatum drew his sword and swung it downwards, blocking his path.

Hodge's eyes never left Blackmane. 'I would not loiter

if I were you, defender.' With that he turned his horse away.

Blackmane's stomach twisted at the sight of Isabel on that horse with tears pouring down her cheeks and blood trailing down her neck. She did not so much as glance in his direction, and he was grateful for the fact. The last thing he wanted to do was add fuel to a fire he would not be there to oversee.

Hodge walked his horse over to Isabel's, taking the reins from her and dragging them up over the mare's neck. He wrapped them around his hand twice, clearly not taking any chances. Then, looking at Tatum, he said, 'Safe travels, Commander.'

Every muscle in Blackmane's body turned to stone as she was led away. The moment she was gone from sight, he turned to the closest tree and slammed his fist into it.

CHAPTER 16

*B*lackmane paced in front of Tatum, knuckles bleeding.

'Just so I'm clear,' the commander said, looking thoroughly confused. 'The woman crying next to the corpses over there is Ita, Isabel's friend who died in a fire five years ago—a fire Hodge started. Except she isn't dead. She was pretending to be dead so Hodge wouldn't find her and kill her—again. And she wants to shoot an arrow into her closest friend's soon-to-be husband's face.' He paused, looking in Ita's direction. 'And in case that's not weird enough, all her other friends are named after things found in nature.'

Hadewaye looked equally as confused by that point. 'You know, I think the longer version of the story is better.'

Alveye, who had been with the reinforcements during the whole thing, appeared through the trees on foot with his horse trailing behind him. He froze when he saw Ita and Rabbit, then looked down at the corpses. 'What did I miss?'

Tatum rubbed his forehead. 'Quite a lot.'

'Did you see Hodge?' Hadewaye asked.

Alveye continued towards them. 'Yes. He informed me that I was going home and offered nothing beyond that.' He gestured over his shoulder and lowered his voice. 'Did *we* kill those people?'

Tatum shook his head.

Blackmane headed over to Ita, who was inspecting Rabbit's wound, and crouched beside her. 'Do you have someone who can take this arrow out?'

Ita nodded. 'But they're a long way from here.'

Rabbit was pale and sweating, obviously in a lot of pain.

'Barbed or non-barbed?' Hadewaye asked, appearing above them.

Blackmane reached for one of the missed arrows poking out of the ground, pulled it out, and inspected the tip. 'Non-barbed.'

'That makes no sense given their enemy doesn't wear any armour, but'—Hadewaye looked at Rabbit and clapped his hands together—'it's good news for you. I can take it out for you.'

Rabbit shook his head. 'No.'

Ita bit her lip. 'It might be safer than leaving it in.'

Hadewaye pointed to a nearby tree. 'Would you look at that? A juggling goat.'

Rabbit looked up, and Hadewaye tugged the arrow out of his leg.

'Fuck,' the rebel grunted.

Hadewaye pressed down on the wound and nodded in the direction of his horse. 'Grab a bandage from my saddlebag, would you?'

'Goats don't climb trees,' Rabbit said, staring at Hadewaye's bloodied hand.

'They also don't juggle,' Hadewaye replied, 'but I'll let that slide, because you look ready to pass out.'

Blackmane returned with supplies, and Hadewaye got to work bandaging the wound. Afterwards, Ita dropped her forehead to Rabbit's shoulder, then looked up at the defenders. 'Thank you.'

Hadewaye handed her a clean bandage. 'You'll need to change it later. You don't want it getting infected.'

'Right, yes. I can do that. Can you... can you help me get him on a horse?' She looked at her dead friends. 'And I'd like to take the others with us too.'

Blackmane could hear Isabel's voice in his head. *'Are you just going to let her travel through the wastelands with an injured friend and two corpses in tow?'*

He went to speak with Tatum.

The commander took one look at his face and said, 'Ah, here we go.'

Blackmane quirked an eyebrow. 'What does that mean?'

'You're about to do that thing.'

'What thing?'

'That thing where I'm over here making a plan, and then you show up with another one that's in complete opposition to mine.'

Blackmane did not deny it. 'I would like permission to remain behind and escort Ita home.'

Tatum gave Alveye an 'I told you so' look. 'No. Hodge has made his wishes very clear. He wants us gone.'

Alveye cleared his throat. 'That said, is it safe for a lady to travel through these parts with two dead companions and one barely holding on?'

Tatum crossed his arms. 'Have you forgotten why we came here in the first place?'

Alveye and Blackmane exchanged a look.

'Don't do that,' Tatum said.

'Do what?' Alveye asked innocently.

He pointed between the two defenders. 'Make me out to be the bastard, unfeeling commander. Someone has to be the sensible one.'

Hadewaye, who had clearly been eavesdropping, wandered over to join the conversation. 'Alveye and I could go ahead, update the warden and King Becket on everything that's happened. We'll simply tell them you had some urgent business to tend to and you're a few days behind us.'

'Great idea,' Tatum said. 'We'll lie to the king.'

Blackmane looked over to where Rabbit was attempting to get to his feet. Ita would never be able to get him on and off his horse without help.

'This is your fault,' Tatum said, pulling Blackmane back into the conversation. 'Of all the women you could have fallen for.'

'I didn't fall for anyone.'

Alveye laughed, then coughed to cover it up.

'What?' Blackmane hissed at him.

'You fell for her immediately,' he said, 'the very first time you saw her standing atop that wall. You, who hates everyone in the world, were brought to your knees by a woman you didn't even know.'

Blackmane opened his mouth to object, then closed it again. It was true. She had quickly gotten under his skin, and lying about it would not change the fact. 'It doesn't matter. It was never going to be anything more than fleeting attraction.' The fleeting part was a lie, but he ran with it anyway. 'She'll marry Lord Lunatic, I'll return to Chadora, and we'll all move on with our lives.'

Alveye tutted. 'I worry about her, though. Hodge is like one of those children who hugs puppies to death, then gets upset even though they're to blame.'

Everyone stared at him.

He looked between them. 'What? Am I wrong?'

Hadewaye shook his head. 'I mean, we're all thinking it, but did you have to say it out loud? The man's just lost the only woman he's ever cared for.'

Blackmane pinched the bridge of his nose. 'Can I stay an extra few days or not?'

Tatum released a noisy breath and looked over at Rabbit, who was now attempting to mount with little success. 'If Hodge finds out we're still here, he'll likely imprison us alongside the wastelanders.'

Blackmane's eyebrows came together. 'If he finds out *we're* still here?'

'Obviously I'm not going to let you traipse through rebel territory alone.' He looked at Alveye and Hadewaye. 'I want you two to head directly to Chadora and give the warden and King Becket a thorough overview of the situation. Explain that we stayed behind to assist a friend of Lady Isabel's. That part is key. And feel free to exaggerate her condition. If the warden asks me upon my return if this woman was pregnant and missing a leg, I'll back that story all the way.' He held up a hand. 'And for God's sake, nobody die. The consequences I'll face will be so much worse if I lose one of you boneheads. Understood?'

Alveye blinked. 'Was that speech supposed to be inspiring?'

Hadewaye smirked at the ground.

'The correct response is "Yes, Commander,"' Tatum prompted.

The pair muttered, 'Yes, Commander,' then headed for their horses.

'You don't have to stay,' Blackmane said when it was just the two of them. 'I can take care of myself.'

Tatum rolled his eyes. 'Like you took care of yourself at Harlech Castle all those years ago when you were shot and fell into a pit of mud?'

Blackmane did not reply.

'Come on,' Tatum said. 'Let's get the man on a horse while he's still able to sit on one.'

They went to join Ita and Rabbit, taking hold of the injured man and lifting him onto the horse. Then they wrapped the dead in their cloaks and tied them to the saddles of the spare horses.

'Thank you,' Ita said, eyeing Walnut's filthy boots that were poking out from beneath the cloak.

'We're going to escort you back to your group,' Blackmane said.

Her brow creased. 'You don't have to do that.'

'It seems any friend of Lady Isabel's is a friend of ours,' Tatum said dryly.

Ita wiped her face, which was still wet with tears from earlier, then said to Blackmane, 'She doesn't stand a chance against him.'

'I know.'

'Never did. He set his sights on her, and there was no stopping him.' She sniffed. 'I'm going to get her out of there and away from him. We're going to get all of them out. We just need some more time.'

He wondered exactly what that plan entailed.

'We'll deal with the dead. You worry about Rabbit,' he said before mounting.

'And if you're struggling,' Tatum said, catching Rabbit's eye, 'I'd prefer to know before you fall from your horse and smack your head on the ground. Understand?'

The rebel nodded.

Blackmane looked over at Alveye and Hadewaye, who were preparing to head off in the other direction. There was an exchange of nods and salutes.

'Remember what I said,' Tatum called to the other defenders. 'Stay alive—so I don't get into trouble.'

The corners of Blackmane's mouth turned up as he nudged his horse forwards.

CHAPTER 17

*I*sabel was as much a prisoner in that camp as any other person locked inside it, which made sitting in a luxurious tent with a tray of hot food all the more ridiculous. It was confirmation that she was stuck between two worlds, and the two guards posted outside were proof that Hodge could feel her slipping to the other side.

'You put me in a very difficult position earlier,' he said when he came in to speak with her. 'Ita's involvement with the St Clare group not only threatens our safety but also jeopardises all we are trying to achieve here.' He sat on the cot beside her. 'She was never an appropriate friend for a young lady, and we are supposed to be presenting a unified front.'

Isabel could barely look at him. 'May I ask you something?'

He moved closer to her. 'Of course.'

She forced herself to meet his eyes. 'Did you set fire to Maddock House?'

The pause before his response confirmed it, not that she needed confirmation. If Ita claimed he had done it, then he had done it.

'Is that what the little witch told you?' He rose and began to pace. 'She disappears from your life—abandons you—then has the audacity to show up and attempt to destroy your happiness by poisoning your mind against me.'

Isabel blinked slowly.

'I should have seen her execution through,' he added.

'She saw you. Through the keyhole.' Her tone was laced with pain.

He turned to her, feigning offence. 'She saw no such thing.'

'You locked the door,' Isabel went on as if he had not spoken. 'I have spent years trying to figure out why that door was locked. Yet the moment Ita told me, it all made sense.'

'You think I would lock two women in a room and set your family home on fire?'

She looked up at him. 'Look around you. You have built a camp that is full of grief and suffering.'

'I have built a solution.'

'Can you not see the damage you are doing to these people? There are families locked in here whose only crime is surviving at a time when most were dying. And this is how they are rewarded.' She stood. 'The rain has stopped. The food has returned. These people should be out there rebuilding their lives. You are taking advantage of their misfortune.' She searched his eyes. 'Can you not see that?'

He stepped up to her—fast, bringing his face close to hers. 'You cannot possibly understand what is happening here, because you have lived the last five years *sheltered* by my father's kindness and my undying love for you.'

'Perhaps you are right.' Her eyes moved between his. 'Perhaps now is a good time to tell you that I no longer wish to be *sheltered*. It is time for me to make my own judgements about the world and life decisions.' She paused because she knew she should not say it. 'Including whom I marry.'

He grabbed hold of her face, squeezing so hard she feared her teeth would shatter. She clawed at his arm, but it was futile.

'I love you tirelessly,' he said, face close to hers, 'and this is how you repay me.' His mouth came crashing down on hers, teeth scraping. She tried to push him away, but he was too strong.

Finally, he broke the kiss and looked at her. 'Think carefully about what comes out of your mouth. Words cannot be taken back.'

Tears fell down her cheeks now. 'I hate you. I hate you for the things you did back then and the things you are doing now.'

His eyes were two flames ready to torch her. 'You hate me? For the things I did back then?' He squeezed her jaw. 'I did that for you!' Spit hit her face. 'I did it for your family! For us!' He released her with a shove.

Her hands went to her cheeks. That should have been the end of it, but apparently she had a death wish. 'I hate your voice, your face, the feel of your hands on me.' She swallowed down the sob in her throat. 'But most of all I hate myself for not telling you that sooner.'

Years of resentment, layer upon layer, suppressed until it had solidified, came pouring out. It had poisoned her for too long.

Oh, the relief.

Hodge was stunned by her confession. Visibly sickened. He blinked a number of times as her words penetrated. 'You are angry. You are angry and trying to hurt me.' He swallowed audibly. 'The woman I know, the one I chose to marry when I was barely a man, would never say those things to me.'

If she had just remained silent, said nothing, she may have been able to salvage the situation. But it was not the day for silence. 'The *woman* you chose to marry? I was *fifteen*. The woman you fell in love with did not even exist yet. She was a figment of your imagination, a fantasy you manipulated into reality.' She laughed. 'And I have wasted five years of my life aiding your delusions.'

His hand met her face with full force—and she had the audacity to act surprised. She had known those words would be too much for him, but she wanted to be sure he understood her. The problem was she had never been struck before and was not prepared for the stinging skin and ringing in her ear that seemed to go on and on. She certainly was not prepared for the shame that swelled inside her or the laughter that erupted from her.

Laughter.

He did not like that.

This time, he took hold of her throat. He was so lost in

his own rage and fear that he barely knew what he was doing.

And the strangest thing happened as his fingers tightened around her throat. The fight left her. She stood there, unable to breathe, with her hands at her sides. She stared him straight in the eye until her vision began to blur. The lack of response must have frightened him because he released her suddenly, as though her skin had burned his hand.

She doubled over, half coughing and half dry retching. He moved to help her, but she raised a hand to stop him. Straightening, she held her throat and tried to breathe normally. He looked down at his hand with absolute horror, as though it were a thing he was not in control of and he could barely believe what it had done.

'My beloved,' he whispered. 'Are you all right?'

Her breaths continued to come in ragged bursts, and she knew speaking would only set her off coughing again. She watched him back away to the other side of the tent, swallowing repeatedly. His anger had dissolved into embarrassment.

'I am going to fix this,' he said quietly. 'I need a moment, and then I am going to fix this.' He looked to the exit. 'There is a path back to each other, I assure you.'

She said nothing.

'I just… I need you to stay here. I cannot be worried about you wandering away again.' He walked over to her, removing his belt as he did so.

'What are you doing?' she croaked.

He reached up and stroked her hair. 'I am sorry. I love you. Give me a chance to fix this.'

She turned away from his touch. He took her hands, surprisingly gentle now, and led her to the centre post. Her face collapsed when she realised what he was doing.

'Shh,' he said. 'Please do not cry. It is only until I return.' He proceeded to guide her hands to either side of the pole and then bound them together with his belt. Now she truly belonged in that camp. In moments, she had gone from straddling two worlds to feeling like a wastelander.

'I will be back soon, I promise,' he said, touching her reddened cheek. Then he turned and exited the tent.

She watched the flap of the tent fall back into place before sinking to the ground.

CHAPTER 18

The defenders waited amid the tall conifers for Ita to return. She had needed to get Rabbit to a medic as quickly as possible, and since she was not permitted to reveal the location of their camp, she told them to wait for her there and she would return with the leader of the St Clare group. The defenders had some questions about the group's plans to free the people in the camp.

Tatum was standing beside his horse, repeatedly throwing a rock into the air and catching it. Blackmane was leaning against a trunk, growing increasingly agitated. He had no idea whether Hodge was treating Isabel like a queen or completely losing his mind over what had transpired. 'I shouldn't have let her go with him.'

'You didn't have a choice.'

'I should have kept her with me.'

'And done what with her? You're a defender of Chadora. She's the woman Lord Hodge has selected to be his wife.' Tatum threw the rock at Blackmane, who caught it. 'Now, I'm the first to admit theirs isn't the healthiest of relationships, but show me a noble match that is.'

Blackmane pushed off the tree, turning the rock in his hand. 'She deserves better than him.'

'I agree.'

'She deserves to feel safe.'

'Every woman does.' Tatum watched him closely. 'You've caught feelings for her. It's natural to want to tear off the head of the man she shares a bed with.'

'She doesn't—' He began pacing. 'You lot always say I'm incapable of feelings.'

'Well, clearly something's changed. Maybe Lady Isabel was placed in your path to remind you that there *is* warmth outside the cold shell you've built around yourself.'

Blackmane pinched the bridge of his nose. 'Or to torture me.'

Tatum studied him. 'Did something happen between you two last night?'

'No.' Blackmane stilled, hesitated. 'She was cold—'

'Ah. And you warmed her up.' Tatum smirked. 'That's rather intimate. Don't you normally just bend your lovers over a bed and tell them not to look at you?'

Blackmane threw the rock back at Tatum—hard—hitting him square on the forehead.

'Fuck,' Tatum grunted, a hand pressed to his head. 'That really hurt.'

The snap of debris underfoot had them both reaching for their weapons.

Ita appeared and raised her hands. 'Only me.'

She had brought the group's leader with her as

promised. The man stopped a safe distance from the defenders.

Tatum looked him up and down. 'I suppose introductions are a bit pointless since you all use aliases.'

The man studied him a moment. 'You can call me Thorn.'

Tatum's eyebrows rose slightly. 'Is there a prickly backstory to that one?'

Thorn stared, not reacting in the slightest.

'Right, well, you can simply address me as Commander,' Tatum said, then gestured to Blackmane. 'And this is Cottontail.'

Blackmane shook his head.

'Twitch here tells me you're trustworthy,' Thorn said.

Tatum quirked a brow. 'Twitch?' Then, realising that was Ita's alias, he added, 'Oh, *Twitch*. Yes, trustworthy.'

Thorn glanced at Ita, who gave him an apologetic look, then continued. 'She tells me you weren't as impressed with the camp as Lord Hodge was hoping for.'

'It's the people in shackles for me,' Tatum said. 'That was a bit of a turn-off.'

Thorn crossed his arms. 'Hodge likes to be in full control.'

Tatum nodded. 'We're interested in your plan to manage that. I'm certain King Becket will also be interested. Maybe there's something we can do to help.'

'Help?' Thorn asked. 'You're going to help the rebel groups you came here to stop?'

Blackmane shifted his weight. 'We weren't sent here to stop anyone. We came to find out what's going on. There's no way King Becket will support what's happening in that camp.'

Thorn looked between them. 'We have ways of getting people out. It's *keeping* them out that's the challenge. Where do we hide sixteen hundred people living in a constant state of fear?'

Neither defender had an answer for him.

'Is your interest in all of this purely to gather intel for your king?' Thorn asked.

Tatum spoke up at that. 'Cottontail here has someone inside the camp he's worried about.'

Thorn looked Blackmane over. 'I thought worry was trained out of you—like every other human emotion.'

Tatum leaned in and whispered, 'I can see where he gets his name from.'

'He's gotten quite attached to Lady Isabel,' Ita explained, the beginnings of a smile on her face.

'I'm not attached to anyone,' the defender replied. 'And I believe the answer here's not to hide sixteen hundred escaped prisoners but to protect them while they live free lives out in the open.'

Thorn appeared amused by that. 'You want me to take on England? Do you know how many men we would need for that task? They outnumber us seven to one, and we have women and children to consider.'

Blackmane was not put off by those odds, but he was also able to kill seven men if the need arose. 'What about the Emlyn group? Do they have the numbers?'

'No one knows anymore. There might be fifty of them or five thousand.'

Tatum frowned. 'And why's that?'

'Because we never see them,' Ita answered. 'They tend to stick farther north and very much to themselves.'

'I'm honestly surprised you haven't joined forces by now,' Tatum said.

Ita shrugged. 'Neither group is very trusting of anyone outside of their own. And we would have to find them first.'

'You don't,' Thorn said. 'They find you.'

Tatum looked between the pair. 'You likely know this already, but defenders are excellent trackers.'

'Can you track ghosts?' Thorn asked.

Blackmane exhaled slowly. 'We don't believe in ghosts.'

'They would have people in those camps too,' Tatum said. 'They would want that place emptied out as much as you do.'

Thorn nodded. 'Of course. They're the reason the second camp isn't open yet.'

They all fell silent a moment.

'Does your king know about what's happening over here?' Blackmane asked.

'We don't have a king,' Ita said. 'He abandoned us during the famine and now wants us locked up for daring to survive.'

Thorn glanced sideways at her. 'We have no way of knowing. We'd have to get past the marcher lords first.'

There was no denying that King Edward II had done some irreparable damage during the final years of his reign.

'Maybe it's time to claim your independence, then,' Tatum said.

Ita laughed. 'And should we build a wall around the wastelands? Raise a pagan flag?'

Tatum waved a finger at her. 'Oh, I see what you did there.'

A large bird swooped between them, prompting everyone to reach for their weapons.

'It's Margery,' Ita said, extending one arm.

The eagle landed, yelping in a way that Blackmane had never heard before.

'What's the matter with her?' he asked.

'She's upset,' Ita said, stroking Margery's back soothingly.

Blackmane narrowed his eyes. 'About what?'

Ita gave him a tired look. 'I may be able to gauge her moods, defender, but I don't speak fluent eagle.'

An uneasy feeling flourished in Blackmane's gut. 'Do you think it has to do with Isabel?'

'Possibly, but it might be as simple as not being able to find her.' She met his gaze. 'I'm not sure whether you've noticed, but they're rather attached.'

Blackmane shook his head as good sense and impulsiveness warred inside him. 'Perhaps I should go to the camp, check on things.'

Tatum whipped his head in Blackmane's direction. 'Absolutely not. If Hodge sees you—'

'He won't.'

Ita stepped forwards. 'I could go with you.'

Thorn glared at her. 'I think we've lost enough people in the past twenty-four hours. Don't you?'

Ita swallowed guiltily.

'Why don't the two of you come with us?' Thorn

suggested. 'We'll continue the conversation somewhere more secure, and you'll have a safe place to spend the night.'

Blackmane nodded. 'I think that's a good idea.' He looked at Tatum. 'You go with them. I'll be back before you know it.'

The commander looked far from impressed by that suggestion. 'Might I have a word with you—in private?'

He led Blackmane away from the group, checking the others weren't listening before beginning. 'I never thought I would utter these words to you, but you need to be logical about this.'

There was no logic when it came to her. 'I just want to check that she's all right before we head home.'

'And if she's not?'

'Then I'll make a sensible call based on the circumstances.'

Tatum laughed. 'Normally I would accept that, because you're unaffected by most things—unless the warden orders you to be affected. That's the way it's been for the five years I've known you. But now? Now suddenly you're having human reactions and forcing me to evaluate the freedoms I give you.'

Blackmane was not ready to back down. 'I can be back within twenty-four hours. I'll stay out of the camp and out of sight. You have my word.'

Tatum released a noisy breath and shook his head. 'Fine. You have twenty-four hours.'

'Did I mention the camp has its own vicar?' Hodge said when he returned to the tent a few hours later. 'Father Digory.'

Isabel lifted her head off the pole, immediately wary of his demeanour. 'No, you did not.'

He dropped down in front of her, face full of fresh hope. 'Marry me.'

She blinked—several times. 'What?'

He took hold of her hands, which were still bound, and said again, 'Marry me.'

She barely knew how to respond. 'Have you lost your mind?'

'On the contrary. I have had a moment of clarity.' He gave her a boyish grin. 'We have delayed this for far too long. I truly believe the best way forwards is to *move* forwards—together. I love you. You love me. It is that simple.'

Except that she did not love him, and she was certain he knew that.

'I have organised everything.'

He was deadly serious. He actually thought she would go along with the insane plan, even after everything that had transpired.

'I just learned that you burned down my house and tried to kill my friend, that you manipulated me and my family so we had no choice but to come with you to Hampstead Keep.' She searched his eyes. 'And now you expect me to *marry* you?'

He let go of her hands. 'What chance do we have if you refuse to let go of past mistakes and grievances?'

Isabel's blood ran a little hotter after those words left his mouth. 'Except that these are not past grievances. These are today's grievances, and tomorrow's grievances. I will likely carry these grievances to my grave.'

His face hardened. 'You will feel differently when I am your husband—trust me.'

'I doubt that.'

'You will!' He rose, then took a moment to compose himself. 'You will,' he repeated, quieter this time. 'I will force joy and light into your heart if I have to.'

She stood also. 'You have spent five years siphoning it from me—willingly.'

His hands went into his hair, and he turned in a circle. He went over to her bag, sifting through it until he found what he was looking for. Then he returned, holding up a dress. 'You can wear this.'

She stared at the gown, feeling sicker with each passing second. 'I do not want to.'

Before he had a chance to raise his voice and make a

scene, the flap of the tent was drawn back, and Yvaine stepped inside.

Hodge rounded on her. 'What?'

Yvaine dropped her gaze. 'Father Digory sent me, my lord. He told me there is to be a wedding and thought I could assist the lady.'

Hodge pinched the bridge of his nose and took a calming breath. 'Yes, good.' He cleared his throat, hand falling to his side. 'Help Lady Isabel change. Fix her hair. Let the guards know when she is ready.' He looked at Isabel. 'I shall see you very soon.' Then he left the tent.

Yvaine waited for his footsteps to fade before rushing over to Isabel and wrapping her arms around her. 'Darling girl,' she whispered. 'What is he doing to you?'

Isabel felt herself begin to tremble but knew she needed to hold herself together. 'We are getting married —tonight.'

Yvaine drew back and looked into her eyes. 'Do you *want* to marry him?'

'No.' The word was barely a whisper.

Yvaine glanced at the exit. 'There is a way out of this place if you dare.'

'The woodpile.'

Yvaine's shoulders fell an inch. 'You found her. You found Ita.'

'Yes.'

'How is she?'

Grieving. And it was all Isabel's fault. 'She is… safe.'

The woman nodded slowly. 'That is all a mother can ask for nowadays.' She fell quiet. 'Will you go to her again?'

'I will try.'

Yvaine loosened the belt around Isabel's wrists. 'I will go in search of flowers for your hair. When I am gone, you are going to slip out under the canvas over there.' She nodded towards the far end of the tent. 'There are no guards at that end.' Dropping the belt to the ground, she began unbuttoning Isabel's dress. 'You are going to the kitchen the long way, behind the sleeping quarters. You will see the guards along the fence line and will be tempted to turn back. Do not.' She picked up the clean dress and began helping her into it. 'If you stay close to the houses, they cannot see you.'

While it felt pointless changing dresses ahead of an escape, Isabel knew it was to protect Yvaine if she got caught. There would be questions.

'When I return with the flowers, I will have to react immediately or the guards will be suspicious.' She walked over to the tray and took the bread from it, stuffing it into the pocket of Isabel's cloak, which was draped over the cot. Then she returned to her. 'Count to fifty before you leave, in case the guards check in on you.'

Isabel searched her eyes. 'We are coming for you. We are going to get all of you out, I promise.'

Yvaine hugged her briefly, then left the tent, informing the guards on her way out that she would be back in a few minutes.

Isabel stood there, her heart pounding in her throat, counting in her head as she eyed her escape route.

Fifty.

She snatched up her cloak and headed for the far end of the tent, tugging at the fabric in various spots until she found the best place to slip through the gap. She peered beneath it before doing so, certain someone would see her, but Yvaine was right. She escaped the tent unnoticed.

Tugging up the hood of her cloak, she looked around to get her bearings, then headed for the fence line as instructed. When she reached the first house, she stopped in the shadows, taking a moment to observe her surroundings. A guard strolled slowly along the fence line, staring vacantly ahead. Drawing a slow breath, Isabel pushed forwards, every muscle in her body tense. She passed the second house without an issue. When she reached the third, she pressed her back against the wall, working up the courage to cross the camp to the other side. She was just about to go when two guards stepped into view, forcing her back into the shadows. Flattening herself against the wall, she held her breath and waited for them to pass.

Now, she told herself. *Go.*

It took all of her self-control to walk and not run out into the open for all to see. Soon, she was back beneath the cover of trees, the kitchen area now in sight. All she could think about was how Hodge would react when he realised she was gone. Who would bear the brunt of his mood? And how far would he go to recover her this time?

Movement above drew her focus to the sky. And there was Margery, gliding silently above her, willing her forwards. It was amazing how much strength Isabel drew from her presence. She could jump a fence if she knew the eagle was waiting for her on the other side.

She was almost to the kitchen when she heard shouting in the distance. Those shouts could have been about anything or anyone, but her feet hurried forwards all the same.

The kitchen was alive with women washing bowls and scrubbing pots the size of sheep. None of these faces were familiar, so she had no reason to trust any of them, but she continued anyway, because there was no turning back at that point. Many cast curious glances her way, but no one said anything as she headed for the woodpile.

Her hands clammed up when it came into sight. What had Ita told her? That if one got a run up, they could use it as a step to reach the top.

She had also said the wood needed to be stacked correctly or it could result in spectacular failure.

There was really only one way to find out if it was stacked correctly.

'Not yet,' a woman whispered, appearing next to her and handing her a pile of forks and a cloth.

Isabel looked down at the items, confused.

A horse cantered by the kitchen. 'I want every guard on alert.'

Isabel recognised Hodge's voice and began rubbing the forks with the cloth, praying her trembling hands would not drop them and draw attention to her. The urge to run was strong with her exit barely thirty feet away, but she waited, knowing she only had one chance to get out—and she needed to get out. She could not help these people from the inside. And she could not marry Hodge.

The woman returned and took the forks and cloth from her. 'Now.'

Isabel took off at a run, eyes on the top of the fence above the woodpile. That was her target. She leapt up onto the pile, as though she had sprouted wings, and died a small death when she felt the wood shift beneath her weight. She kept her focus, though, reaching. One hand caught the fence. The other missed, but she managed to swing herself back to try again. It worked, and she grabbed hold of it.

Never in her life would she have thought she could get over that fence from that position, but pure fear was the ultimate fuel. She walked her feet up the fence, ignoring her stinging hands as splinters pierced her soft skin. She got one elbow up, then the other. Biting back a groan, she pushed herself up until her hips sat level with the top of the fence.

'Halt!' boomed a voice behind her.

She did not waste time looking over her shoulder to see if the person was speaking to her. Holding her breath, she swung her legs over and dropped blindly down the other side, hands clawing at the air as she tried to judge the distance to the ground. She saw it at the last moment, softening her knees just in time to prevent serious injury. She fell forwards, landing on her hands and knees, where she remained for a few moments in shock. But there was nothing quite like the shouts of angry men from the other side of the wall to get one moving again. Scrambling to her feet, she took off at a run.

The numbing fear, combined with darkness and low-lying branches intent on taking out her eyes, made for a challenging course. She knew she needed to head north until she reached the road and then follow it east. The problem was she did not know if she was headed north and did not have the luxury of time to stop and figure it out. She had to rely on the boundary fence for guidance, the very fence she needed to get away from.

Margery glided down beside her.

'Tell me this is north,' Isabel panted.

The eagle lifted into the air, disappearing into the trees on her left.

Isabel pulled up and turned in a circle for a few breathless moments, realising she had accidentally lost sight of the fence anyway. She decided to follow Margery.

No sooner had she begun to run again then she heard the gentle rumble of hooves.

Horses.

There were horses coming her way.

She stopped once more, trying to decide whether to run or hide. But hide where? Behind a tree? *Up* a tree? Could she even climb a tree? Certainly not quickly. But she also could not outrun a horse.

'Isabel!'

Her blood turned cold as Hodge's voice reached her. He was close—much too close.

All logic abandoned her, replaced with primal fear. She took off after the eagle, despite having lost track of her again. She simply ran.

'Isabel!' Hodge shouted. 'I know you are out here!'

Was it just her imagination or was he closer than the last time he had called her name?

She slowed, struggling to hear the horses over her thudding heart.

'My beloved.'

That was forty feet away at most.

She stilled, frozen in place, with no idea which direction the voice had travelled from.

A hand clamped over her mouth at the same time an arm caught her by the waist. She screamed but was forced to swallow it.

'Not a sound,' a familiar voice whispered into her ear. It was Blackmane.

He swung her to the other side of him and retreated behind a wide trunk just before horses came into view. Isabel was trembling all over, her chest heaving from her running efforts. Blackmane was a striking contrast of calm stillness. He kept a hand firmly over her mouth, the other pinning her to him.

'Isabel,' Hodge said. 'I know you are close. I can feel you.' He stopped his horse barely twenty feet from them. 'Please. Let us not do this. Return with me now, and we shall figure this out together.'

Blackmane made it clear via his tightening grip that she was not to take Hodge up on that offer. A long, drawn-out silence followed as Hodge waited for her to show herself. She focused on quietening her breathing, afraid he would hear her.

'I want men combing every inch of land within a three-mile radius of the camp,' Hodge said to the guard riding next to him.

'Yes, my lord,' the guard replied as he turned his horse around. Then he cantered away.

Hodge remained where he was for some time, looking around and listening. They waited him out. What else could they do?

Finally, he pushed his horse into a trot and continued

south—or possibly west. She really had no idea at that point.

When they could no longer hear the horse, Blackmane removed his hand from her mouth, one finger at a time. The moment the pressure on her ribcage eased, she turned in his arms and buried her face in his uniform. This man, whom she barely knew, was beginning to feel like the only safe place she had left.

'Are you all right?' he asked.

She nodded.

He hooked a finger under her chin and lifted her face so he could see her eyes. 'I'm going to get you out of here, but I need you to do exactly what I say.'

Another nod.

He took hold of her hand. 'Let's go.'

CHAPTER 20

*I*t would have been so easy to shoot that crazed man from his horse, then cut his throat for good measure, but the warden's orders echoed in Blackmane's mind. So he let the man ride away, then headed north to the dense part of the forest where his mare was tethered. Isabel did well in keeping up, though he felt her beginning to tire during the second mile.

'Not too much farther,' he said.

Soon the forest would be crawling with guards, and they needed to be well outside the three-mile radius before then.

'I am fine,' she lied. The first words she had spoken since he found her.

A pair of horses approached at a canter. Blackmane pulled her into the brush, and she huddled against him, holding her breath as they passed. He was tempted to shoot them when they circled back, but dead soldiers would clue them in that she was helped, and the three-mile search would quickly broaden.

When the sound of horses faded to a distant thud, he rose and took her hand once more. She responded with a sharp breath.

'What's the matter?' he asked.

She shook her head. 'It is nothing. A few splinters.'

He looked down at her hand but could not see much in the dark, so he made a mental note to deal with those later when they were safe.

They ran the last mile. Whenever she tripped, he pulled her upright, and she would resume running again without saying a word. When they reached the horse, he let go of her hand, and she grabbed hold of his arm.

'Where are you going?'

He noted the panic in her voice. 'I need to fetch a large branch.'

'What for?'

'They'll try to track you. We need to make that as hard as possible for them.' He pulled out his knife and went to cut off a large branch.

'What are you going to do with that?'

'Remove our tracks.' Mounting, he reached for her with his spare hand, pulling her up onto the horse behind him. She held on tightly as he kicked the mare into a canter. The leafy end of the branch dragged along the ground behind the horse.

'Do you want me to hold it so you can concentrate on riding?' she asked.

'No.' It would be too painful if her hands were full of splinters. 'No more talking for a while. I want you to tap me if you see or hear anything. Can you do that?'

'Yes.'

'And let me know if you need to stop.'

'I will not need to stop.'

She might have been useless with weapons, but she had the heart of a wastelander.

They rode for around four hours, only slowing down when his horse began to tire. Soon after, he felt the weight of Isabel's head on his back. He glanced over his shoulder. She was definitely tiring but was not ready to admit it.

Around half an hour later, her hands slipped from his uniform, and she began to slide sideways. Blackmane dropped the branch and caught hold of her. She woke with a start.

'Sorry,' she muttered, straightening herself.

'There's a stream up ahead. We'll rest there.'

The stream was barely a trickle, but it was enough for the horse to drink and for him to fill his waterskin. He brought it over to where Isabel stood shivering. 'Here.'

She drank, then handed it back to him. 'Now what?'

He walked over to the horse and began removing things. 'Now we rest for a few hours. We'll continue at first light.'

He felt her eyes on him the whole time he was moving about. He did not bother with a fire, not only because he did not want to give away their location but because he knew she was more likely to sleep without one.

'Why did you come back?' she asked after a long silence.

He gestured for her to sit down on the bedroll, then dropped down beside her, drawing his knees up. 'Your bird showed up making alarming noises. Ita seemed worried.'

She looked up at the black sky. 'She is such a smart girl.'

'It certainly appears that way.'

Remembering the bread Yvaine had stuffed into her cloak, Isabel fetched it out. 'I brought us dinner.'

He looked down at the bread in her hands. 'You go ahead.'

She tore it in half. 'We will share it.'

'I've already eaten.'

'I doubt that.' She held it out for him to take. 'I will not eat unless you do.'

He reluctantly took it, and they ate in silence.

'How bad are the hands?' he asked.

She looked down at them. 'I guess we shall find out when the sun rises.'

He reached for one, running the tips of his fingers over her open palms, pausing at the sharp bubbles of skin. 'What happened?'

'I had to climb over the fence.' She paused. 'It was not as easy as Ita made it sound.'

'I don't recall her saying it was easy.'

'You likely would have leapt over it without need of hands.'

He watched as she stifled a yawn. 'Lie down. Try to sleep. I'll wake you when it's time to go.'

She did not lie down. 'What about you? When will you sleep?'

'Later.'

She did not move. 'I am truly sorry for dragging you into this mess. You should be on your way home by now, not stuck here with me.'

He brushed a finger down his nose. 'I wasn't about to leave you in that place… with him.'

She shook the blanket open and lay down on the bedroll, moving over to one side and covering herself. 'Will you rest with me for a moment?'

He watched her from a safe distance. 'I don't think that's a good idea. Not after last night.'

'What was wrong with last night?'

'A lot of things.'

'You were simply keeping me warm.' Her eyes were liquid in the dark. 'And tonight there is no fire at all.'

Knowing he could not let her freeze when she was asking him for warmth, he lay beside her, face to face, his body pressed to hers.

'Is that better?' he asked.

She shook her head.

'What do you need?'

'Can you put your arm around me?'

When he did not move, she reached for his hand and dragged it across her body until his fingers grazed her back. She emitted the softest breath when they pressed against her spine.

She was killing him.

'Is that better?' he asked again.

And once again, she shook her head. 'My face is cold.'

He had a physical reaction to those words.

Undeterred by his silence and lack of action, Isabel brought her mouth closer to his. 'Your breath is warm.'

Her words hit his lips, making every inch of him pay attention. 'Isabel—'

'Ryder.'

He searched her face. 'I'm going back to Chadora.'

She continued to study his face. 'Then we do not have much time left together, do we?'

He swallowed.

'I did not know it could be like this,' she said.

'It?'

'We have not even kissed yet, and I feel all light-headed and hot.'

She had definitely said *yet*.

'Every time he touches me, I want only to move away.' Her leg moved against his beneath the blanket. 'And every time you touch me, I cannot get close enough.'

His restraint dissolved, and he closed the gap between them, kissing her. He was aiming for gentle, but there was nothing gentle about it. The act was fuelled by hunger and frustration, and he expected her to draw back in shock, recoil, reprimand him. Then he would hate himself a little more for it.

But she did not draw back. Isabel inhaled the kiss and reached up to draw him closer. They kissed this way for a number of minutes, mutual pent-up tension working its way out of their bodies. Then the energy between them began to settle, their hands wandering beneath the blanket.

Now he was gentle.

Now he could kiss her the way she deserved to be kissed.

'My neck is cold,' she whispered into his open mouth.

He trailed soft kisses down her throat, warming every inch of skin with his breath, before returning to eye level. 'Better?' he whispered.

'Why did you stop?'

'You know why.'

She ran her thumb across his wet lips. 'That was a good kiss.'

'It was.' He brought her icy hands to his stomach to warm them.

'The kind of kiss they write songs about.'

He pushed back the hair that had fallen over her face and tucked it behind her ear. 'Now the truth comes out about the kinds of books you read.'

She did not smile as expected.

'He lost control tonight,' she whispered. 'In a way that shocked us both.'

'Hodge?'

A nod.

'Did he hurt you?'

She swallowed. 'Yes.'

Blackmane's body tensed involuntarily.

'He thought he could fix it by marrying me—right there in the camp.'

It took a moment for Blackmane to process that. 'Is that why you ran?'

Another nod before her eyes sank shut. 'Will you sleep beside me?'

'No.'

'Will you at least lie beside me?'

'No.'

Her eyes fluttered open. 'No?'

'But I'll keep watch over you.'

Her eyes sank shut again, and sleep took her.

Blackmane gave himself two minutes. Two minutes to

study her face and savour her sleepy breaths. Two minutes to swim in her scent and keep her warm.

When the two minutes were up, he climbed out from beneath the blanket and tucked it tightly around her, then kept watch over her for the rest of the night.

CHAPTER 21

*I*sabel woke to warm fingers brushing her cheek. She forced her heavy eyes open and found Blackmane seated next to her, framed by grey light.

'What happened to your face?' he asked, his voice like ice.

She pushed herself up into a seated position. 'I already told you what happened.'

'He did this?'

She nodded.

'And the marks on your neck?'

'Like I said, he scared even himself.'

'I don't give a shit what he felt.' He held up her arms between them. 'These are fresh. He tie you up as well?'

The marks were barely noticeable. He must have been studying her closely before she woke. 'He wanted to make sure I did not go anywhere.'

He gently lowered her arms before standing up and going over to the horse. 'We need to get moving.'

She watched his rigid posture from the back. 'Are you angry?'

'Yes.'

'At me?'

'Not at you.'

She hugged her knees. 'Love makes people do crazy things.'

He walked over to her and snatched up the blanket. 'Love. Right.'

She stood and began to help him. 'I left. What more do you want?'

'To break his face, for a start.' He jerked the bedroll off the ground. 'He doesn't get to do that again.'

He was clearly feeling helpless, and she could see how uncomfortable he was in that state. 'If it helps, I plan on staying as far away from him as I can.'

He nodded. 'Show me your hands.'

She held them out so he could see the splinters.

'These aren't splinters,' he said, going to fetch his medic kit. 'You have entire sticks wedged beneath your skin.' He took out a small metal instrument, which he used to grab the end of the splinters, gently pulling them out one at a time.

'Yours would have held up significantly better,' she said, attempting to lighten the mood.

'Not much gets through a defender's calloused palm—except maybe a sword.' He picked up his waterskin. 'Here.'

She held them out so he could pour some water over them, wincing as he did so.

His gaze flicked up to meet hers. 'Sorry,' he said quietly.

Wounds cleaned, he secured the last few items, then did a final check of the girth.

'So, now we find Ita and Tatum, and then you go home?' she said to his back.

He nodded. 'That's right.'

She walked to the front of the horse, stroking the mare's face as she looked up at the sky. There was still no sign of Margery. 'I need to get word to my family about everything that has happened. I know Hodge appears to adore my mother and brother, but I worry he will use them as pawns against me.'

He glanced in her direction. 'I think that's a valid fear. Do they have somewhere safe they can go? At least until the dust settles?'

'My uncle has a small farm a few hours east of Hampstead Keep. The best part is I do not think His Lordship knows anything of it.'

Blackmane paused what he was doing. 'Good. You should go there too. Be with your family.'

She stared back at him. 'Except that I wish to remain here in Carmarthenshire. I want to help free the people in the camp.'

He prepared to mount. 'There's going to be fighting. You want to stay for that?'

'I do not want to, but I will.'

He looked straight at her as he landed in the saddle. 'You can't fight.'

'I do not need to fight to be of use.'

He pinched the bridge of his nose and drew a breath. 'Have you forgotten what it was like when we were attacked the other day? How helpless you were? You had to hide under a horse because you had no way of defending yourself.'

His words stung. She was beginning to tire of people pointing out how useless she was. 'I know I must seem pathetic in the eyes of a defender.'

'Don't put words in my mouth.'

'Unless I have the ability to kill five men with one swoosh of my sword, then hide and stay out of everyone's way, is that it?'

'One *swoosh*?'

She took a step towards him, pointing in the direction of the camp. 'I promised Yvaine I would come back for her, that she would walk free. I intend to keep that promise.'

'The camp's the other way.'

She immediately dropped her hand to her side, heat filling her cheeks. Neither of them spoke for a moment.

'We want the same thing,' he said, breaking the silence. 'Everyone wants to see those people free, but not everyone can help. I know you don't want to hear this—'

'You are right. I do not want to hear it.' She adjusted the folds of her cloak. 'I think I have had enough of men telling me what I can and cannot do for now.' Her eyes began to well up. 'I am tired, hungry, and cold—but mostly hungry.' Her hand went to her stomach. 'I cannot thank you enough for your assistance last night. And this morning.' She lowered her voice. 'And this past week. But now I think we should go our separate ways.' With that, she started walking, praying she was going in the right direction. She heard Blackmane cursing repeatedly under his breath as he dismounted and came after her on foot.

'We're going to the same place,' he said, 'and you want to travel separately?'

'What I want is a few moments of peace after a very difficult week.'

'So you're going to walk to the place that you have no idea how to get to?'

'I was raised here, defender. I might not know my directions, but I know my landmarks. And Margery will guide me along the way.'

'It's at least eighteen miles from here.'

'These boots are surprisingly comfortable.'

Blackmane looked down at them. 'Maybe for the first five miles. Then you'll have more blisters than you can count.'

She picked up her pace.

'I gather you know all the local water sources too?' he continued.

She rolled her eyes at that. 'Do not pretend you know that. You found the stream back there because you heard the running water. I have ears too.'

'The difference is I know how to get water from other sources if there's none to be found.'

'Yet another way you are superior to me. Congratulations.'

He caught hold of her arm. 'Stop. You can't walk eighteen miles with Hodge in pursuit. You want to feel useful. I get it.'

She tore her arm free and was about to respond to that, but he whipped his head around to look behind him, going deadly still.

Isabel peered nervously past him. 'What is—'

He clamped a hand over her mouth, then ushered her behind a nearby tree. He gestured for her to be quiet and remain where she was, then slowly retrieved his bow and quiver. Weapon loaded and aimed, he shouted, 'Show yourself. Come out with your hands where I can see them.'

No one appeared.

Isabel listened intently, but there was not a thread of noise to grab hold of.

A few moments passed, and she remained silent as instructed. But then she saw movement. It was like the trees were coming to life around them.

Large men in matching grey cloaks stepped into view, their faces hidden by their cloaks. That seemed to be the way they wore them post-famine, always faceless to intruders. They held weapons of all kinds: longbows, axes, swords, knives, hammers. Even chains. She wondered how she had not seen them, not heard them approach.

It appeared they had accidentally found the Emlyn group.

The string of Blackmane's bow was so taut she was sure it would snap beneath his fingers before he had a chance to shoot anyone.

'Not a step farther,' the defender called to them, 'or I will start shooting.'

They were hardly going to be scared off by one defender and an unarmed woman, but she admired Blackmane's confidence nonetheless.

Nobody moved forwards, but nobody laid down their weapons either.

Blackmane glanced over his shoulder to where more

people stood observing them. 'We pose no threat unless you start a fight. We're simply passing through and can do it quickly if that's your preference.'

How he managed to remain so calm she would never understand.

'You're a little far from home, defender,' someone said. It was difficult to tell who had spoken. 'And a little outnumbered to be barking instructions, don't you think?'

Blackmane swung his weapon in the other direction. 'Who said that? Show yourself.'

One man stepped forwards and pushed back the hood of his cloak.

The string of Blackmane's bow went slack.

Isabel looked between them, immediately recognising the similarities. Same thick, dark hair. Same piercing stare. Same height, build, and sharp-edged jaw.

'Tolly,' Blackmane breathed.

Tolly looked him up and down a few times, then shook his head in disbelief. 'Hello, brother.'

*H*e was alive. Or he was a ghost. Since Blackmane did not believe in ghosts, that meant he was alive.

Tolly raised a hand, a gesture to the others to lower their weapons. They did so without question. 'I guess that explains why I haven't been able to find you. You've been hiding behind walls all this time.'

Blackmane struggled to process what he was saying because he was still getting his head around the fact that his brother was alive. 'What are you...?' His throat closed. 'I watched you leave on that ship.'

'I left on it. I just didn't stay on it.'

Blackmane looked around at the other men. 'Tell your men to put their weapons away.'

Tolly sheathed his sword but said nothing to the others. 'Are you going to put yours away?'

'Not before they do.'

Tolly studied him for a long moment. 'You know, that's a big ask. Historically, defenders haven't treated us very well.' He crossed his arms, waiting.

Blackmane looked around, weighing his options.

Isabel reached out and touched his arm. 'He is your brother. There is no need for arrows.'

'It's not my brother I'm worried about.'

Tolly looked Isabel over. 'This your wife?'

Blackmane shook his head and reluctantly lowered his bow.

'That's a relief given the state of her.' Tolly's eyes narrowed on the marks on her throat. 'What's your name?'

'Don't answer that,' Blackmane said.

Tolly's gaze returned to him. 'She can't tell me her name?'

Blackmane looked around at the men watching them. 'Are you part of the Emlyn group?'

Tolly appeared amused by that question. 'Much has changed in the past five years, hasn't it?'

'You grew up, for one.' He paused. 'And joined a rebel group, it seems.'

Tolly shrugged. 'As did you. You just have fancier uniforms and more money than us.' One corner of his mouth lifted. 'But you haven't changed a bit. Still as serious as ever. Still carrying the weight of the world on your shoulders.'

Margery chose that moment to appear, swooping down between them, prompting everyone to raise their weapons again.

'The eagle belongs to the lady,' Blackmane said, nodding towards Isabel.

Tolly frowned as Margery returned. Isabel extended

her arm so the eagle could land, but she continued to swoop instead. A worried expression settled on Isabel's face.

'What's wrong?' Blackmane asked.

She looked around past the men surrounding them. 'I think Lord Hodge might be coming.'

Tolly's brows dropped. 'Hodge?'

She nodded.

'How do you know it's him?' Blackmane asked.

'Because she will not come to me when he is around. I think she is here to warn me.'

Tolly signalled to his men, and they retreated silently into the trees, seemingly disappearing into thin air. 'One of you want to tell me what the hell is going on?'

'He is looking for me,' Isabel said.

Tolly stared at her for a moment. 'Oh shit. You're Lady Isabel.'

The sound of horses approaching at a canter had Margery disappearing also.

'We have to go—now,' Blackmane said, taking Isabel's hand and pulling her towards the horse.

Tolly exhaled loudly. 'You want to tell me why a Chadorian defender is on the run with a marcher lord's betrothed, or should I not ask?'

'Better you don't ask,' Blackmane replied.

Cursing, Tolly said, 'Get your horse and follow me.'

'Where?'

Tolly angled his head. 'Somewhere he won't find you.'

Blackmane had little choice but to trust him at that point. They would struggle to outrun that many horses, and hiding was no guarantee. Keeping Isabel safe *and*

Hodge alive would be ambitious. He grabbed hold of his horse's reins. 'Let's go.'

The three of them ran through the trees. Blackmane looked around for the rest of the Emlyn group but found no sign of them. Then a woman appeared in front of them, gesturing to Tolly with her hands. He seemed to understand what she was saying and gestured something back. It made sense that they had found ways to communicate without words over the years. She then stepped forwards and took Blackmane's horse. Again, he was forced to trust that at some point he would get it back.

Tolly checked his surroundings, then whipped out a knife before crouching and tapping it on a nearby log. A moment later, it began to roll, and the section of earth beneath it lifted at the same time.

The pair leaned forwards, peering into the dark hole. Isabel then took a giant step back. Tolly jumped down first, then looked up, his expression making it clear that they only had one chance to follow him. Blackmane guided Isabel back to the edge of the hole and gestured for her to jump. She hesitated for only a moment, then dropped down. Tolly caught her, and then Blackmane followed.

Everything went dark.

No one spoke as a rumble of hooves passed overhead. Isabel's hand found Blackmane's in the dark, and his fingers closed around hers. Of course she was afraid. She had just been thrown into a black hole, and the man she was fleeing from was right above them.

When the thunderous noise overhead faded, Tolly said, 'Give me a moment.'

They heard him shuffling around, and then there were sparks from a flint, sending Isabel scrambling closer to Blackmane. Pale light filled the room, cast from a candle Tolly was holding. It gave Blackmane a chance to gauge their surroundings. It was amazing that they could stand up while underground, a vast contrast to the maze of tunnels that had once connected the boroughs inside Chadora's walls. This one opened out to spacious rocky pathways that could be navigated without the need to duck one's head. There was no way it was man-made.

'Are we in a cave?' Isabel asked, peeling herself from Blackmane.

'Yes.' Tolly lifted the candle high so they could see. 'This way.'

Blackmane kept hold of Isabel's hand, his other resting on the hilt of his sword. They followed him down a wet path to a large space with water trickling down one wall. It took Blackmane a moment for his eyes to adjust properly, to realise there were people on the other side of the cave—lots of them. Men, women, children of all ages. Some were seated on woven mats preparing food. Others were sewing. Children were playing a game with rocks in an area marked out by charcoal.

'Do you live down here?' Isabel asked when she noticed younger children asleep on blankets along one wall.

'For now. We try not to stay in the same place for too long.'

A young boy, around ten years old, abandoned his game and ran over to Tolly. 'Do you want to play with us?'

One of the older girls came after him. 'Can't you see

he's busy?' She eyed the strangers cautiously before leading him away.

'I'll play later,' Tolly called after him. 'Their mother was captured two weeks ago and taken to the camp.' His voice was quiet now. 'The women do a great job caring for all the children between them.'

Isabel looked around. 'How many are there?'

'Eighty-three at present. We were originally trying to make sure the children remained with their mothers at all times, so that even if they were captured, they would at least be together. But when we found out they were being separated from their parents and caged like farm animals, we decided to keep the children underground as much as possible. This area's mostly occupied by the remaining families.' He pointed down a path. 'The soldiers you saw earlier sleep down there.'

The boy returned to Tolly again. 'Can you play now?'

Isabel bent down to his height. 'I could play with you, if you like?'

The boy sized her up, clearly not trusting the kind offer. 'Do you even know how to play?'

She shook her head. 'No, but you could teach me.'

He considered that for a long time before finally nodding. 'The first rule is no throwing rocks at people's heads.'

'Excellent first rule,' Isabel said as she followed him.

Blackmane's eyes never left her.

'They're not good with new people,' Tolly said. 'Encounters with strangers don't usually end well for them.'

Blackmane watched as she was handed a rock and

listened carefully to the rules of the game. He noticed the other children kept well back from her, some even retreating to the safety of a familiar adult. It was difficult to watch.

'I took a risk in bringing you down here,' Tolly said. 'There's a reason we don't let people from outside the group in—even people we think we know.' He looked at Blackmane. 'I need to know I can trust you.'

'You can trust her.'

Tolly's eyebrows lifted. 'But not you?'

'I'm trustworthy until I receive orders to the contrary.'

Tolly exhaled through his nose. 'You really are a defender.'

Blackmane did not reply. He was silent while Isabel took her first throw. It hit one of the women sewing. Isabel's hand flew up to her mouth, and then she rushed over to check that the woman was all right, apologising profusely.

'She's not great at the rock game,' Tolly observed.

'No, she's really not.'

His brother looked at him. 'You going to tell me what you're doing in the middle of the wastelands, alone with Hodge's soon-to-be *wife*?'

'I think it's safe to say the wedding's off.'

'You have anything to do with that?'

Blackmane shook his head. 'Hodge gets full credit there. I'm taking her to a friend.'

'And where's this friend of hers located?'

'All over the place. She's part of the St Clare group. They move around a lot, like you. It's a miracle you don't cross paths more often than you do.'

'We make a point of staying out of each other's way.'

Blackmane tore his gaze from Isabel. 'I think that needs to change. It's time to get those people, those children, out of that camp.'

Tolly met his gaze briefly. 'That's a big ask of people with trust issues.'

'You have the trust of everyone here.'

'Which is why I can't afford to break it.' He paused. 'Even if we could get all those people out, then what? These caves barely fit our group.'

'Who says you have to hide?'

'Logic.'

'You would no longer be just a group of people running away. You would be a kingdom—fighting.'

Tolly laughed. 'A kingdom? Have you forgotten where you are, defender? You're in the wastelands, the forgotten kingdom, left to self-destruct. We have no leader, no army, no heroes.' He paused before adding, 'No walls.'

Blackmane gestured around them. 'But you do have caves.'

A nod. 'Today we have caves. Tomorrow, who knows? If there's one thing I've learned these past five years, it's that everything is temporary. Everything you have can be taken away in an instant.'

Blackmane felt the pain in that statement, and guilt whirled inside him. 'You don't need walls and an army to win a war, but you do need heroes. I've met plenty of those these past few days.'

Tolly turned to stare at him. 'Why are you encouraging this? You hoping we all die to save you the hassle of killing us?'

'King Becket's a good man. He'll not sit idle while innocent people are locked in camps designed to benefit the rich.'

'He won't go to war with England either.' Tolly chuckled softly and rubbed his forehead. 'I've missed arguing with you. Five years.'

Blackmane did not respond straight away. 'I thought you were dead.'

Tolly nodded slowly. 'Figured as much. I sailed back, you know. Couldn't find a grave with your name on it, but that didn't mean much back then. They were burning bodies in mass graves.'

Blackmane looked at him. 'You sailed back to Ireland?'

'I waited six months.' He swallowed. 'Then I figured if you ever came looking for me, it would be here in Wales. I worked at the port for a while, until the ships stopped coming in.'

'Then decided to join a rebel group?'

Tolly's mouth turned up. 'It's funny hearing phrases like "rebel group" and "Emlyn ghosts". We're just a bunch of desperate people who figured out we could stay alive in a pack. The only difference between us and the people in the camp is that we're not ready to give up yet.'

'And you have matching cloaks.'

'That part's important.'

Blackmane smirked. After a beat of silence, he said, 'Come meet with the St Clare people. Have a conversation. That's it.' When Tolly did not respond, he added, 'The alternative is you live like this forever.'

The muscles in his brother's face tightened. Then he gave a reluctant nod. 'All right. One meeting.'

*U*nsurprisingly, Isabel was not very good at the rock game. She was aware of the women watching her the whole time, no doubt worried she might suddenly pull a knife on their offspring or drag them off to the camp while they were not looking. She was also aware of Tolly and Blackmane slowly relaxing into each other's presence. While the shock for both of them must have been enormous, she was warmed by the fact that they had found each other after all these years.

'Where are your children?' the boy asked, handing her the rock for her next turn. 'In the camp?'

Her heart pinched. 'I do not have any children.'

'Is that your husband?'

'No.' She glanced over at Blackmane, who was watching her as closely as the women were, but for a different reason. He was the furthest thing from her husband. He was a defender of Chadora. And *she* had no intention of ever living behind walls again. Not that he had asked her—or even hinted at it as a possibility.

Blackmane said something to Tolly, then walked over to where she was standing. 'Who's winning?'

'Me,' said the boy. 'She's not very good, but neither was my mother. She was good at making bread, though.' He looked back at Isabel. 'Do you make good bread? He might marry you if it's really good.'

Isabel's cheeks flooded with colour. 'I am a very average baker. I am certain the defender can do much better if that is part of his criteria.' She glanced awkwardly at Blackmane, who was watching her with a serious expression.

'I'm taking Tolly to meet with the St Clare group. I need you to stay here.'

That explained the serious expression. 'Why? The whole point is to get me to Ita. Then you get to go home.'

He exhaled. 'The point is to keep you safe, and the safest place for you right now is here in this cave.'

She shook her head. 'You cannot exclude me from this. I am part of it whether you like it or not.'

'I'm not excluding you. I'm simply asking that you remain here while Hodge is combing the forest looking for *you*.'

'I'll take care of you,' the boy said. 'You'll still miss him, but at least you won't be alone.'

Isabel felt her heart crack. It was unfathomable what these children had been through at such a tender age. 'Thank you.'

'I'll be back as soon as I can,' Blackmane said. 'Do not leave these caves under any circumstances. You under-stand me?'

She stared at him a moment, tempted to argue, then sighed. 'Fine.'

Blackmane placed a hand on the boy's shoulder. 'What's your name?'

'Huw, sir.'

Blackmane clapped him on the back. 'Take good care of her, Huw.'

She watched him return to Tolly, then glance a final time in their direction before they headed for the exit.

One of the women came over to her. 'You want to have a wash while you wait for him?'

Isabel could only imagine what a mess she must have looked like. 'That would be wonderful, thank you.'

'Let me find you something to wear, and then I'll show you where to go.' She went over to one woman who was sewing and returned with some folded garments. 'Not as fancy as the things you're wearing, but at least they're clean.'

Isabel took them from her. 'Thank you.' Generosity from a stranger who had so little to share was proof that the spirit of Carmarthenshire was not dead. This was what they were fighting for, the chance to live like this but above ground, where all the children could play in the sun and make as much noise as they pleased.

'We will play again later,' she told Huw before following the woman.

They headed down a narrow path with a low ceiling, ducking their heads for a few paces. She was relieved when the cave opened up once more. The woman used the candle she was holding to light another one, illuminating a pool of water.

'Don't expect it to be warm,' the woman said, 'but it's private, so you can have a proper wash.' She went to leave.

'What is your name?' Isabel asked.

The woman looked back, hesitating. 'Genevieve.'

'I am Isabel, but you can call me Belle.'

Genevieve gave her a weak smile. 'The children know not to come here. Wash, sleep.' Her gaze fell to Isabel's marked neck. 'Cry. There's nothing you can say within these walls that they have not heard before.' With that, she headed back in the direction she had come.

The moment Isabel was alone, exhaustion hit her like a boulder. She slumped down next to the stone ledge holding the water, resting her head against it. Her hand went to her throat. Everything was fine. She was fine. She would have been a lot less fine if she had stayed at the camp with Hodge. Her eyes sank shut, and she allowed herself a few moments to rest before…

Isabel woke hours later with a start, her only gauge of time having passed being the pain in her neck from sleeping in one position on a rock pillow for much too long. And thirst. She was so thirsty.

Crawling over the stone ledge, she scooped up handfuls of water, drinking greedily. When she could drink no more, she stripped off her dirty clothes and threw them into the water before wading in after them. She stopped when she was waist deep, enjoying the sensation of the cool water on her skin. She scrubbed her clothes clean, wrung them out, and laid them flat on the ledge to dry. Then, taking a deep breath, she dropped down into the water.

It was cold in a refreshing, nourishing sort of way. She

scrubbed her hair and face clean, then spent time staring up at the roof of the cave, imagining stars shining down on her.

More time slipped by.

Only when she began to lose feeling in her lips did she stand up, preparing to exit the water. Naturally, Blackmane chose that exact moment to step around the corner. He stilled when he saw her, gaze falling briefly before turning around.

'Sorry,' he said. 'I just came to check on you.'

Isabel sank back down beneath the water's surface, heart pounding against her ribcage. Yet when he went to leave, she called out, 'Wait.'

He stilled but did not look back. 'What's wrong?'

Nothing was wrong. She simply wanted him to stay. 'Are you not going to have a wash while you are here?'

He half looked over his shoulder. '*Now?*'

'You can barely see anything in this light.' Her cheeks heated at the lie. 'I will keep my back turned until you are in the water.'

Silence.

'I want to know how the meeting went.'

He sighed, then made his way over, making a point of not looking at her. When he began to remove his weapons, she did as she had promised and turned away from him, listening for his entry into the water the whole time. Eventually, she heard gentle splashes behind her.

'Are you in?' she asked.

'Yes.'

When she turned, only his head and the top of his muscled shoulders were visible. Her eyes moved over him, pausing on what appeared to be an arrow scar on his shoulder. Everything below the water's surface was blurry. They watched each other, five feet of safety between them. Then Blackmane disappeared underwater for a moment, rinsing his hair and face as she had done. She wondered if his eyes were open or closed and whether the visibility down there was better or worse. The thought was not as unsettling as it ought to have been.

He resurfaced after a few moments, wiping a hand down his face.

'Better?' she asked him.

He brushed water from his hair. 'Better.'

Isabel swallowed. 'So, what happened?'

Blackmane ventured a foot closer. 'They've agreed to work together to get everyone out of the camp—and soon.'

Hope soared inside Isabel. 'How soon?'

'The St Clare group already has a tunnel dug that reaches all the way to the fence line where the children are confined. They had planned to use it to get them out first, but then Hodge started violently hanging escapees, so their plans came to a halt.'

Isabel reduced the distance between them to two feet. 'So they will get the children out of harm's way first, and then what?'

'Then the fighting begins. It'll be messy but necessary.'

She regarded him. 'And where will you be while all of this is taking place?'

'In Chadora, as ordered.'

She drifted towards him until her bare knees brushed his. 'Is Tatum here?'

'Yes.'

'Are you leaving today?'

He nodded.

Her heart sank all the way to her stomach. 'And still you do not reach for me?'

'I've gotten myself into enough trouble this week.'

She found his hand beneath the water and threaded her fingers through his. 'You do not reach for me, but you do not retreat either.'

He licked water from his lips. 'Don't you remember what happened last night when you played this game?'

Her skin heated at the memory. 'Why do you think I am keen to play again?'

His gaze fell to her lips, then lower. 'Exactly how much trouble are you trying to get me into during one assignment?'

She closed the remaining distance between them and reached up to touch his wet hair. 'If this is goodbye, then naturally I am going to try to keep you here for as long as I can.'

He caught her by the waist and pulled her closer—but not too close. 'While I appreciate the farewell, I think it's time for you to get out of the water.'

The sensation of his hands on her bare skin made her eyes sink shut. 'I do not want to get out of the water or get dressed. I want to stay here, with your hands on me, and pray you are tempted to kiss me again.'

Blackmane's hands slid to her back, a shaky breath coming from him. 'Then *I'm* going to get out of the water.

Because if I don't, you're going to end up doing things you regret.'

She opened her eyes and looked at him. 'I could never regret anything that happened with you.'

He searched her eyes. 'When I leave, you'll despise me for everything that took place in this cave. And I'll despise myself for letting it happen.'

She climbed onto his lap, met with heat and sensation.

'Belle.' Her name came out on a strangled breath.

'I want you to show me the rest.' Colour filled her cheeks. 'Unless you do not want to. Then absolutely, we will both exit the water and sensibly put on our clothes.'

He dropped his mouth to her neck, kissing once, twice. 'Do you understand what you're asking for?'

She nodded.

'I need words,' he said.

'Yes. I understand.'

His arms tightened around her, teeth scraping gently on her skin, sending shivers of pleasure along her spine.

'You want me to be the man who ruins you?' he asked.

She took hold of his face, forcing him to meet her eyes. 'You think *this* is what ruins a woman? Hodge completely destroyed me without ever removing one item of clothing.' She dropped her forehead to his. 'I do not want you to ruin me. I want you to fix what he broke.'

His eyes were darker than the water they swam in. 'I want to kill him.'

She swallowed. 'I know.'

Blackmane drew her close until she was flush against him, then descended on her.

CHAPTER 24

*I*sabel lay curled against Blackmane, her body limp.

'I can't believe I'm saying this, but we need to get dressed,' Blackmane said, his voice rumbling against her shoulder.

Goose bumps broke out down her arm. She was so content there, trapped beneath his heavy leg, that she thought she might never put clothes on again. But Blackmane had other ideas. Sitting up, he passed her the pile of folded clothes Genevieve had given her, then reached for his uniform.

'I'm going to take you to Ita. She'll meet us a few miles from here before sundown. Hodge should be on his way back to the camp by then.'

Isabel reluctantly sat up and tugged on the dress. Eyeing the scar on his shoulder, she reached out, touching it. 'Where were you when this happened?'

'Departing Harlech Castle—in a rush.'

She buttoned her dress while he tugged on his shirt. 'Was Tatum with you?'

'Yes.'

'And Alveye and Hadewaye?'

'Yes.'

'Did they save your life?'

He slid her boots in front of her. 'Why do you ask?'

She loosened the laces. 'I am simply trying to better understand you.'

'And what have you figured out so far?'

She stood, combing her hair out with her fingers. 'That you are very loyal to those who have earned the privilege.'

He did not respond.

'Your king, your comrades, your family.' She began plaiting her hair. 'And then there is me.'

He looked up while buckling his belt. 'What does that mean?'

'It means everything is as it should be.' She forced a smile.

He regarded her a moment. 'Don't tell me you're regretting what we did already.'

'No.' Her reply was instant. 'I was simply pointing out the hierarchy of things.'

He nodded slowly. 'And what about you? There's your family, Ita, Yvaine, Margery. All the people in that camp. Your destroyed house. Where do I fall?'

She searched his eyes.

Before she could reply, Tatum's voice echoed down to them. 'Blackmane!'

Something in his tone had the defender on instant alert. He quickly strapped on his weapon. 'Let's go.'

They made their way back along the narrow path to the main part of the cave, where a few of the women were now tearing skins off rabbits.

'Wait here,' Blackmane said.

Isabel followed his line of sight to where Tolly and Tatum stood, talking in hushed voices. An uneasy feeling flourished in her stomach. When Blackmane reached the others, Tatum handed him a piece of parchment. He read it, then quickly folded it in half.

Ignoring his clear instructions, Isabel walked over to find out what was going on.

'What is that?' she asked.

Blackmane tucked the parchment into his pocket before turning to her. 'I told you to wait with the other women.'

She looked at Tatum. 'Is it to do with my family?'

The commander shook his head. 'No.'

Losing patience, she stepped up to Blackmane and fetched it from his pocket herself. The fact that he did not try to stop her confirmed the note had something to do with her. Upon opening it, she immediately recognised Hodge's handwriting.

One every hour until she is returned to me.
- The Earl of Hereford

Isabel felt like she had stepped into freezing water. Then hot water. She read it again. 'One what every hour?' she asked, looking up at Blackmane.

'One dead,' he said quietly.

The nausea hit her hard. 'One *person?*'

The smallest nod.

She read it again, then again. 'Where did you get this?'

No one replied.

She looked between them all. 'Where?'

Blackmane shifted his weight. 'It was attached to one of the corpses.'

Her face collapsed. 'One of them? How many are there?'

'My men found three,' Tolly said. 'But that was close to an hour ago.'

An hour *ago.* 'Where?'

'A few miles from here,' Tatum said. 'He must suspect you're in the area.'

She pressed a hand to her stomach, taking a moment. 'Can you take me there, please?'

Blackmane shook his head. 'Absolutely not.'

'I am not a prisoner. I am free to leave,' Isabel replied. 'Please, open the door.'

Blackmane drew a breath and nodded to Tolly.

'We'll all go,' Tolly said. 'The forest is crawling with soldiers right now.'

The sunlight was disorientating as they climbed out into it. They walked a short distance to collect their horses from a woman who somehow knew to expect them, then rode the rest of the way, Isabel on the back of Blackmane's horse, dreading what was to come. The three men watched their surroundings carefully, never speaking a word between them.

When the horse came to a stop, Isabel looked around,

then sucked in a breath when she spotted one of the corpses. A woman suspended fifteen feet in the air. Isabel slid from the back of the horse and walked towards it, stopping when she spotted another corpse twenty feet away, hands and feet bound with rope. She looked around and found two more.

'There are four,' she said.

Tolly shifted in the saddle. 'One every hour.'

Isabel pressed a hand to her chest, sure her heart was about to burst through it.

'We can't stay here,' Tatum called to her. 'Not if there are soldiers coming and going.'

Isabel was staring at the third corpse, a woman whose face was covered by dark hair. She took a few steps closer, eyes narrowing on the swollen ankles and brown boots—brown boots with pointed toes.

A burst of heat shot through Isabel. She clapped a hand over her mouth and fell to her knees.

Blackmane leapt from his horse and ran to her, dropping into a crouch beside her.

'Are you all right?'

Hot tears streamed down Isabel's face as she stared up at Yvaine.

Blackmane looked from her to the corpse. It took him a moment to recognise the woman. 'Oh shit.' He gestured to Tolly. 'Cut that one down and bring her with us.'

Tatum loaded his bow and took aim at the rope, slicing through it on the first go.

Tolly caught it before it hit the ground. 'All right. Let's go.'

Blackmane pulled Isabel to her feet and led her back to

his horse. A moment later, the group cantered away from the tiny graveyard.

'Where to now?' Tatum asked.

'To meet Ita,' Isabel said, struggling to form words. 'She needs to see her mother.'

Tatum looked over at the corpse. 'Well, this just keeps getting better and better.'

'We're going to lose light soon,' Tolly said.

Isabel dropped her head to Blackmane's back. 'Then we better ride fast.'

It was not an easy thing to watch Ita's face light up with joy when Isabel rode into sight, only to dissolve into devastation when she spotted her dead mother draped across Tolly's horse.

'Leave us,' Isabel said before dismounting. 'Please.'

Tolly laid the corpse on the ground, and the three men led their horses away over to where Thorn stood with his own horse. The four men watched from a distance as Ita gathered her dead mother in her arms and rocked her back and forth. Isabel's attempts to comfort her were futile.

'I am so sorry,' she kept saying over and over, as if she had tied the noose and hung the woman from a tree herself.

'What happened?' Thorn asked.

Blackmane handed him the note. The St Clare leader read it, then handed it back.

'This has to stop,' he said.

Tolly glanced at him. 'We have to stop it.'

Thorn watched the women for a moment. 'She'll have to go to the camp until we do.'

Blackmane stiffened. 'What the hell are you talking about? She's not going anywhere near that place.' He looked to Tatum for support, but the commander only looked down at his feet. 'We'll figure out another way.'

'We?' Tolly asked. 'You're about to return home, remember? We'll be the ones figuring a way through this mess.'

Thorn sniffed. 'We all know if she goes back in there, she'll be the safest person in that camp.'

'You don't know that,' Blackmane said.

Thorn lifted his eyebrows. 'I didn't say she would get off easy, but at least she would be alive at the end. Meanwhile, while we stand here debating this, someone else is being killed while he waits for her.'

'He is right,' Isabel said behind him.

Blackmane whipped his head around, not realising she had wandered over to them.

'I need to get to the camp.' She looked over to where Ita was still rocking her mother. 'Right now.'

Blackmane took a step towards her, and she took a step back.

'I am not asking your permission,' she said. 'The sooner I go, the fewer people will die.'

Tatum cleared his throat. 'Not to play devil's advocate here, but there's a lot of sense in what she's saying. Lord Cuckoo is prepared to burn the world down in order to get her back, and her return will soothe him in the interim.'

Blackmane stared at him like he was a traitor. 'Or maybe he accidentally kills her—like he almost did last time.' He looked back at Isabel. 'Go comfort your friend. She needs you.'

Isabel searched his eyes. Then, with a defeated nod, she returned to Ita.

'How quickly can we get those children out?' Thorn asked.

'We estimate two hundred children,' Tolly said. 'One at a time utilising a single tunnel. It'll take all day, but more realistically, it'll end up being as many as we can before someone notices they're missing.'

'That's a lot of hours,' Thorn replied. 'A lot of corpses hanging from trees.'

Blackmane blinked slowly. He hated the thought as much as any of them. He simply was not prepared to sacrifice Isabel for the cause.

'And when the children are out, the fighting begins,' Tatum said.

Thorn crossed his arms. 'The challenge there is getting enough people inside at one time to make a real impact.'

'We have a little defender trick that'll help with that,' Tatum offered.

'I didn't think you were *allowed* to help with anything,' Tolly said. 'Aren't you supposed to be neutral?'

Tatum brushed a hand over his head. 'I don't see an issue with us casually mentioning the technique before departing.'

They had to leave for Chadora. They should have left two days ago. Yet the timing felt very off. Blackmane wanted to stay to ensure Isabel did not do anything reckless and his brother did not die—again.

He glanced over at Ita, who continued to calmly rock her mother. But someone was missing from the picture now.

Isabel.

He turned, searching for her.

'What's wrong?' Tatum asked.

Blackmane turned in a full circle. 'Where's Isabel?'

They all looked around.

'She can't have gone far,' Thorn said.

Blackmane had an image in his head of her being snatched up by a soldier while they stood there talking, but then he realised Ita's horse was also missing.

He made a dash for his mare.

'Talk to me,' Tatum said, running after him.

Blackmane leapt onto his horse. 'She's gone to hand herself in.'

'You need to let her go,' Ita called to him. 'I know it's scary, but if it keeps a few more people alive, then it'll be worth it.'

Blackmane pressed his teeth together. 'He nearly killed her.'

'And now she knows what he's capable of,' Ita replied. 'She's smarter and stronger than you think. We're all here for the same reason—to save lives.' She paused. 'Let her do her part.'

Blackmane shook his head repeatedly, eyes going to Tatum.

The commander nodded once. 'It was her choice to go.'

How was he expected to do nothing when her scent remained on his skin, the memory of her arched beneath him barely a few hours old? But Tatum was right. It was her choice, and he had to respect it.

He exhaled long and hard, then dismounted, walking circles for a minute. His feet stopped, and he looked at the others. 'All right. You have until the end of the day tomorrow to get her out, or I'm going in.'

Tatum rubbed his forehead. 'I guess we're staying another day.'

*I*sabel returned to the area where they had cut Yvaine down, waiting amid the dead for some-body from the camp to arrive. She did not have to wait long. A pair of guards appeared minutes later, a horse trailing behind them with a dead man bound to its back. He was number five. Five people were dead simply because Hodge refused to be separated from her.

'Well, well, well,' said one of the guards. 'Who do we have here?'

She raised her chin. 'I think you know who I am. Now, escort me back to the camp so this insanity can stop.'

The other guard chuckled. 'On your horse, then. We don't have much light left.'

She did as she was told. 'How do we get word to His Lordship that I am on my way so no more people die?'

'We don't,' the second man said.

The guards proceeded to escort her to the camp, barely speaking throughout the journey. Isabel felt sicker with every passing hour.

It was dark when they finally arrived, and two torches burned either side of the gate.

'Incoming!' called out one of the guards as they neared the entrance to the camp.

A moment later, Isabel heard the scrape of the drawbar being removed, and the gate split down the middle. They opened it wide enough for the horses to slip through before immediately closing behind them.

'Tell the executioner that Lady Isabel is here,' the man said to the guard inside.

Isabel stopped her horse and asked the man, 'How many dead?'

He looked her up and down before replying. 'Eight.'

She gripped the pommel of the saddle. 'Eight?' Three more people had died waiting for her to arrive.

The drawbar slid back into place behind her, and she followed the waiting guards. She was aware of the prisoners watching her as she made her way to the tents at the back of the camp but did not dare look in their direction. She was too afraid of what she might see on their faces. They knew exactly who she was and what had taken place in her absence.

Hodge emerged from his tent when he heard the horses, eyes locking on her. She had no idea what to expect from him, whether he would be beside himself with remorse or lost in his own rage. His eyes moved slowly over her, taking in her appearance from head to toe.

'What on earth are you wearing?' he asked, sounding almost repulsed. 'You look like an absolute peasant.'

She had given no thought to what she was wearing or

how he would react to seeing her dressed like a waste-lander. Of course he would not like it. He had tried so hard to erase that part of her. She did not bother replying.

He walked over to her horse, offering his hand. She stared down at it, feeling disgust at the thought of touching him. But this was the choice she had made, to return to him, to appease him until the gate was opened for all to leave. She could make this hard or easy on herself. So she took his hand and dismounted.

When her feet touched the ground, Hodge turned her to face him, looking deep into her eyes. 'Your actions have driven me to places I never thought I would go. I did what I had to. I hope you understand that.'

Again, she said nothing.

His soft, clammy hand enclosed hers, and he led her into his tent, gesturing for her to sit at the table.

'I would prefer to stand as I have been sitting for hours.'

He watched her a moment. 'There is something different about you.'

She swallowed.

He poured her some water from the jug on the table. 'You made it surprisingly far without a horse. Your feet must be a sight.'

She had been expecting these kinds of questions. 'I have Ita's horse.'

His eyebrows rose. 'I suppose it should come as no surprise that she was waiting to help you.'

'No, it really should not. She is a very loyal friend.' As far as he was aware, the defenders had returned to Chadora, and she wanted to keep it that way.

'I am surprised she supported your returning to me.' He handed her the cup.

She watched him over the brim as she drank. When she was done, she handed him the empty cup. 'One of the women you hanged was Ita's mother.'

His eyebrows rose. 'I did not even know she was living in the camp.' He paused to think. 'I gather she was the woman who aided your escape?'

'All she did was remove the belt from my wrists.'

'Which started this whole nightmare. She is the reason I almost lost you.'

Isabel blinked away the image of Yvaine suspended from a tree. 'She was a cook in our household for more than twenty years. She was my mother's friend and a beautiful human being.'

He appeared unmoved by this revelation. 'Am I expected to remember all the faces of your past?'

She looked away. 'That woman helped raise me.'

'I assure you she did not die because she was Ita's mother. Perhaps if she had identified herself—'

'She was afraid you would kill her. A valid fear, it turns out.'

He gave her an exasperated look. 'What a mood you have arrived in.'

'I just left Ita with her mother's corpse.'

He put the cup down and stepped closer to her. 'So you are angry and once again determined to carry past grievances into our future?'

She blinked. 'I found her hanging from a tree mere hours ago.'

'And we both know that me standing here telling you I

am sorry will do little to ease your suffering. You are a very sensitive woman. I understand that. So tell me what you need from me.'

She regarded him. 'Tell me what you want from me.'

His expression softened. 'You already know. I want you as my wife, as the mother of my children. I want you forever—and soon. The waiting has been pure torture, and I stand by what I said yesterday. It is not good for either of us.'

From another man, under different circumstances, those words might have been romantic. But from Hodge, after what he had done, they were grotesque.

'It did occur to me, after your sudden departure, that perhaps I had gotten a little carried away with the idea of marrying you here in the camp,' he continued. 'It is only natural that you want your family to bear witness to our union.'

She ran with that notion. 'Yes. They would be most disappointed to miss it.'

Hodge linked his hands behind his back and began to pace. 'To be honest, this entire journey has been a disaster. From Trahern being killed to the defenders looking down their noses at me, as though their morals are superior. We all know they are nothing but ruthless killers. Then Ita showed up…' He tutted, then turned back to her, wagging a finger in her direction. 'And this place brings out the worst in you. You have been a different person since we left those walls.'

Funny, she had never felt more like herself. The waste-lands had brought her back to life. Of course he did not like that. He needed her contained.

'So,' he said, clapping his hands together, 'I think we should head home as soon as possible and leave all this toxicity behind us.'

That was not where she thought the conversation was going. 'But you have things you need to take care of here.'

'Nothing that is more important than us.' He closed the distance between them. 'I am committed to restoring our love.' His hands went to her waist. 'We shall leave for Hampstead Keep tomorrow.'

His hands made her skin want to crawl off her body. 'Tomorrow?'

'I do have a few things to take care of in the morning, but I really think the sooner the better. Remaining here feels like an invitation to fate to throw more obstacles in our path.'

The groups needed time to refine and implement their plans. Once she was back behind the walls of Hampstead Keep, there would be no chance of freedom for her.

'I would like you to spend the night with me tonight,' he said.

She stepped out of his hold. 'No.' The word came out with more disdain than she had intended.

He chuckled. 'Relax, my beloved. Your virtue will remain intact until we are wed, I promise you that.'

The man was in for the shock of his life if that wedding ever took place.

'I simply wish to hold you while we sleep.' He walked to the corner where her bag was located. 'I had your things brought in. Normally I would give you privacy to change, but given what happened yesterday, I will be staying in the tent this time.' He dropped the bag at her feet, then turned his back to her. 'Take as much time as you need.'

She stared at him for a moment, then looked down at the open bag. It was clear from the placement of things that he, or possibly someone else, had been through it. With no other choice, she fetched out a nightdress and changed into it.

'Decent?' he asked.

She hugged herself. 'Yes.'

He walked over to the cot and stripped down to braies and an under tunic, then climbed into bed. 'Come,' he said, like he was commanding a dog.

She glanced over at the lit candle. Normally she would insist that it be put out, but her fear of lying in the dark with him outweighed her fear of the tent catching fire.

'You can blow it out if you like,' he said.

She shook her head. 'No. It is fine as is.'

He held the blankets open to her, waiting. Everything about this moment felt wrong, but she went to him anyway, lying down on her side at the far edge of the cot. She went rigid as he tucked the blankets around her, then buried his face in her hair. His arm went over her, and everything inside her recoiled.

'I love you,' he whispered.

She responded with silence.

Thankfully, he fell asleep within minutes, without further expectations. There was no way she could have kissed him. The mere sensation of him breathing into her hair was already more than she could bear.

Seven hours she lay there, blinking and staring up at

the roof of the tent, while he breathed loudly in her ear. True to his word, he held her all night. *All night*. His arm grew heavier and heavier with every breath she drew.

She did not know what the next day would bring. She simply prayed that she was strong enough to survive it.

CHAPTER 26

The plan was not without its faults, but it was the best play they could pull off with the time restraints they had. Blackmane wanted Isabel out yesterday but was forced to settle for the following day instead.

They worked overnight, completing the tunnel into the children's area. Men and women formed a line from the mouth of the tunnel, passing pails of dirt back and forth along it. They emptied them far from the camp to avoid attracting the attention of guards passing through the area. Not taking any chances, they set up a perimeter of soldiers to ensure they could work without the stress of being discovered.

They broke through the surface on the other side of the fence a little before dawn. The hole was no larger than a cup, widening to three feet below. They could not afford to draw the attention of the guards or the children who would arrive when the sun rose. Once everyone was settled for the day, someone would go in and widen the hole so they could begin the process of extraction.

'We need someone who the children will trust,' Tolly said. They were seated high up in the branches of a hornbeam, fifty yards back from the fence, waiting for the children to arrive. 'I thought perhaps Ita could do it.'

'Afraid not,' Blackmane said. 'She's away on a special assignment. But I'll do it.'

Tatum ran a hand down his face. 'Firstly, it's annoying that children do, in fact, like you when most adults don't. But secondly, we're supposed to be neutral observers.'

'I'm not going to kill anyone.'

Tatum laughed. 'If I had a shilling for every time I've heard that.'

Thorn looked Blackmane up and down. 'Do you think the children will trust you in that uniform?'

Blackmane shrugged. 'They'll respect me.'

'We might have to settle for that,' Tolly said. 'At the very least, he'll hold their attention long enough to share our plan.'

Thorn sat up a little straighter, peering through the branches. 'Here they come.'

All four men looked towards the camp, watching in silence as children entered the enclosure in single file, some carrying infants seemingly too young to be separated from their mothers.

'Ready for stage one?' Tatum asked.

The men nodded and began to climb down, except for Thorn, who remained where he was. He would be their eyes above.

When they reached the bottom, they headed to the

mouth of the cave, where the first runner was waiting. His job was to take the child to the safe zone when they surfaced.

'There's not a lot of airflow in there right now,' Tolly said, 'but it'll improve when you open up the other end.'

Tatum clapped him on the back. 'Don't forget to smile for the children.'

Blackmane ignored him as he removed all of his weapons aside from one dagger, then picked up the trenching tool and tucked it into his trousers. He climbed down into the narrow shaft, dropping onto his hands and knees. The tunnel was around one hundred and fifty feet long, and it took him close to five minutes to reach the end. The air inside was foul and damp, the darkness the most difficult part. He had to use one hand to feel out his surroundings until he eventually reached a wall of dirt at the other end. He looked up, eyes narrowing on the small circle of light above. He waited for the signal that the guards had left the enclosure.

Clang, clang, clang.

Out came the tool, and he started to dig, guiding the dirt away from his face. He paused when he saw many curious faces peering down into the hole. It would only be a matter of time before one of the guards noticed the odd behaviour.

He tore the remaining edges away with his hand and looked between the faces. 'I'm here to get you out. All the children first, then the rest of your families. To do that, I need someone to be my second-in-command.' Blackmane's voice was just above a whisper. 'Which one of you knows what that means?'

'Are you a defender?' asked one of the girls. She was watching him with intense curiosity rather than fear.

'Yes I am.'

'Are we going to Chadora?' asked a boy.

'No.'

One of the girls, probably around five, brought her face close to his. 'Do we get a sword?'

'Absolutely not.' He focused again on the first girl who had spoken. 'You. Will you be my second-in-command?'

She angled her head, thinking. 'Do I have to do exactly what you say?'

He nodded. 'You also have to ensure that everyone else does exactly what I say.'

She appeared pleased by that thought. 'And punish those who don't listen?'

'I'm certain everyone will listen to you. What's your name, soldier?'

'Wynne, sir.'

'How old are you?'

'Seven.'

He nodded. 'Optimal age for this position. Now, listen carefully, because I'm only going to say this once. First thing, I need everyone to move away from this hole so as to not draw the attention of the guards. Have them do whatever they normally do and pretend nothing's happening over here.'

The girl looked around at the children pressed together around the hole. 'You heard the man. Off you go, before I start lopping off fingers.'

The area cleared out quickly. He had chosen well.

'I want you to bring me the youngest child in the

enclosure, and I'm going to take them through the tunnel. Others will come through after me, and it's your responsibility to have the next youngest ready to go.'

'But I don't know everyone's age.'

'That's all right. Go by size. You can bring me the smallest child in here, all right?'

She looked around, eyes wide. 'You mean the babies?'

Blackmane's stomach fell. 'There are babies in here?'

She nodded.

Apparently they were not prepared to lose their workers for too long. 'Yes. Bring me one of the babies.'

Wynne disappeared from sight, returning a minute later awkwardly holding a baby who was no older than six months old.

'Her mother cries every morning when the guards take her. Then the baby cries all day. I brought you the noisy one first.'

That revelation extinguished any doubts he was having in that moment. They would get the mother out, and the two of them would never be separated again.

He took the infant and tucked it against his chest. 'Have the next one ready, all right?'

'Yes, sir.'

The journey back through the tunnel took twice as long with the baby. Without a hand free to navigate, he frequently brushed against the walls, resulting in dirt crumbling down around him. At least there was better airflow now. Still, by the time he reached the other end, he was sweating profusely, and the baby was crying.

Everyone appeared shocked when he emerged and offered up the infant.

'Are you fucking joking?' Tatum said, taking the crying infant from him and handing it to the runner. 'Someone find a wet nurse.'

'We're going to need more than one,' Blackmane added.

The runner tucked the baby against him and took off. One of Thorn's men dropped down into the shaft, preparing to leave.

Blackmane clamped a hand on his shoulder. 'Any problems, ask for Wynne.' Letting go, he added, 'And by no means give her a weapon of any description.'

The man gave him a puzzled look before getting down on hands and knees and heading off through the tunnel.

Tolly jogged up to where they stood. 'Was that a baby I just saw?'

Blackmane nodded. 'There are more on their way.'

Tolly cursed under his breath. 'Am I still not allowed to kill the man responsible?'

'You can kill him,' Tatum said. 'We just can't *let* you kill him. Best wait until we're back behind Chadora's walls to do it.'

Tolly walked away muttering something about defenders.

They got more efficient as time passed, managing to get twelve infants out in the first hour. The problem was they had roughly one hundred and eighty children to go, which at their current pace would take them another fifteen hours.

'We don't have fifteen hours,' Tolly said when he returned. 'We have six hours at best until mothers come looking for their children, and then we're going to have some problems.'

Blackmane glanced in the direction of the camp. 'We can make up time with the older children, take them through three or four at a time.'

'Good point,' Tatum said. 'We'll tie them together with a rope if we have to. That way no one gets lost or left behind.'

Tolly nodded. 'Let's get them out.'

For the next three hours, men climbed in and out of the tunnels, returning with as many children as they could coordinate at the time. That number varied depending on the emotional state of the children coming through. Naturally, some of them were scared, especially because they did not know the state of the children on the other side.

They were around one hundred and forty children in when a whistle sounded from the tree above, signalling that a guard had entered the pen.

'Shit,' Tatum said, picking up the bars and tapping them together. 'Who's in there?'

'One of mine,' Tolly replied, staring hard at the tunnel.

Tatum placed the bars down. 'They're going to notice that many missing children.'

'We don't know what the situation is,' Blackmane said, 'only that someone entered the enclosure. Maybe one of the cooks bringing food.'

'Or a mother coming to feed her child,' Tatum said.

A second whistle sounded, different to the first. The three men looked at each other. It was the signal to collapse the tunnel. The problem was they still had a man inside, which meant there was likely a child inside too.

'Come on,' Tolly said under his breath, beginning to pace.

Tatum and Blackmane retrieved their bows, loaded them, and pointed them at the hole.

Another whistle sounded. *Collapse the tunnel.*

'It's been too long,' Tatum said. 'We need to stick to the plan.'

Tolly drew his sword. 'Give him a moment. He'll make it out. I know he will.'

Blackmane and Tatum exchanged a look.

A tense minute passed before they heard someone approaching. The defenders took aim when they saw movement at the bottom. It was Tolly's man. He lifted a boy up to them, and a runner came forwards to take him.

'I heard the signal,' the man in the tunnel said. 'I only had time to get one.'

Tatum reached for him, pulling him up, while Blackmane kept his arrow trained on the dark hole. He was about to tell them to collapse the tunnel when a face appeared at the bottom. Thankfully, he hesitated long enough to recognise Wynne. She stood up, eyes wide with fear. She had followed them through the tunnel. He reached for her, pulling her up onto the ground beside him.

'Are there any more of you in the tunnel?'

She shook her head, eyes welling up. 'I'm so sorry, sir.'

A cold sensation travelled down Blackmane's spine. He looked over at Tolly. 'Collapse the tunnel—now.'

A runner appeared, taking Wynne by the hand and

dragging her away. Others ran forwards with shovels and began digging into the dirt and smashing their heels into the edges. An arrow burst from the darkness below, striking one man through the chest. The two defenders fired arrows into the hole, one after another, giving whoever was inside no more chances to do anything other than retreat. There was a cry of pain as one arrow hit the target, and then the mouth of the tunnel began to collapse as men continued to dig and push at the dirt. Eventually, they were forced to step back to avoid ending up in the hole. The walls of the tunnel collapsed, sending a cloud of dust up into the air. Then everything went still.

Blackmane looked over at Tolly, who was crouched beside the dying man, then at Tatum. 'It's time for stage two.'

CHAPTER 27

*I*t was time to emerge from their hiding places and draw their swords.

'Planks ready!' Tolly shouted.

Tatum brought his fingers to his mouth and whistled up at Thorn, confirming they were going in. That whistle echoed from tree to tree until it had circled the entire perimeter of the camp and made its way back to them.

'Let's go!' Tolly shouted. 'Move!'

Men emerged from the trees at a run, twenty-foot planks balanced on their shoulders as they ran straight for the camp walls. Every able-bodied wastelander followed.

'Remember,' Tatum said to Blackmane, 'Thorn's going to retrieve Isabel. You're not to go anywhere near Hodge. We get the children out and leave the fighting to them.'

'I remember.' Though he did not like it.

'Shoot only from the shadows,' Tatum added. 'We're aiming for discreet.'

Blackmane gave him a casual salute before following the others.

239

They taught the plank technique to defenders early in their training. It was effective for small walls. Anything over fifteen feet would be a challenge. One end of the plank went to the top of the construction, the other to the ground. Two men would follow close, one with pegs and the other with a mallet. These were used to secure the wood in place. The moment they stepped back, two men carrying the second plank would run to the top of the first, securing the other half of the bridge in place. They did not always have the luxury of pegging the other side. In fact, often the second plank would be dragged away by the occupants, forcing the intruder to jump if they wished to enter. Usually, if enough planks landed at the same time, a few would manage to survive. They only needed a few entry points.

So, every fifty feet along the fence line, planks simultaneously hit the ground on the other side. Chaos erupted inside the camp.

The remaining children were the first priority. Two of the wooden bridges landed inside the enclosure, and Tatum and Blackmane were first to cross. They immediately took cover, their job to guard the fence and protect those who followed them in, whose sole purpose was to get the children to the runners waiting on the other side.

But the children were not there.

Tatum watched the fence down his arrow. 'They knew we were coming.'

'What now?' Blackmane asked, gesturing to the others to draw their weapons.

Tatum headed for the open gate. 'Now we hunt.'

The pair exited the children's pen and entered what

could only be described as a battlefield. Not only had the rebel groups successfully penetrated the camp, but the prisoners, realising what was happening, had joined the fight.

Tatum stopped one of Thorn's men as he went to run by. 'Direct all the women to the children's enclosure,' Tatum said. 'The runners will take them to the safe zone.'

A camp guard came for Tatum as they resumed walking, sword raised to strike him. Blackmane shot him through the neck.

'So much for being discreet,' Tatum muttered. 'The warden's going to have our heads when he finds out about this.'

Blackmane was firing arrows left and right at that point. 'I'm technically in the shadows due to the angle of the sun.'

Tatum put his bow away and drew his sword. 'I may as well fight properly if we're in trouble anyway.' He looked around. 'Where would you hide sixty-odd children?'

Blackmane's eyes kept drifting in the direction of the guest tents at the end, hoping to glimpse Isabel. She would likely be in hiding with Hodge, under heavy guard.

Tatum clicked his fingers in front of Blackmane's face. 'Are we focused here?'

Blackmane cleared his throat. 'What about the sleeping quarters?' He raised his bow and shot another camp guard behind Tatum. 'Or the gallows?'

'That's rather dark.' Tatum turned and drove his sword through the guard's stomach. 'Though I wouldn't put anything past Hodge at this point.' He looked around. 'Let's start with the sleeping quarters.'

They weaved their way through the fighting, trying very hard to not be a part of it and failing miserably. Every now and then, Blackmane would load his bow and discreetly fire an arrow into a guard's back if the prisoner he was fighting appeared to be at a disadvantage.

'I saw that,' Tatum would say.

The guards would have a chance to surrender once the wastelanders had control of the camp. Then Tolly and Thorn would send them marching east—with Hodge in tow.

There was no guard outside the first house, so Blackmane went straight through the door, bow poised as he turned in a full circle. 'Empty.'

They continued through it, exiting via the door at the other end. There was a guard standing outside the second house. He startled when they appeared, eyes widening. Blackmane pointed an arrow at his face and said, 'You have one chance to run.'

The man backed up all the way to the door, then took off towards the road.

Tatum pushed the door open, and Blackmane rushed in, gaze sweeping the length of the room. He stopped and listened. Nothing. He looked over his shoulder at Tatum. 'Lucky number three?'

They headed to the exit.

Charging out the door on the other side, they almost knocked down a guard posted there. The man turned, sword swinging at Tatum. The commander disarmed him in three moves, then kicked him in the stomach. The guard landed on his back. They would have let him live if he had not drawn a dagger from his feet and come at them again. Blackmane shot him through the heart, gifting him a quick death.

'No guard outside the third house,' Tatum noted.

Blackmane watched the guard draw his last breath before looking up. 'Let's take a look inside.'

They stormed into the final building, turning in circles as they made their way to the far end. They combed every inch of the house to make sure they had not missed anything, lifting mattresses and throwing blankets all about the place.

'Maybe the gallows isn't such a crazy suggestion after all,' Tatum said.

Blackmane looked back in the direction they had come. 'Let's go back to the second house.'

'Why? It was empty.'

Blackmane met his eyes. 'Because it was guarded.'

They headed back the way they had come, following the path back to the second house. They quietly pulled the door open this time. Blackmane entered first, finding it as empty as it had been before.

Tatum looked around. 'Should we start slicing the mattresses open?'

Without replying, Blackmane walked slowly through the house, boots landing softly on the hardwood floor. He felt the weight of someone watching him. Pausing, he dropped his gaze to the ground, then slowly leaned his weight on his front foot. The floorboard creaked. His gaze travelled along it to the joins.

'Cover me,' he said to Tatum.

The commander ran forwards, sheathing his sword and loading his bow.

Blackmane gestured to the floor, and Tatum replied with a nod. The defender stepped back and drew his dagger, sliding it between two pieces of wood. They were loose.

He lifted one, and Tatum took aim at the gap in the floor. At first Blackmane could see nothing but shadows, but once his eyes adjusted, he made out little faces staring up at him.

Blackmane dropped to his knees and cautiously peered inside. 'There you are. Everyone all right?'

No one spoke.

'Any guards down there with you?'

Nothing.

Tatum kept his arrow trained on them. 'Be careful.'

'You all ready to get out of here?' Blackmane asked. 'Go find your parents?'

No one moved.

The men exchanged a confused look.

'I know you're scared,' Tatum said, 'but someone needs to start talking.'

One of the boys glanced at the girl next to him before saying, 'They said if we made a sound, they would hang us next to our fathers.'

Blackmane reached out to the boy. 'That's just something scared people say. Come on. Let's get you out of here.'

Tatum pulled up another board to widen the gap, and then the pair lifted the children up and out of the ground. 'Probably safest for them to wait in here until the camp's secure. Wouldn't want them getting caught in the crossfire.'

Blackmane nodded in agreement.

The sound of the door opening had him reaching for his weapon, but it was only Thorn.

Blackmane drew his eyebrows together. He was supposed to be retrieving Isabel.

'Where is she?' Blackmane asked him.

Thorn glanced at Tatum, which made Blackmane's stomach twist into knots. It was bad news.

'Where is she?' he asked again.

Realising what they were doing, Thorn walked over to help. 'I don't know.'

Blackmane stiffened. 'What do you mean, you don't know?'

Thorn lifted a little girl out and placed her safely on the floor beside him. 'Hodge made it out.'

The words hung heavy in the air between them. That was impossible. Utterly impossible. The man was about as handy with a sword as Tatum was at doing his own laundry. 'How the hell did they get out?'

'Apparently they left for Hampstead Keep an hour before we attacked.'

Blackmane linked his hands atop his head and turned in a circle. Of course he had taken her to Hampstead Keep. He would be in full control of her there. 'I have to stop them.'

'Nope,' Tatum said immediately. 'If you go, someone will wind up dead. It's the only way that ends.'

'Not necessarily.'

Tatum took a step towards him. 'You can't get to her without getting through him. Tell me I'm wrong.'

If they made it back to Hampstead Keep, she was never leaving there again. 'I'll figure it out on the way.'

'You're not going,' Tatum said calmly, 'and that's final.'

Blackmane stared at him. 'Really? You're going to tell me to stay? Do nothing?'

'Don't give me that horseshit. We've done plenty, much more than we were ever allowed to.' He gestured to the children. 'Look around you.'

Blackmane pinched the bridge of his nose. 'I swear to you, before Belenus, if you let me go, Hodge will return to Hampstead Keep alive.'

Tatum's jaw tightened. 'You don't even know which way they went.'

'I'll track them.'

There was a long silence before Tatum threw his hands in the air in defeat. 'Fucking love.' He shook his head. 'I better not regret this.'

*B*lackmane took the most direct route, knowing Hodge would be keen to get her back behind walls as quickly as possible. That meant he had to move quickly to make up for lost time.

He rode at a steady canter, eyeing the hoof tracks on the road without knowing if he was following the right ones. At least he did not have to worry about random rebel attacks anymore. They were all a little preoccupied at that time.

An hour into his journey, he noticed Margery circling overhead. He slowed his horse to a walk and watched her a moment. She was hovering directly above him. Shaking his head, he raised one arm in the air and waited to see what she would do. She surprised him by flying down and landing on him, eyeing him warily from the farthest point on his arm.

'How do we do this?' Blackmane asked the bird. 'Because you have no idea what I'm saying, and I have no idea what you're thinking.'

TANYA BIRD

The eagle jerked her head left and right, studying him
from every possible angle.

'I know you don't want her going back to that place
either. Where is she?' He released a breath and looked
heavenward. 'And now I'm talking to a bird.'

Margery spread her wings and flew off but returned a
moment later as though waiting for him.

Blackmane kicked his horse back into a canter. 'If
you're going east and I'm going east, then we may as well
go east together.'

A short time after, Margery dipped left and disappeared into the trees. Blackmane brought his horse to a
halt and stared after her. He could not afford to lose time
by participating in a wild-goose chase. Or, in this case, a
domesticated-eagle chase. He had an hour of sunlight left
at best.

He was about to proceed east when Margery reappeared, landing on a branch up high and glaring down
at him.

'Am I supposed to trust you? Just follow you into the
forest and hope you know what you're doing?'

Margery responded by flying off again. Cursing under
his breath, Blackmane left the road and headed into the
trees after her.

He followed the eagle north for a while, watching the
sun continue to sink. Just when he was beginning to think
he had made a big mistake, he emerged onto a road.
Margery landed on a low branch nearby with what looked
an awful lot like an 'I told you so' expression. She was
waiting to see what he would do next.

Blackmane glanced both ways down the road, then

looked down at the ground. He counted six sets of fresh hoofprints headed east. The corners of his mouth lifted. 'I guess you're not just a pretty face after all.' He looked up at the eagle. 'After you.'

Off she flew, this time rising high into the sky before hovering.

Blackmane's horse was tiring, so he continued at a trot now. That was fine, because he could tell by the spacing of the prints that the party ahead of him was moving at a walk. He suspected he was close when Margery disappeared from sight. That was as near as she would get to Hodge. Blackmane could not blame her after their encounter.

He decided to get in front of the group, because Hodge was more likely to stop if Blackmane was physically in his way. He veered his horse right into the trees and continued at a fast walk, listening for any noise up ahead. Nothing. He decided to return to the road and saw the tracks were gone. At some point, the group had left the road also.

'What are you up to, Hodge?' he muttered as he looked around.

He crossed the road and trotted into the trees, but a few minutes later, he stopped again. A familiar feeling came over him. He realised he was no longer the one doing the hunting.

Letting go of the reins, he raised both hands. 'My bow's on my back. My sword's sheathed. Let's talk.'

At first, silence. Then finally a horse walked into view.

Hodge.

'I thought I made it clear that you were no longer a welcomed guest in Carmarthenshire.'

Blackmane slowly lowered his hands, resting them on the pommel of his saddle. 'Word in the woods is that you're no longer a welcomed guest in these parts either.'

Hodge watched him carefully from twenty feet away. 'All right. I will take the bait. Clearly there is something you wish to tell me, defender, so go ahead.'

'The wastelanders started a war today. Judging by your composure and the steady speed at which you're travelling, I'm guessing you haven't heard.'

'What in heaven's name are you rambling on about, defender?'

Blackmane looked around for Isabel, but she was nowhere in sight. 'I'm saying that your father's noble idea to build a camp for the people of Carmarthenshire has run its course.' He paused. 'Sometimes these ideas just don't work, not because people resist being rehabilitated but because they never needed it to begin with. It's over.' It was undeniably enjoyable watching the colour drain from Hodge's face. 'You'll need to find another way to make money.'

Hodge's face twitched. 'You expect me to believe that rebels have taken control of my camp in the short time since I left?'

'I don't expect anything from you. I didn't come here for that.'

'Then what are you doing here, defender?'

Blackmane searched the trees behind Hodge. 'I came to collect one of the prisoners.'

'Well, I am sorry for the wasted journey, but there are no prisoners here.'

'I'm talking about Lady Isabel.'

A faint smile settled on Hodge's face. 'You know, I do not blame you for taking a fancy to her. She is truly lovely and would seem all the more enticing to a barbaric man like yourself. I was aware of your interest, from the very first day. I noted the way you kept a *special* eye on her during our short time together. I tolerated your presence because I had to. But now your heroic gestures are really starting to get on my nerves.' He brushed a finger down his nose. 'So let me be very clear about something. Lady Isabel returns to Hampstead Keep of her own free will. She is safe, and she is no longer your concern.'

'If that's true, then I'll wish you both well and be on my way. But I'm going to need to hear it from her mouth.'

Hodge's smile broadened. 'Always the protector. I worry, however, that you might be drastically overstepping. The fact that you are here without your comrades says a lot.'

'You don't have to worry about me. I'm very capable on my own.'

Hodge chuckled lightly and looked over his shoulder. 'Bring her out.'

A few moments later, four guards emerged from the trees, Isabel tucked between them. Her eyes were sunken with fatigue, her face a pale contrast against the vibrant green dress she was wearing. She held his gaze for a moment before looking at Hodge.

'My beloved,' Hodge began, 'Blackmane here has

ridden all this way to check on you. Is that not terribly considerate of him?'

She did not reply.

'I was just telling him how much you are looking forward to being reunited with your family at Hampstead Keep.' He adjusted his hands on the reins. 'Can you *imagine* how devastated they would be if you did not return as planned? Lady Gwenore and Everard are two of our biggest advocates.'

Isabel kept her eyes down and mouth closed. The control this man still had over her blew Blackmane away. But this time, that smug expression on his face was not justified.

'You sure about that?' Blackmane asked, looking him straight in the eye.

'Which part, defender?'

'The part about them being your biggest advocates.' He paused for effect. 'And the part about them being at Hampstead Keep.'

Isabel lifted her gaze, eyes showing life for the first time.

Hodge's expression darkened. 'You have no authority over any person within my estate. The only way those two would leave Hampstead Keep would be at my request.'

Now it was Blackmane's turn to look smug. 'That may have been true when you left, but a lot has happened since then, *my lord*. One of those things is that Ita Chapman was found alive and well—despite your best efforts. Another is that her mother was hanged to her death at your request.'

Hodge shifted in his saddle. 'Events that need to be explained in person so they are not misconstrued.'

One corner of Blackmane's mouth lifted. 'I agree. That's why Ita borrowed a horse and made the journey to Hampstead Keep—before her mother was even buried. She knew they would want to know as soon as possible so they could make arrangements to leave before you returned.'

Isabel pressed a hand to her chest and exhaled a shaky breath. Her relief was palpable.

Hodge's eyes glazed over. 'Even if I were to believe you, this changes nothing.'

'This changes everything,' Isabel said, speaking for the first time. '*Everything*. It is as if the shackles have been cut from my feet and hands.'

Hodge stared at her, his expression unreadable. The defender kneaded the leather reins between his fingers as he waited to see how the earl would react to this news.

'Like a knife to the heart,' Hodge said. 'But even still, I forgive the vile words that come from your mouth.' He looked back at Blackmane. 'That is *true* love, defender. Love of the rarest kind. Forgiveness is key.' He raised his chin. 'Now, I suggest you turn around and go back to Chadora while I am still calm enough to let you leave.'

'I am coming with you,' Isabel said urgently, pushing her horse forwards.

One of the guards caught the rein of her horse. Blackmane resisted the urge to slice the man's arm off at the shoulder.

Hodge pressed his eyes closed, his patience reaching the end of its tether. 'Do not make a scene. I beg of you.'

Opening his eyes, he narrowed them at Blackmane once again. 'Last chance to ride away, defender. After that, I will not be held responsible for what my guards do.'

'You're rarely held accountable for anything, are you?' Blackmane replied.

Hodge rolled his eyes heavenward.

'Now, here are my terms,' Blackmane continued. 'Your guards can either hand the lady over to me, or I can take her from them. For the sake of your men, I suggest the former.'

The heat from Hodge's glare intensified. 'You are grossly outnumbered, and you and I both know that if any harm comes to me at your hands, it will spell disaster for that little kingdom hiding behind its walls.'

Blackmane nodded slowly, then looked around at the guards. 'Sorry, boys. It appears your fierce leader is prepared to sacrifice all of your lives in the name of love.'

A few tense moments passed before Hodge said, 'Your time is up, defender.'

The guards reached for their weapons, but Blackmane had a knife in hand before any of their swords left their sheaths. He threw it, piercing the sword hand of the man closest him. A beat later, he had his bow loaded and pointed at the same man. 'Stop now and you can all leave here alive.'

The men looked at the guard clutching his bleeding hand, then at Hodge.

'Kill him,' Hodge said, not backing down.

Blackmane fired the first arrow through the neck of a guard. Two others retrieved their bows during that time. He shot one in the stomach and leaned back to avoid an arrow from the other, momentarily flattening himself against the horse's rump before springing upright again and taking out the shooter. He dropped another arrow into place and took aim at the fourth guard. The man dropped his weapon and raised his hands.

'Good choice,' Blackmane said.

Hodge had retrieved his own bow during this time and now had it pointed at Blackmane's head.

'Stop,' Isabel said, walking her horse closer to Hodge's.

The earl ignored her. 'Do you give no thought to the people you kill, defender? These men have families waiting at home for them.'

Blackmane was defenceless in that moment, because the only way to prevent himself from being killed was to injure or kill. 'Every one of these deaths lands squarely on your shoulders. You had a chance to save all of them. Be sure to mention that to their families.'

The string of Hodge's bow tightened.

Isabel moved her horse closer still. 'My lord. Look at me. Please.'

Hodge did not look at her. 'Then perhaps I will see you in hell, defender.' His lips curled into a snarl as he released the arrow.

Blackmane leapt from his horse, amazed when the arrow did not hit him on the way to the ground. He rolled once and got back on his feet as quickly as possible. The plan was to disarm Hodge—if he could reach him without dying.

He fixed his eyes on the earl, then froze when he saw Hodge's panicked expression.

His gaze snapped to Isabel. He had not seen her ride

forwards. She looked straight at him, and he knew some-thing was very wrong. His eyes travelled down to the arrow lodged in her shoulder, and all the air left his lungs.

She was the reason the arrow never hit him.

For a moment, he could not move. He simply stared at the arrow protruding from her, vaguely aware of Hodge shouting. Maybe words. Or maybe just an anguished cry. Then she began to fall.

That was the moment Blackmane remembered he could move, act, help. Some feeling returned to his limbs, and he took off at a run towards her, catching her on the way down. He lowered her gently to the ground, and she stared up at him with wide, terrified eyes. He was vaguely aware of Hodge leaping from his horse, of him reloading his bow and pointing it at Blackmane. Isabel gripped his cloak, as if to warn him. He did not know if he had it in him to lay her on the ground, to walk away from her, to *fight*.

Thankfully, he did not have to.

An arrow pierced Hodge's hand, his scream making Blackmane look up. Tolly appeared through the trees, coming to a stop in front of Hodge. When the remaining guard dismounted and snatched up his weapon, Tolly shot him through the neck.

'I'm allowed to kill you,' he said as he looked Hodge over. The earl was clutching his hand, tears spilling down his reddened face. 'All right. Keep it down. It's just a small hole through the hand.' He looked over at Blackmane. 'Can you get her to the camp?'

Blackmane nodded and gathered Isabel in his arms

before rising. 'We're going to get you some help. You stay awake, do you hear me?'

There was the snap of wood as Tolly broke off the end of the arrow lodged in Hodge's hand, then another scream as he pushed it through the appendage and out the other side.

'See?' Tolly said. 'That wasn't so bad, was it?' He frowned at the blood. 'Oh. Let's see if we can find something to stop that bleeding.' First, he went to help Blackmane onto one of the guard's horses, which was far less tired than the one he had arrived on. 'I'll deal with Hodge. You go.'

Another nod from Blackmane.

'Is it bad?' Isabel asked him, still gripping his cloak.

The question tore at his heart. 'You're talking. That's good. Stay awake now.'

Her eyes closed. 'All right. I'll stay awake.'

He glanced at his brother before swinging his horse around and galloping off in the direction of the camp.

CHAPTER 29

'Please. I do not want to go to Hampstead Keep,' Isabel pleaded. She could not keep her eyes open when there was a fire burning in her chest, shoulder, and arm.

Blackmane repositioned her against him. 'No one's going to Hampstead Keep. I'm taking you somewhere safe. I just need you to stay awake until we get there.'

She could do that. She could stay awake if he asked her to. But a breath later, she was drifting off again.

'Belle.'

She just needed a small rest, some sleep to recharge. Then she would do everything he needed her to do.

'Belle.'

It was so much effort to come back to him. 'Mmm?'

'You still awake? Just resting?'

She was vaguely aware of the rocking motion of the horse they were riding on. It was not ideal when trying to remain awake. 'Yes, resting.'

'But you're all right?'

Of course she was all right. His arms were the safest place on earth.

'How's the pain?'

So many questions. It was almost as if he wanted her to stay awake.

She attempted to gauge her pain level and failed. It was likely consistent with being hit by an arrow. 'Better when my eyes are closed.'

Warm lips pressed against her forehead. That made her want to open her eyes, to look up at him, but everything felt so heavy.

'Keep them closed if it helps,' Blackmane said. 'We're nearly there. But I need you to wake up when we get there.'

She thought she nodded, but she must have only done it in her head because Blackmane said her name again. 'Belle. Will you wake for me when we get there?'

She forced her eyes open. It took all of her strength, but she did it for him. His face was a blur. 'Yes. When we get there.'

'Good.'

Then, what felt like three seconds later, she heard, 'Belle, I need you to wake up.' Warm fingers pressed against her neck. 'Come on. You said you would wake up, so wake up.'

She was no longer on the horse. Everything was still now.

'Isabel, I need you to open your eyes and look at me.'

That was a new voice, a female one. Familiar, maybe. She blinked her eyes open to see who it was. It was Genevieve, the Emlyn woman from the caves.

'Is the arrow out?' she asked.

Genevieve appeared relieved, and she turned her attention back to the wound, poking and prodding. 'Give her something to bite down on.'

With enormous effort, Isabel turned her head, looking for Blackmane. He appeared above her, brushing hair back from her face. She had never seen him so anxious. His face was beaded with sweat. 'I told you I would wake up.'

He bent, touching his forehead to hers. 'You did. I need you to bite down on this for me. Can you do that?'

'Yes,' she said with no idea what she was agreeing to. But if he needed her to do it, she would.

A moment later, she tasted leather.

Leather?

Pain exploded through her shoulder again, like she had been shot a second time. She screamed through gritted teeth, surprised she had it in her.

'I need pressure on that,' Genevieve said.

Blackmane moved to the other side of Isabel. Her eyes followed him. She needed to see his face to know everything was all right.

'It's out,' he said. 'You did great.'

Isabel felt hot tears slide down her temples before her eyes sank shut.

~

'Belle.'

That was Ita's voice singing her name. There was

instant comfort in hearing it, like stepping into a warm bath.

'Open your eyes,' Ita urged. 'Look who's here to see you.'

Isabel slowly peeled her eyes open and found an eagle mere inches from her face.

'See?' Ita said, sitting on the edge of the bed. 'I told you she wasn't dead.'

Margery turned her head back and forth, studying Isabel.

'I agree.' Ita nodded. 'She does look like she's been run over by a wagon three times and left to bleed out, but we must remember what my mother always used to say. Some thoughts are *inside* thoughts. Let's not make her feel any worse.'

Isabel went to speak, but her tongue was stuck to the roof of her mouth. It took a moment to work everything loose. 'Water, please?'

Ita rose to fetch it. 'As much as I'd enjoy watching you spill water all over yourself, we should probably get you sitting up first.' She slid her hand beneath Isabel's back and gently raised her up, stuffing a pillow behind her in the process.

Isabel looked down and saw one of her arms was in a sling.

'Genevieve recommended you keep that on for a few days to avoid the temptation of using it and potentially reopening the wound.' She poured some water and brought it to Isabel's mouth.

Isabel emptied the cup, then looked around the unfamiliar room. 'Where are we?'

'Talgarth. They've turned the whole town into an almshouse for the injured.' Ita smiled mischievously. 'We did it, you know. We took the camp. The remaining guards were marched to the border.' She glanced out the window. 'And now everyone is moving about out in the open, above ground, without fear of being captured or having to pack up one's life with a moment's notice.'

Isabel watched Margery settle herself in the blankets, then rested her head back against the wall. It was amazing how exhausting the act of sitting still could be. 'Did you really remove my family from Hampstead Keep?'

'They removed themselves, really. I was just the messenger.' She returned to the bed. 'Though I think it took them a moment to accept what I was telling them.'

Isabel blinked up at the ceiling. 'Did they go to my uncle's?'

'I believe that was the plan, yes.' She took Isabel's hand. 'It might be a while before you see them again, given the state of things.'

Isabel lifted her head. 'The state of things?'

'I mean with the border now in place. Plus, King Edward announced a temporary travel ban between England and Wales.'

Isabel relaxed against the wall again. 'So long as they are safe, I suppose.'

'Your mother is going to hate living on a farm.'

'No question.' There was a spell of silence before Isabel asked, 'How did you get here so quickly?'

Ita laughed. 'I didn't get here quickly. You slept for three days.'

Isabel's head popped up again. '*Three days?*'

Ita suppressed a smile. 'Genevieve was able to rouse you enough to swallow some water, so she was happy with that.' She went to pour Isabel another drink. 'I'm under strict instructions to force-feed you fluids when you wake up. How's the pain?'

'Fine,' she lied. 'So everyone is out of the camp?'

'Every last person. I don't think Lord Hodge will be returning any time soon—especially with a sore hand.' She made a pouty face. 'You know what a whiner he is.'

Isabel thought back to their last encounter. She could only remember snippets. 'Someone shot him. Through the hand?'

'Yes. Much to everyone's disappointment. No idea why Tolly didn't shoot him in the face and be done with it. I guess he was trying to prevent his brother from getting in trouble.'

Ryder.

If three days had passed, he would be back in Chadora by now.

'He's been waiting for you to wake,' Ita said, reading her mind—and panicked expression. 'But he can't stay. If they don't return soon, everyone back home will presume they're dead.'

She needed to go find him. 'Can you help me up?'

'Up? No way. You're supposed to remain in bed.'

Isabel gave her best pleading expression. 'Please? He is the reason I am alive.'

'Actually, he's the reason you got shot.'

The sound of footsteps approaching had Isabel looking to the door. Blackmane appeared a moment later, heavy boots stopping in the doorway as he took in the scene before him. The disapproving scowl was instant.

'You're not trying to get up, are you?' He stepped inside, looking accusingly at Ita.

Ita raised her hands. 'I told her no.' She looked back at Isabel. 'I'll go let Genevieve know you're awake. I'm sure she'll want to check in on you.' She moved past Black-mane and exited the room.

The defender waited until they were alone before speaking again. Isabel noticed he remained close to the door.

'How are you feeling?' he asked.

'Thirsty.'

He walked over to the table, filled her cup, and handed it to her. 'You really should be lying down.'

'I am all right sitting up.'

He retreated to the wall and leaned against it, watching her with a serious expression. 'You really shouldn't have done that.'

It took her a moment to realise what he was referring to. 'Stop the arrow?'

He nodded.

'I told you I would.'

He held her gaze for a long time before finally looking away. A long silence followed. When her cup was empty once again, he stepped up to take it from her.

'I have to return to Chadora,' he said.

'I know.' She kept her eyes on Margery. 'Will you be coming back?'

'That depends on—'

'Your orders,' she finished. Her chest hurt, but she did

not know if it was from the injury or the fact that he was leaving. 'When?'

'The horses are saddled. I wanted to make sure you were all right before we left.'

The pain in her chest worsened. 'What if I go downhill again or the wound becomes infected or something?' She was well aware of how ridiculous she sounded.

He cleared his throat. 'The arrow missed all of your vital organs, and you're in safe hands.'

Her eyes began to sting.

'I don't want this to be awkward,' he said.

She finally looked up at him. 'This is not awkward. This is heartbreaking.'

Nothing changed on his face. Perhaps his heart had finally calloused too.

'It was always going to end with me leaving.' His voice was so quiet.

She swallowed repeatedly. 'I know. But do you have to make it look so easy?'

He rubbed his forehead. 'You think some big emotional display will help us?'

It was his tone that she found most distressing. It was as though Blackmane had already departed and left a faceless defender in his place.

'What about your brother?' she asked, digging for an emotional response from him. 'You will be leaving him behind also.'

'Yes.'

She brushed a stray tear away, embarrassed that it had escaped. 'You could take him with you. I am certain King

Becket would not wish to separate you from the only family you have left.'

There was a flicker of some emotion on his face, but it was gone too fast for her to identify.

'This is his home now. He'll stay and protect it.' He watched her a moment. 'I can't just bring him back to the barracks.'

She nodded. 'You are right. He is needed here.'

A tense moment passed, made worse by the fact that Isabel could now hear horses out front. Their time was up.

Blackmane glanced out the window. 'Keep an eye on that wound. Any odour or change in colour, let Genevieve know right away.'

Her throat burned. 'Thank you.'

'For what?'

'For giving me my life back.'

He nodded once. 'Take care of yourself.' Then he was heading for the door.

'Why did you not ask me to go with you?' The words tumbled out of her, all choked up.

He paused in the doorway and looked back at her. 'You want me to take you from your home—for the second time? Separate you from your family? From Ita?'

'No—'

'You want to live behind walls again?'

'No.' She shook her head. 'But I want *you* to want that.'

He looked out the door. 'I'm not him.' Then he stepped through it, disappearing from sight.

Panic rose in her. She tried to stand, to go to the window, to lay eyes on him again. But suddenly the pain in her chest was everywhere at once. It was not heart-break she was experiencing but a complete shattering of mind and body. She could not stand up, despite how badly she wanted to. She could not even call out to him. Her hands went over her face as a sob tore from her throat. She could not even cry properly. It was all silent heaving and rolling nausea.

Arms went around her, familiar and safe—but they did not belong to Blackmane.

'I'm here,' Ita whispered, holding her tightly. 'I'm here, and I'm not going anywhere.'

*B*lackmane could feel Tatum watching him as he mounted his horse. He was waiting for him to say something.

'I guess we'll talk about it later?' Tatum said, riding up next to him.

Blackmane did not respond.

Glancing over his shoulder, Tatum asked, 'She knows you're leaving? Permanently?'

'What happened to talking later?' Blackmane was resisting the urge to look back at the house. He had heard the retched sob as he walked away, and he had kept walking.

'Shame you didn't get to say goodbye to Tolly.'

Blackmane blinked slowly. His brother was off protecting the borders, which was much more important. 'There's always next time.'

The pair fell silent.

Talgarth was swarming with injured and displaced people trying to find information about missing family members. They would have preferred to stay and help out for a few weeks, but orders were orders, and they had consequences of their own to face back home.

The return journey to Chadora took two days, and Blackmane barely spoke a word the entire time. Tatum managed to fill the long silences with long ramblings that Blackmane had learned to tune out. By the time they reached Chadora, he was exhausted and eager to be away from people for a while. But first they had to face the warden.

Shapur Wright rolled into the barracks like a dark storm, hands on his hips as he looked between them. 'What the hell happened?'

As commander of their unit, it fell upon Tatum to answer. 'I got everyone back here safely, and Hodge returned home alive, sir—as ordered.'

The warden stared him down. 'Did you forget the part about the eastern camp getting ambushed? What about the guards who were slaughtered? Or the wastelands being overtaken by rebel groups again? The English locked out of Carmarthenshire while you two wandered freely through it?'

Tatum went to speak.

'Shut your mouth,' Shapur said before he had a chance. 'I know what you are going to say, and I have already heard it from Alveye and Hadewaye—who arrived home nearly a week ago, by the way. You should have returned with them. The delay only confirms your involvement in this war you had no business being in.' He looked between them. 'I sent you there to *observe*. To keep Lord Hodge *safe*.'

Tatum cleared his throat. 'My understanding is that he's safely inside the walls of Hampstead Keep.'

'With a hole in his hand and minus the woman he is to marry!' Shapur shouted. 'Where is she?'

'Home,' Blackmane said.

The warden's gaze darted to him. 'Yes. I heard all about your part in that. Lord Hodge is requesting your head. He is ready to go to war for this woman.'

'With one hand?' Blackmane asked.

Shapur's eyes flashed, and his mouth flattened into a line as he stepped up into the defender's space. 'You are treading on thin ice, Blackmane. Remember where you came from and what we have handed you.'

Blackmane swallowed.

Shapur looked back to Tatum. 'You are hereby stripped of your command.' He reached out and tore the gold pin from his cloak. 'You better thank Belenus that I am not throwing both your arses outside the gate. Now get out of my sight.'

The men saluted before turning and heading straight for the wash area. They waited until they were a good distance away before speaking.

'That went about as well as I expected,' Tatum said.

Blackmane glanced over his shoulder. 'Were you expecting to be stood down?'

'When you made the comment about Hodge going to war with one hand I was.'

It was out of character for Blackmane to talk back like that. Usually he chose silence when being reprimanded. 'Sorry.'

Tatum waved the apology away. 'Don't be. It was a good joke. Wrong audience, perhaps—and bad timing.'

They were almost to the washroom when Alveye and Hadewaye jogged up to them, looking displeased.

'What happened?' Alveye asked. 'You said you would be a day behind us. Next thing we hear, you're waging a war against England.'

'That's one version of the story,' Blackmane said.

Hadewaye fell into step with Tatum. 'How did you manage to walk away from that conversation with the warden unscathed?'

'Not unscathed,' Tatum replied. 'He took my pin.'

Alveye frowned. 'But left your head, which is the perplexing part.'

'I just got used to calling you Commander,' Hadewaye said.

Tatum clapped him on the back. 'The deep respect you build for a superior will never go away.'

'Where's Isabel?' Hadewaye asked, looking over at Blackmane.

'Carmarthenshire. Where else would she be?'

Hadewaye thought about that. 'I don't know. I thought perhaps you would bring her here with you.'

Blackmane's chest tightened. 'She can barely sit up, let alone ride a horse.'

'We heard she got injured in the... crossfire,' Alveye said, jogging a few paces to catch up. 'So that's it? It's over between you two?'

Blackmane picked up his pace.

'I really liked her,' Hadewaye said. 'She was caring and

funny, and she brought out those things in you.' He looked around at the others. 'Did you all notice that?'

Blackmane looked heavenward. 'Can someone shut him up before I stab him?'

'She was smart too,' Alveye added.

Blackmane drew a long breath.

'And beautiful,' Tatum said. 'If you're into that doe-eyed, fair-haired sort of look. Personally, I prefer brunettes.'

Blackmane shook his head. 'We're done with this subject.'

Everyone fell silent when they reached the wash area. Alveye and Hadewaye settled themselves on barrels to watch the training field, visibly happy to have their friends back, while Tatum and Blackmane stripped down to wash.

'So the whole camp is empty?' Alveye asked. 'Every child out?'

Tatum nodded. 'Every child.'

'What's their plan now?' Hadewaye asked. 'Besides making sure Hodge and his men stay away.'

Tatum headed to one of the tubs and climbed in. 'Hopefully both kings realise the people of Carmarthenshire pose no threat and only wish to be left alone. Thorn and Tolly plan to meet with them both, eventually.'

Hadewaye looked in his direction. 'Do you think either king will agree to meet with someone named Thorn?'

'I imagine they'll resort to their proper names at some point,' Alveye said. 'You two will have to keep your heads down for a while and let all this play out. The warden will be watching you like an eagle.'

Hadewaye winced. 'Might be too soon for eagle mentions.'

Blackmane tried very hard not to listen to anything being said around him. He would have preferred to never talk again if that were an option. The way through these feelings was to focus on work and to bury the previous few weeks deep in his mind. That was how he had always gotten through. The routine of work and training until his fingers bled and legs gave out would keep his mind steady and moods even.

Reaching for the washcloth, he scrubbed hard at his skin, washing away any part of the wastelands that still clung to him. When every inch of him was clean, he submerged himself in the water and let the cold freeze the memories of her.

'Should we be worried?' he heard Alveye ask Tatum as he surfaced.

Blackmane stood, water running off him. 'No, you shouldn't.' He reached for a towel and wrapped it around himself before going to collect his uniform and boots. 'I think I'll go train, get my hours in.'

Hadewaye's eyebrows shot up. 'What are you talking about? You just got back. Not even the warden's expecting you to train today.'

Without saying another word, Blackmane headed for his room.

CHAPTER 31

The scar had reduced to a coin-sized bump just above her heart. Isabel's hand went to it whenever she paused throughout the day, eyes going south to the road that connected Maddock House to the rest of the world. It was in these moments that she thought of him. Not the man who had shot her but the one she had taken an arrow for. And she would have done it again without hesitation, despite all the pain it caused. Both physical *and* mental.

It was incomprehensible that she could miss a person whom she barely knew this much. They had only gotten days together. A few weeks at a stretch. A handful of meaningful conversations. And one afternoon to sample what could have been. The emptiness left by him was not rational, and months later, she was struggling to fill it.

It was during one of these moments that Ita rode up the very road she had been watching, holding a letter in the air.

'It's from your mother,' she called.

Isabel ran out to meet her. It had been two months since any mail had gotten past the marcher lords. In the process of shutting out the world, they had found themselves cut off from it. Funny, that. Isabel's biggest fear was that Lord Hodge would intercept correspondence to her family and use it to gain information. She did not want him knowing where her mother and brother were. The sooner her family made it to Carmarthenshire the better.

'Is it sealed?' Isabel asked as Ita stopped the horse in front of her.

'It was, until it reached the border.'

The wastelanders were not taking any chances.

Isabel took the letter from her friend and opened it to read.

Ita dismounted and waited exactly three seconds before asking, 'Well? Are they coming?'

Isabel's hand went over her mouth, and then she emitted a relieved breath. 'They are going to wait a few more months for things to settle, and then they will relocate to Maddock House in the spring.'

A smile spread across Ita's face. 'That's perfect. We'll have a house for them to live in by then.'

They looked over at the pile of freshly cut trees behind them. Maddock House would never be the grand house it had been, mostly due to lack of materials, but it would stand in exactly the same spot it once had. These kinds of rebuilds were happening throughout the region as people got to work restoring their homes and communities. But since a large majority of the men were away protecting the borders, it fell upon the women to do the bulk of the labour. They were more than happy to, however.

Isabel's chest felt light with hope.

Margery flew down and landed on a nearby post, and the women walked over to shower her with attention.

'Rabbit showed me how to use a trowel,' Ita said. 'We only have a small amount of stone to work with, but I thought I'd teach you how to mix and lay mortar.'

The day before, Rabbit had taught the women how to use an auger, and they had spent the day drilling holes into wood. The day before that, they had spent six hours hammering wooden pegs into the ground. Isabel's hands had been covered in blisters by the end.

'There is something else I would like to learn how to do,' Isabel said, playfully catching hold of Margery's beak.

'Oh? What's that?'

'I thought maybe you could teach me how to use a bow.'

Ita frowned. 'What for? You have Margery to hunt for you.'

'It is not only for hunting. It is for protection too.'

'And you have me for that.'

Isabel looked back at the road again. 'Be that as it may, I would still like to learn.'

Ita watched her for a moment. 'You're quite safe here, you know.'

'I know.'

Hodge was rumoured to be lying low after losing favour with King Edward. The king had withdrawn his support after certain details about the camp surfaced, in particular the part about produce being shipped else-where for profit instead of being given to the people growing it. They had all hoped for a much bigger consequence, but the country still needed its marcher lords to insulate the border.

'Of course I'll teach you,' Ita said. 'Rabbit can help too.'

Isabel found it amusing that all this time had passed and yet they were unable to break the habit of using aliases.

'Let's get started on the mortar,' Ita said, tying up her horse.

Isabel glanced again at the road.

'I can't tell if you're waiting for Hodge to show up or Blackmane to return,' Ita said as they strolled towards the building site.

Isabel's eyebrows came together. 'What do you mean?'

'I'm talking about the way you watch the road.'

Isabel looked up as Margery flew overhead, landing by the tools. 'Do you think he ever thinks about me?'

Ita threaded her arm through Isabel's. 'Hodge? Absolutely. Blackmane? Also absolutely. I'm guessing you're asking about Blackmane.'

'A man trained in the art of forgetting.'

'I happen to know for a fact that you are unforgettable.'

Isabel gave her a sceptical look. 'The difference being that you had fifteen years of memories to erase, and he had two weeks.'

'The time is irrelevant. It took my parents minutes to fall in love, and their feelings only strengthened over the years.'

Isabel glanced sideways at her friend. 'When did you get so wise?'

'I didn't. I was simply trying to make you feel better.

What do I know about love? All the men in my life view me as a sister and would likely be appalled at the thought of anything more.'

'I doubt that. More likely they are afraid to attempt anything because you usually have at least two weapons on you at all times.'

Ita released her arm and walked over to where the tools sat. 'Well, maybe you're not the only one afraid that Hodge will return.' She picked up the trowel and inspected it before handing it to Isabel. 'I'm sorry he left.'

'Hodge?'

Ita pinched her playfully. 'Blackmane. While I admit to being initially surprised by your taste in men, I soon saw how deeply you cared for each other.'

Isabel stared hard at the tool in her hand. 'There was too much against us, too many reasons why it could never work. And one day I plan on accepting them.'

'A little pining in the meantime is relatively harmless, so long as it doesn't interfere with your ability to work.' Ita winked at her.

Isabel hoped that was true. 'All right. Show me what to do.'

'You ready to get dirty?'

Isabel's gaze drifted a final time to the empty road. 'I am ready.'

CHAPTER 32

*B*lackmane pulled himself from the icy water and stood on Flat Rock, looking back at the mainland. He fed off these quiet moments, rare snatches of time, away from the clashing weapons and noisy dinners and all the other things that made up his life. All he could hear at that moment was the autumn wind catching his ears and the thudding of his own heart after a long swim.

He gave himself a few minutes to catch his breath before returning to shore. Normally, a cliff climb was done as a team, but Blackmane had done it solo that day. Tatum stood atop the wall, watching him, making sure he did not drown or fall from the cliff face. Blackmane did not object, knowing he would do the same if the roles were reversed.

The sea kicked up against the rock, sending a spray of water over him. What better cleanse was there? He dove into the turbulent sea and began the swim back, rolled side to side by the waves as he fought to steer clear of the sharp rocks. Thankfully, he made it back to the mainland in one piece before climbing to the top without incident.

When he reached the ledge at the top, he paused to catch his breath, then took hold of the rope and began the final climb up. When his feet finally hit the wall walk, he looked around for Tatum, surprised to find Tolly instead, leaning against one of the embrasures and looking out to sea.

'Tolly?'

His brother looked in his direction, a smile reaching his lips as he straightened. 'Hello, brother.'

Blackmane walked over to where he stood, eyes raking over him. He looked strong and had colour back in his face, no doubt due to spending more time above ground.

'I guess the rumours about your training are true,' Tolly said. 'That was one hell of a drill.'

Blackmane glanced in the direction of Flat Rock. 'It's a decent amount of work. What are you doing here?'

Tolly leaned on the embrasure again, looking around. 'We met with King Becket.'

'Ah.' Blackmane crossed his arms. 'How did it go?'

'I like the man. He's intelligent, and he listens. Those are rare traits in a king.'

Blackmane nodded slowly. 'Did you meet the warden?'

'Terrifying man.'

A soft chuckle came from Blackmane, his first in months. 'True.'

'King Becket seems in favour of our move towards independence,' Tolly said. 'Not surprising given we stand in the way of all your inland trade routes.'

'Like you said, he's intelligent. He's also a peaceful man, which works in your favour.'

Tolly watched the water for a few moments. 'At least we won't be forced to meet again on the battlefield.'

'I'd prefer not to kill you.'

Tolly's amused gaze slid to him. 'I'd like to think you would let me live.'

'Hopefully we never have to find out.'

A few seconds of silence passed before Tolly said, 'I saw Isabel a few days ago. She's back in Llanelieu.'

Simply hearing her name spoken aloud made his pulse quicken. He was pleased to hear that she had returned to her home village, though. He had so many questions but was not sure if he wanted all the answers. 'She seem well?'

'Physically, she's fine. She's rebuilding Maddock House.'

He had expected that. There was no other home she would have settled for other than the one taken from her.

'And when I say she's rebuilding Maddock House, I mean she's doing the labour herself. Ita and Rabbit are helping, of course, but she was sawing wood when we arrived, covered in dust.'

The corners of Blackmane's mouth lifted at the visual. She would be living her best life with no one around to tell her no. 'What about her family?'

'They'll be joining her soon. The tricky part is getting through without Hodge noticing. There are fears he'll try to intercept them.'

'Valid fears, no doubt.'

'He might be staying out of the wastelands, but he isn't giving up on her. Our sources tell us he has men placed all along the border, waiting for them to emerge from hiding.'

Of course he did. He would not miss an opportunity like that. 'Probably better they stay where they are for now.'

'Isabel's concerned he'll widen his search. Unfortunately, there's nothing we can do about that.'

Blackmane shifted his weight. 'I guess that's what you meant by physically fine. Mentally, not so great.'

Tolly studied him intently. 'She asked about you. Wanted to know if I'd heard from you.'

He had thought about writing to Tolly but had struggled with what to say. 'Well, if she asks again, you can tell her I'm fine.'

'And are you?'

Blackmane swallowed. 'Yes.'

His brother sighed. 'For the record, I liked her for you.'

Blackmane had liked her for himself too. 'She can do a lot better than a hardened defender.'

'That's not what she sees. She sees a loyal, protective man who will go to extraordinary lengths for the people he loves.' He looked out to sea. 'Even forcing them onto a ship in the hope of saving their life.'

'An act you hated me for.'

He nodded in agreement. 'As a child, I did. But as a man...'

Blackmane's throat began to burn. 'I should have gotten on that ship with you.'

'You really should have. But instead, you stayed to care for the dying, knowing every second spent in their company meant a higher chance of you contracting the pox.' His eyes returned to Blackmane. 'I think that makes you a catch.' He stepped back from the wall. 'She gets it. She's not bitter about your leaving. Your life's here. Your friends are here.' He gestured towards the barracks. 'That terrifying warden is here.'

Blackmane nodded. 'He's a tough man to leave behind.'

The corners of Tolly's mouth lifted, and then he looked over his shoulder. 'I have to go. Thorn's waiting for me at the stables. I didn't want to go without seeing you.' He looked back at Blackmane. 'Don't be a stranger. I know I'm not much of a draw, but no one will shoot you if you want to come visit sometime.'

When his brother went to leave, Blackmane said, 'You're wrong. You're enough of a draw.'

Tolly wet his lips and glanced out to sea a final time. 'Take care of yourself, brother.'

A nod. 'You too.'

Blackmane watched him walk away, chest pinching as Tolly disappeared into the turret. He stood there for a full minute, not nearly exhausted enough, watching the water pool at his feet, then went to clean himself up.

CHAPTER 33

*I*sabel stood with Ita in front of Maddock House, the hood of her cloak pulled up to protect her ears from the cold, wintery air, staring up at the roof.

'It is definitely even?' she asked.

'Definitely.' Though Ita sounded less sure than the last time Isabel had asked the question. 'But even if there was a *slight* height difference, which there isn't, it's an excellent thatched roof for a first effort.'

Isabel nodded in agreement. 'Even if the left side was a *little* higher than the right side, which it is not, it is not so drastic that anyone would notice.'

'Agreed. We've been standing here for the past half an hour, actively searching for faults. It's only natural that we would start to imagine them.'

Isabel let out a relieved breath. 'You are quite right. We are viewing it through rather critical eyes. It is fine.'

'More than fine.'

The sound of footsteps had the women looking over their shoulders. Rabbit approached, eyeing the roof as he walked.

'What do you think?' Ita asked.

He stopped beside her, crossing his arms as he stared up at the newly finished house. 'The left side's higher than the right.'

Ita jabbed him with her elbow.

He made an 'oof' sound, then raised his hands. 'What?'

'You could have commented on our excellent technique instead of pointing out its flaws.'

'Lied, you mean?'

Isabel's chest deflated. 'But it is salvageable, yes?'

'Everything's salvageable in the wastelands,' Rabbit replied. 'I can give you a hand, if you like?'

Isabel knew there was no point dwelling on their disappointment. 'We would appreciate that, thank you.'

Margery flew down and landed on Ita's shoulder, looking around. Isabel reached out to pet her, but her attention was diverted by the sound of horses. Initially, she had found that sound alarming, but the wastelanders had proven over the previous seven months that they were more than capable of keeping the border secure. They were filled with a fierce determination that no king or lord was brave enough to test.

'Is that Tolly?' Ita asked as the horses drew closer.

Isabel narrowed her eyes on the man riding at the front of the group. 'It is.' Normally, she looked forward to his visits, but the speed at which he approached induced a healthy amount of anxiety. This was not a social visit.

As she watched him, she could not help but notice how much he looked like Blackmane when he wore that serious expression. A familiar sadness crept in around the edges of her soul.

'Why does this feel like bad news?' Ita said beside her.

A sick feeling settled in Isabel's stomach.

Rabbit walked out to meet the horses. 'Perhaps he has news of your family.'

That was what she was worried about. It had been over a month since her mother and brother had written to say they would soon be departing for Maddock House. A delay of some kind had been expected as they waited for her uncle to organise safe passage across the border. But Isabel's biggest fear was that there was no such thing as safe passage anymore.

The group of horses came to an abrupt stop ten feet away. Tolly dismounted and headed straight for Isabel. Her stomach tightened as she read his expression.

'Do you have news of my family?' she asked before he had even reached her.

'Yes.' Tolly gave her an apologetic look, confirming it was not good news. 'They're alive and well.'

Isabel's heart slowed right down as she braced for the 'but'.

'They're at Hampstead Keep.'

It was as though he had thrown a pail of icy water over her. Simply the name of the castle spoken aloud was enough to make her vision blur. Ita took hold of her hand and squeezed.

'I'm guessing they didn't go there willingly,' Rabbit said.

Tolly shook his head. 'Hodge has been keeping a close eye on who crosses the border for many months. Your uncle sent your mother and brother as far south as he could get them, but Hodge still managed to intercept.'

Ita shook her head. 'Of course he did. The man's a leech.'

Isabel pulled her hand free and stepped away from the group, taking deep breaths in an attempt to clear her mind. There was a way through this. They had not gotten this far only to fail this close to the finish line. She turned to Tolly. 'How did you find out? Did my uncle send word or did Hodge?'

'Hodge. He sent a letter addressed to you. The border guards flagged it.' He reached into the pocket of his cloak to retrieve it, then held it out to her.

Isabel took the letter. 'He was always going to make his move eventually. I had simply hoped it would be *after* my mother and brother were safely in Carmarthenshire.' She unfolded the parchment and began to read.

> *My beloved,*
> *After many months of reflection, I feel it is time for us to*
> *talk. Please join me and your family at Hampstead*
> *Keep.*
> *Yours,*
> *H*

Even his handwriting made Isabel feel ill. She closed the note and looked at Ita. 'I have to go.'

'You can't be serious,' Ita replied. 'He's laying a trap for you. If you go there, he will never let you leave.'

'And what do you suppose he will do if I do not go?'

Ita bit her lip. 'I still think it's more dangerous to play his games.'

Isabel looked at Tolly. 'We all know what he is capable of. My family is only safe there for as long as he has the upper hand.' She sighed. 'What is the best way to proceed?'

Frustrated by the conversation, Ita stepped away.

'I think arriving with a large group would be a mistake. I could escort you there to speak to him.'

'I'm obviously coming with you,' Ita called to them.

Isabel shook her head. 'Absolutely not. You are another pawn he can use in his game. I cannot be worried about you too.'

Rabbit glanced over at the paddock where the horses were grazing. 'I'll saddle your gelding.' Then he headed off in that direction.

Ita emitted a frustrated groan, which made Margery fly off.

'I am sorry to drag you into this mess,' Isabel said to Tolly. 'There are probably a million more important things you should be doing right now.'

'I'm more worried about my brother hanging me from the closest tree when he finds out I took you straight to Hodge.'

Isabel dropped her gaze, palms heating. 'Let me pack a few things. I will be with you shortly.'

~

Blackmane was seated in the mess hall, having just finished his second bowl of stew. The harder he trained, the hungrier he was. Thankfully, the famine was far enough behind them that rationing was finally a thing of the past. Defenders were now permitted to eat whatever they needed to in order to perform at their peak. He was considering going back for his third bowl when Tatum strode into the room and looked around. Spotting Blackmane, he walked over and sank down onto the bench seat beside him.

'I have a letter for you.' He wrestled it out of his pocket and slapped it down on the table next to Blackmane's bowl. 'I hope you appreciate me not reading it on the way here. Very tempting when there's no seal.'

'The fact that you want to be acknowledged for that says so much about you.' Blackmane had received a few letters from Tolly over the past few months, but they were always sealed, and this was not his handwriting. His eyes went straight to the signature at the bottom.

'Who's it from?' Tatum asked.

It took Blackmane a moment to reply. 'Ita.'

Tatum's brow creased. 'I didn't realise the two of you were still in contact.'

'We're not.' Blackmane read quickly, the parchment creasing beneath his grip. 'Bastard.'

Tatum appeared taken aback. 'I know she can be a tad bossy, but—'

Blackmane rose abruptly, shoving the note into his pocket as he stepped away from the table.

'Where are you going?' Tatum asked.

'To see the warden.'

Tatum winced. 'This can't be good.'

Blackmane fled the mess hall, ignoring the questions that followed him out. He went straight to the warden's quarters, knocking and then entering without waiting for a reply.

Shapur looked up from the table he sat behind. 'You are supposed to wait until you are invited in after knocking, defender.'

'Apologies, sir. I've received some news from Carmarthenshire and require a few days' leave.'

Shapur stared at him. 'For what purpose?'

He did not dance around the facts. 'My brother and Isabel Maddock have gone to Hampstead Keep, and I fear they might be in danger.'

Shapur rose slowly. 'You have a lot of nerve barging in here with this request. Now, get out before I have you locked up.'

Blackmane did not move. 'I'm happy to go alone.'

Shapur's eyes narrowed into slits. 'Are you trying to start a war?'

'Actually, I'm trying to prevent one. Lord Hodge is holding Lady Gwenore and her son at Hampstead Keep against their will. Swift and discreet action could prevent this from building into a fight that will halt all chains of supply to Chadora.' He paused. 'I just need four days.'

The tips of Shapur's fingers pressed against the wooden table. 'Fine. You leave Chadora discreetly, and you are back in four days.'

Blackmane's lungs relaxed. 'Yes, sir. Thank you.' He turned to leave.

'Blackmane.'

The defender stopped and waited.

'I want Hodge in one piece at the end of the four days. Understand?'

He nodded. 'Yes, sir.'

*I*sabel stood in front of the moat that enclosed Hampstead Keep, watching the gate lower before her. Armed guards observed the pair from above, and Tolly watched them right back. The gate touched the ground a few feet in front of their horses. Hodge stood on the other side, his face illuminated by orange light cast from the torches on either side of him.

'My beloved.' His voice carried across the bridge to her.

She felt only anger and disgust as she stared at him and had to assume it showed on her face. 'My lord.'

'I see you brought a friend,' he said, displeasure clear in his voice.

Isabel glanced sideways at Tolly. 'This is Tolly Blackmane, my escort.'

'Oh, I know who he is.'

Tolly glanced up at the guards as he asked, 'How's the hand?'

Hodge held it up and wriggled his fingers. 'As good as

new.' He let it fall to his side before adding, 'I appreciate you getting Lady Isabel here safely.'

'I plan on getting her home safely too.'

Hodge's lips turned up. 'You are free to wait out here if you have nothing better to do.'

'Actually,' Isabel said, 'I think this is far enough for both of us.'

Hodge's eyebrows lifted slightly. 'I thought you would be keen to see your family.'

And so the game begins.

'Where are they?' she asked, content to play for now.

He glanced over his shoulder. 'In their quarters, waiting to eat.'

'In their *quarters*?'

'Yes.' He feigned confusion at her question.

Anger flickered inside her. 'The thing is, they do not have quarters at Hampstead Keep, because they do not live here anymore.'

That only made him smile. 'Everything is as they left it, and they have settled in rather well.'

She stared at him, his disillusions unsettling. 'I want to see them.'

'So come see them.'

She shook her head. 'No. I want you to bring them out.'

'You want me to drag them out into the cold?'

'Drag them? No. A simple request will suffice. I imagine they will be keen to see me also.'

He watched her for the longest time before finally nodding. 'Very well.' Turning to one of the guards, he said, 'Bring Lady Gwenore and her son down to the gate.'

A few tense minutes passed, the men glaring at one another while Isabel stared at the pommel of her saddle. Finally, her mother and brother appeared, the guard in tow. The sight of them made Isabel's chest tighten and eyes burn, but she pushed all of her emotions down. That would have to wait.

'Belle,' her mother said, her voice trembling.

Everard was glaring in Hodge's direction.

'Are you both all right?' Isabel asked, looking between them.

'No,' Everard replied. 'None of this is all right.'

Hodge ignored the boy. 'Now that we have established that everyone is well, shall we go inside? I believe roast chicken is on the menu, and I know that is one of your favourites, my beloved.'

'I think we are a little past endearments,' she said. 'You may call me Isabel.'

He drew a slow breath. 'Very well.'

It was frustrating having her family so close but being unable to reach them without appeasing him first. Her cold eyes bored into him. 'What do you want, my lord?'

'Right now? Dinner.'

She blinked slowly. 'You are wasting both our time. Tell me what you hoped to achieve by luring me here.'

He tilted his head and regarded her for a long moment. 'That place has changed you. You have lost your warmth and kind spirit.'

'That place has not changed me. *You* changed me. You *broke* me. It is going to take some time to heal and regain the warmth you siphoned from my very bones.'

Her mother dropped her gaze while Everard continued to glower at Hodge.

'Clearly we have a lot to discuss,' Hodge said.

'Then speak fast' was Tolly's reply. 'We have a long ride back to Llanelieu.'

Hodge looked between the pair of them. 'This is the company you choose to keep now?'

Isabel nodded. 'Yes. Now tell me what needs to happen in order for you to let my family go.'

'Go?' Hodge laughed. 'They just got here. We are finally all together again, as we were before.' He waved her in. 'Come inside. Please. This is silly.'

She wanted to scream at him, but that would help no one. 'I do not want to come inside. I do not want to eat roast chicken with you.'

Hodge frowned. 'Now you are being incredibly ill-mannered.'

Isabel pressed her eyes closed as she realised they had reached *that* part of the game. 'If you want me to come inside the castle, you will need to let them leave.' She opened her eyes. 'You do not get both.'

Everard's glare cut to her. 'What?'

'I echo that sentiment,' Tolly said.

Her eyes went to him. 'We both know what this is. It is a simple exchange.'

Gwenore's face fell. 'We will not leave without you.'

Naturally, Hodge remained completely silent, content to let this part play out.

'Who do you want at your dinner table?' Isabel asked him. 'Me or them?'

Gwenore's chest was rising and falling hard, and Everard looked ready to charge at Hodge.

'If you come inside, he will never let you go,' Everard said.

'Do you think you will be safe here if I ride away? You are old enough to gauge what is going on here.' Her gaze drifted to Hodge. 'I am waiting for your reply, my lord.'

He seemed to like that, relishing in the temporary power he had been missing for so long. 'While I shall miss their company, if they choose to leave and skip dinner, then that is their choice.'

Isabel looked tiredly at Tolly. 'Would you please escort my mother and brother home?'

He looked understandably torn. 'Are you sure about this?'

'Very sure.' Her eyes returned to Hodge. 'Please fetch their horses.'

The earl's lips curled up as he turned and nodded to the waiting guard.

'Belle, no,' Everard said. 'I will stay instead. You take mother, and I will—'

'He does not want you.' Her eyes drifted up to the armed guards above. 'You will go and take care of our mother. Do you hear me?'

He was fuming, but he must have known she was right because he did not object again.

Hodge cleared his throat. 'Remember, Hampstead Keep is always open to you. You are welcome any time.'

'I think their social calendar is going to be quite full moving forwards,' Isabel said dryly.

A few tense minutes passed as they waited for the

horses to arrive. Gwenore was wiping at her face, and Everard could not keep his feet still.

When the horses arrived, her mother was helped onto one of them, and Everard snatched the reins of the other but refused to mount. The guard ushered them both through the gate and along the bridge, and Isabel had no choice but to cross it too. She gave her brother a reassuring smile as they passed each other. He was so angry. Maybe at her, or maybe at the situation. It did not matter. Isabel met her mother's gaze and saw something in her eyes she had never seen before—remorse. No words of any kind were exchanged because there was nothing left to say.

Isabel was comforted by the fact that Tolly was waiting on the other side for them. He would ensure they got safely to Maddock House.

'Shall we?' Hodge said when she reached him, gesturing to the castle.

Isabel looked back at the others, watching Everard mount his horse before looking at Tolly. The soldier nodded once, then turned his horse away.

She felt numb from head to toe.

Only when they were gone from sight did she step past Hodge and slowly make her way towards the castle.

CHAPTER 35

*I*t took Blackmane two days to reach Llanelieu. He was stopped at a patrol point along the way, where he spent two hours answering questions about what he was doing, where he was headed, and who he knew. He did try to be patient and give them what they needed in order to feel secure enough to let him pass, but that patience wore thin after a while. Question time finished with two men at the end of two blades while Blackmane calmly explained to the third that if he intended to go on a killing spree, he would have started with them.

'I would have shot you from that tree,' he told them. 'You would never have even known who killed you.'

When the three men were calm enough, Blackmane put away his weapons and politely asked if he could leave. The red-faced men let him go.

While many villages remained abandoned, occasionally he would pass through one where rebuilding was taking place. It was good to see men hammering in fence posts and ploughing fields, to see women hanging laundry, and children playing nearby.

It brought a sense of hope.

He stopped a man carrying a lamb, walking on the other side of the road, and asked for directions to Maddock House. When he arrived there, he found Ita working in the vegetable garden. She rose, dusting off her dress before coming out to meet him.

'Welcome to Maddock House, defender,' she said, sounding worn out.

He eyed the uneven thatching on the roof. 'Any news?'

'Lady Gwenore and Everard arrived here this morning.'

He searched her eyes. 'I gather by your expression that Isabel did not return with them?'

Ita shook her head. 'It seems a deal was struck. She agreed to stay in exchange for their release.'

The fire burning in Blackmane's stomach flared. 'Tolly let her go with him?'

Ita swallowed. 'She chose to go.'

Blackmane nodded, teeth pressing. 'Right.'

His brother exited the house, followed closely by Lady Gwenore and Everard. One look at Blackmane's face had Tolly raising his hands.

'Before you get angry—'

Blackmane's fist hit Tolly's face before he had a chance to finish that sentence. 'I'm already angry. What the hell were you thinking?'

Tolly straightened and held on to his jaw. Blood painted his teeth. 'I see that.'

Gwenore stood frozen with a hand over her mouth

while Everard stepped between them, pushing his chest out as far as he could.

'It is not his fault, defender,' Everard said, bringing volume to his voice. 'She did it for us. Hodge left her no choice. He is a right bastard. I cannot believe it took me so long to see it.'

'That is enough of that language,' Gwenore said, hand going to her forehead. 'Take the defender's horse down to the water trough.'

Everard shook his head, then stepped up to take Blackmane's mare, leading her over to the trough.

'He's right, though,' Ita said. 'This isn't Tolly's fault.'

Someone had to bear the brunt of Blackmane's anger in Hodge's absence. His eyes narrowed on Gwenore. The fact that she was safely at the house her daughter had rebuilt with her own hands did not sit well with him. 'I'm surprised to see you here. Few mothers would have the resolve to leave their daughter behind with a man like that.'

Tolly looked over at him. 'Easy, Ryder.'

Blackmane continued to stare at Gwenore. 'There's a long history of her putting her family's needs above her own safety, isn't there?'

Gwenore set her mouth. 'You are drawing all kinds of conclusions from a handful of observations. These kinds of situations are always more complicated than they seem.'

He crossed his arms. 'When I was at Hampstead Keep, all those months back, I noticed bruises on your daughter's arms. Over the next few days, I witnessed Hodge grab her, shout at her, and manipulate her. We were then separated for a short period. In that time, he tied her to a post with his belt, hit her in the face, and choked her.' He paused, noting Gwenore's trembling lower lip. 'I learned a lot about their relationship from those handful of observations. Tell me, what did you learn about their relationship during your five years of observing them?'

She blinked, and a tear rolled down her cheek. 'With God as my witness, I never saw him be violent with her.'

'But I know you saw the evidence. Bruises like that are hard to miss.'

She looked down, swallowed.

He nodded. 'That's what I thought.'

'I did not know the extent of his... moods.' She paused. 'All I heard from him was how much he loved her, how he wanted to take care of her.'

'Oh, we all bore witness to his outpourings of love.' He glanced at Ita. 'But I don't know a single person who felt comfortable seeing it.'

'I thought things would improve after they were wed,' Gwenore admitted.

'You mean you *hoped* things would improve. For the sake of your son, no doubt.'

Gwenore looked away. 'Despite what you think of me, defender, I am keen to get my daughter out of there. I want her safe.'

Ita hugged herself and exhaled. 'I don't see how that's possible.'

Blackmane was far from defeated. 'I'm going to Hampstead Keep. I'll find a way.'

'I am coming with you,' Everard said, returning to the group. He let the mare graze.

'Absolutely not,' Gwenore said.

'He will need some help, Mother.'

Tolly reached out and squeezed the boy's shoulder. 'I'm going with him. Rest easy.'

Blackmane studied his brother's tired face. 'You just got back from there and look ready to fall down.'

'That's because you punched me in the face.'

'He did get *some* sleep,' Ita said. 'He nodded off in his chair mid-meal and didn't wake until he heard your horse approaching.'

'I was just resting my eyes.'

Ita frowned. 'While pretend snoring?'

Blackmane had no choice but to accept the help because he needed it. 'An army of two, then.'

'What exactly is your plan?' Ita asked.

Tolly rubbed his jaw. 'You're assuming he has one.'

'Defenders always have a plan,' Blackmane replied. 'They just rarely work out.'

Ita gestured to the house. 'At least come in and have something to eat before you leave.'

Blackmane did not feel right dining in Isabel's home while she was trapped with Hodge. 'Thanks, but I need to get going.'

'Then I'll pack you something to take with you,' Ita said, disappearing into the house.

Everard ran to fetch Tolly's horse.

'Tell me you can get her out of that place,' Gwenore said, sounding more like a concerned mother now.

At least she finally appeared to be grasping the danger Isabel was in.

'I'll do my best.'

CHAPTER 36

*I*t was chilling to step inside her old quarters and find everything as it was before she left. The bed made. Her clothes still on hangers. The cage in the corner, so painfully symbolic. And the feathers she used to collect still hung from the bedhead.

It was as though she had never left.

For the next three days, Isabel remained in her quarters. She declined every invitation from Hodge, until he became so fed up that he yelled through her door, 'If you do not eat with me, then you do not eat at all.'

So she went without food.

She sat on a stool by the window, watching the sky and trying to think of an exit that would not end with her dead. Margery had not been to visit, and it felt quite deliberate.

'Evening, my lady' came the voice of her new maid as she entered the bedchamber.

Isabel glanced in the girl's direction. Paige was a

bubbly young lady who had obviously been hand selected by Hodge.

'Shall we get you ready for dinner?' Paige chirped.

Isabel laid her head on the windowsill. 'Can I eat in here?'

Paige crinkled her nose. 'Afraid not. Please, I cannot bear to see you wasting away before my eyes.'

Isabel was silent for a long time. 'How long does death via starvation take?'

Paige sighed and walked over to her. She held a jug of water with steam rising from it. 'I brought some hot water so you can have a wash.'

'Thank you.'

Paige filled the basin, casting worried glances in her direction the whole time. 'Please, my lady. One meal. One conversation. Give him something, and I am certain he will give you something in return.'

Isabel blinked. *What do I have to lose?* 'Fine.'

Upon hearing that, Paige sprang into action, flitting about the room like an excited bird, laying out garments and fetching jewels. She helped Isabel undress, then brought the basin of water over and set it at her feet.

'I've laid out a gown for you to wear.'

Isabel glanced at the dress, one of Hodge's favourites, then over at the table where the jewels sat. Emeralds. 'Did he instruct you on hair too?'

Paige nodded. 'He said you wear it pulled back.'

She hated it pulled back and always ended the night with a headache.

'And pink lips,' Paige added.

Isabel pressed her eyes closed. 'May I ask you something?'

'Of course.'

'When did His Lordship employ you?'

'A few weeks back.' There was excitement in her voice. 'If someone had told me a month ago that I would be a lady's maid to the future Countess of Hereford, I would not have believed it.'

A month ago, Isabel would not have believed it either. He really had thought of everything.

She washed and put on the dress. She let Paige brush her hair and smooth it back into a painful bun. On went the emeralds and pink paint. Then it was time for dinner.

A guard escorted her to Hodge's private quarters. He was not pleased to see her but rather agitated.

'Finally,' Hodge said when she stepped into the room. 'I am surprised you can even walk after foolishly starving yourself.' He gestured for her to take a seat at the small table. 'Wine?'

'No, thank you.'

He immediately began loading her plate with food. 'Well, eat up.'

She stared down at the mountain of food, feeling more sick than hungry. Picking up her cutlery, she cut off a small piece of beef, barely tasting it as she chewed.

'Look at the state of your hands,' Hodge said. 'Labourer's hands.' He tutted. 'I cannot tell you how saddened I am by the sight.'

She looked down at them. 'These hands have been useful for the first time in years.'

'Doing what, exactly?'

TANYA BIRD

She met his gaze. 'Rebuilding the house you burned down.'

He swallowed his mouthful before responding to that. 'I am surprised any building is taking place right now, given all of the men are busy terrorising people who come within a mile of their bogus border.'

Oh, how she hated him. 'The men are working hard to keep us safe.'

He watched her across the table as he cut into his food. 'I am curious about something. Does this protection go all the way around Carmarthenshire, or is it only the English who are not welcome?'

She recognised jealousy in his tone. 'The protection is all the way around, but as you can see by the fact that I am eating dinner with you right now instead of at home with my family, the real threat continues to be in the east.'

He set his cutlery down and leaned back in his chair. 'I cannot help but wonder if a certain defender has made his way through this… impenetrable ring.'

'And why would you wonder about such things?'

'Because I would hate to think that you were taken advantage of by a man.'

She stilled. 'Really? Because history would suggest otherwise.'

His jaw ticked as he reached for his cup and took a long drink. He sniffed before placing it down again. 'I know you are missing your family right now, so I will let that slide.'

It was early, but she was already *so* tired of him. 'What do you hope to gain from keeping me here? I will never willingly marry you, never love you, never forgive you.

And I am not sure how much polite conversation I have left in me.'

He nodded slowly. 'You know, I have done a lot of reflecting over the past few months. I have been re-evaluating my purpose and what I want my legacy to be. I have accepted my failure to bring Carmarthenshire back under King Edward's rule, but I refuse to fail in my home life as well.' He looked deep into her eyes. 'We are destined to be together. I knew it from the first time we met. However, I am unable to convince you that your future is here with me.'

She pushed her plate away. 'My lord, if we were truly destined to be together, then I would not need convincing. You can hold me inside these walls for as long as you like, but that will not change the fact that there is no future for us.'

He did not speak for a minute. 'If not with me, then with whom? Blackmane? The man you took an arrow for?'

She looked away on an exhale. 'I am not talking about him with you.'

Hodge leaned forwards. 'First, I had the torture of waiting to find out if you were alive. Then I had the torture of imagining you with *him*. I had to write to the warden in Chadora to put myself out of my misery.' He straightened. 'Though learning the two of you were apart offered little comfort, because I know first-hand that an absent person can still occupy the entirety of one's mind.' He reached for his cup, tapping his finger on the stem. 'What was it about him? His strong physique and handsome face? Or was it the fact that he read a book once?'

She shook her head and went to stand. 'I think this dinner is over.'

He slammed his fist against the table, making everything atop it rattle. '*Months* I have waited to have this conversation. The very least you can do is listen.'

She lowered herself back into the chair and stared at him. 'Let me go home.'

'To him?'

She shook her head, exhausted.

'To the *wastelands*? Every comfort you can dream up is right here in this castle.'

She wet her lips. 'You think this dinner is comfortable? You think this conversation, these questions, are *comfortable*?' She began pulling pins out of her hair. 'I assure you none of this is comfortable.'

He stared into his cup. 'We cannot fix what is broken in a few nights.'

She slammed the hairpins down onto the table. 'You are not listening to me. I do not want to fix this.'

He rose abruptly, chair scraping so loudly that Isabel flinched. He leaned across the table, fingertips pressing into it. She thought he might strike her, but instead, he marched over to the door, yanked it open, and said to the guard outside, 'Lady Isabel is ready to return to her quarters.'

She took the exit while it was on offer and fled the room.

CHAPTER 37

*B*lackmane and Tolly watched the castle beneath a setting sun from the safety of the trees. Hodge must have been expecting company, because every hour, two guards would ride out and do a lap of the tree line.

'I think we need to have a little chat with one of the guards,' Blackmane said when the bridge lowered again.

'Only one?' Tolly asked.

Blackmane nodded and swung his horse around. They cantered east, following the men for a while before splitting up. Blackmane loaded his bow and took aim at the larger of the two riders, shooting him through the neck. The other guard watched his comrade fall from his horse, then, panicking, dug his heels in, preparing to flee. Tolly appeared, blocking his exit and drawing his sword. The guard was forced to pull up, looking over his shoulder as Blackmane trotted up to join them. He immediately raised his hands, confirming to Blackmane that he had kept the right man alive.

'We need some information,' Tolly said. 'And you're going to give it to us.'

The guard looked between them with a worried expression. 'I don't know anything—'

'Isabel Maddock,' Blackmane said. 'You know that name, don't you? That's why you're out here looking for men like us?'

His expression confirmed that was exactly what he was doing. 'Of course I know her. She's lived at Hampstead Keep for years.'

'But then she left, didn't she?' Tolly said.

He seemed unsure how to answer that. 'She was away for a period.'

'She *left*,' Blackmane said, leaving no room for argument.

The guard remained silent.

Blackmane kept his arrow trained on the man. 'The only reason you're still alive is because of the information you have—remember that.'

He let out a resigned sigh. 'What do you want to know?'

'Is she unharmed?' Blackmane asked.

There was a beat of silence. 'Yes.'

'You hesitated.'

'She's unharmed.'

Blackmane studied him. 'But?'

The man wrestled with his response for a moment. 'But she's been refusing food.'

'For how long?'

'I don't know all the details. They had dinner. There was a fight. Now he won't let her eat unless she eats with him.'

Blackmane knew she would sooner starve than share a table with him. 'And where is she at present?'

'In her bedchamber.'

'The one she was in before she left?'

The guard nodded, then looked nervously between them. 'Are you going to kill me now?'

'No,' Tolly said. 'We need you for this next part. What's your name?'

'Morris.' He was sweating now. 'If I help you, I'm dead anyway.'

Tolly frowned. 'You haven't even heard the plan yet.'

The guard made the sign of the cross on himself. 'God help me.'

Blackmane put his bow away and moved closer to him. 'So here's what's going to happen. You're going to take me into custody and lock me up.'

Morris blinked and looked between them, as though trying to gauge if they were serious. 'Lock you up where?'

'Hampstead Keep has a dungeon,' Blackmane said. 'I paid it a visit last time I was there.'

Morris was staring at him like he was mad. 'Is this some sort of trick?'

'If it was,' Tolly said, 'do you think we would tell you?'

The guard exhaled noisily. 'I've got a bad feeling about this.'

Blackmane began removing his weapons. 'I assume you strip prisoners of their weapons when you take them into custody?'

'Yes. They don't hand them over willingly.' He reluctantly took the weapons Blackmane handed to him. 'How do you know I won't tell everyone what you're up to the moment we set foot inside?'

'Because doing this my way means you're alive at the end,' Blackmane replied. 'If you mess up your small part in this, I'll cut your throat with your own weapon in front of all your comrades, then kill a lot of other people too.'

The man swallowed. 'So I lock you up, and then what?'

'That's the end of your part,' Tolly said. 'You don't have to worry about the rest.'

Blackmane walked his horse closer and held his hands out to be bound. 'You were on patrol, and I killed your friend here. You captured me and locked me up. It's that simple. Any more questions?'

Morris wiped sweat from his brow and asked, 'Can I borrow some rope?'

The pounding on the door was giving Isabel a headache. 'I just want to talk' came Hodge's voice through it.

She continued to ignore him.

'I simply want you to join me on the terrace for something to eat.'

She pressed her eyes closed. 'And I told you, I am not hungry.'

'Open the door!'

She drew her legs up and waited for him to give up and leave, but he did not. Instead, the pounding turned to kicking. She covered her ears.

'Go away,' she called to him.

The kicks grew more intense until the door finally burst open, sending a spray of wood in all directions.

Isabel shot up from where she was seated and stared wide-eyed at the mess he had made.

'Listen,' he said, marching into the room.

She backed right up to the window.

'My lord!' came a voice in the corridor, making Hodge pause. A guard appeared in the doorway, looking around at the damage.

'What is it?' Hodge barked.

The man glanced at Isabel before speaking. 'You were right to keep eyes outside the walls. We came across two men while patrolling the area. My comrade was shot, but I managed to detain one of the men. I thought you may wish to question him.'

Hodge took a few steps towards him. 'You captured a wastelander?'

'A defender. Goes by Blackmane. Came sniffing around exactly like you said they would.'

Isabel's hands went limp at her sides. *Ryder.* He had come to Hampstead Keep. She went from elation at the mention of his name to despair at learning he had been captured in the same breath. He was here, in this castle— but he was also in grave danger. Hodge hated him and now had the perfect excuse to be rid of him for good.

But captured? She could not imagine Blackmane being captured by anyone, let alone the guard standing before her.

All the muscles in Hodge's face hardened. 'You brought a defender inside the walls? Into my *home*?'

The man shifted his weight. 'As a prisoner, my lord. He's locked in the dungeon.'

'Idiot.' Hodge ran a hand down his face. 'Nobody captures a defender that easily. You have been played.' He headed for the door. 'Take me to him at once.'

Hopefully Hodge was right and this was part of his plan.

The earl went to leave, then paused, remembering the door could not be locked.

Isabel suppressed her first smile in days. 'I bet you wish you had waited for me to open it.'

Jaw working, Hodge turned to the guard and said, 'Lock her in my quarters. Do not leave her alone under any circumstances.' With that, he marched out into the corridor.

Blackmane knew he did not have a lot of time until Hodge showed up asking questions, and he was not hanging around to answer them. He would have every guard in the castle parked outside his cell within minutes, because he knew exactly what he was up against. For now, Blackmane only had one guard to deal with.

He began to pace the length of the cell, acting nervous and restless while slowly working a small blade from the sleeve of his uniform. He only had one chance to get out. The moment the blade touched the flesh of his palm, he turned and flung it. It slipped easily between the bars, striking the guard in the throat. Ideal, because the only noise the man could make was that of a man suffocating on his own blood. While the man sat dying, Blackmane unbuckled his belt and removed the two prongs from it— the belt had been designed that way specifically for the purpose of picking locks.

He was through the cell door in under a minute, rushing over to the now-dead guard and stripping him of his weapons. With a sword in one hand and a knife in the other, Blackmane ascended the narrow stone steps to the light-filled room at the top. He had the advantage of knowing his way around the castle, including where all the guards were posted. It always helped to pay attention.

The defender moved silently and meticulously through the corridors of the castle, stepping into the shadows whenever he encountered someone. It was better for everyone if he hid rather than left a trail of corpses in his wake.

When he reached Isabel's quarters, he knew she was not in there because there was no guard posted at the door. In fact, the door sat ajar, and on closer inspection, he realised it had been busted open. His teeth creaked. Where the hell had Hodge taken her? Perhaps with him. That would be the smartest thing to do. Or maybe he had locked her in his quarters.

He took off at a jog in that direction. He was halfway there when he encountered a guard coming the other way. There was nowhere for him to hide, so he threw his sword at the man, striking him in the chest. Blackmane caught him before he hit the ground, attempting to keep the floor clean, and dragged him to the side. He tugged the weapon free and wiped it on the guard's trousers before jogging away, continuing to the end of the corridor and peering around the corner. And who should he find outside Hodge's bedchamber door other than Morris himself. That was problematic, as he had promised to let the man live. He stepped out into the open, and Morris whipped his head in Blackmane's direction.

'How did you…? You know what? Never mind.' He nervously glanced both ways down the corridor. 'Surely you know I can't let you inside this room. If you don't kill me, then His Lordship will.'

'Not if it looks like you put up a good fight.' Blackmane stepped up to him fast, slicing open Morris's arm before the man even had a chance to draw his sword.

'Shit,' Morris grunted.

'It's just a surface wound,' Blackmane said, 'but you're going to want to apply pressure.' He tried the door handle, but it was locked.

'You *cut* me.'

Blackmane searched the bleeding guard for keys. 'I *saved* you. You should be thanking me.' He found the keys in a trouser pocket. 'Thanks,' he said before going to unlock the door.

'You'll never make it out,' Morris said. 'His Lordship is probably on his way. This corridor will be swarming with guards in a moment.'

Blackmane knew that. 'Don't you have a wound to tend to?' He pushed the door open and looked around the oversized room. Isabel stood against the far wall, staring at him with a look of pure disbelief.

'You know how this goes,' he said, stepping inside. 'I need you to do exactly as I say.'

She nodded. 'All right.'

He tucked the knife into his belt and extended one bloodied hand in her direction. She ran to him, but instead of taking his hand, she wrapped her arms around his neck and whispered, 'He is going to kill you.'

Blackmane breathed in her floral scent. 'Only if he gets the chance.'

As if on cue, he heard footsteps coming at a run—lots of them.

Isabel stepped back from him, and he turned to lock the door. 'Gather all the linen and garments you can find,' he instructed.

She ran straight to the bed, tearing the covers from it. While she was doing that, Blackmane jammed a chair beneath the doorhandle, then got to work knotting all the linen together.

'Are we going out the window?' she asked.

'Yes.'

The door handle rattled, and then Hodge's voice boomed, 'I know you are in there, Blackmane. Hand her over to me, and in return, I will not force her to watch your death.'

'He will break the door,' she whispered.

Blackmane secured one end of the garment rope to the bed and tossed the other end through the window. 'Get on my back, quickly.'

She ran to him and climbed onto his back.

He climbed out the window, pressing the soles of his boots into the wall. 'Hold on tight.' He then lowered them all the way to the ground while Hodge continued to shout above them.

When they reached the bottom, Isabel climbed off and looked around. 'How are we going to get over the wall?'

He took her hand and ran towards the wall. 'We're going to climb the stairs, like civilised people.'

She did her best to keep up with his fast pace. 'And when we reach the top?'

Thankfully, Blackmane did not have a chance to reply, because two guards emerged from the turret ahead and came for them. 'I'm going to let go of your hand, and you're going to stay right behind me.'

She nodded.

He continued at the same pace, drawing his dagger so he was once again armed with two weapons.

'Halt!' one man shouted.

Blackmane cut his way through, then glanced over his shoulder to ensure Isabel was behind him as they neared the stairwell. 'That's it. Keep up.'

They flew up the steps, greeted by guards at the top. It took Blackmane longer than usual to take them down because he had to account for Isabel behind him. When all the guards were dead, he sheathed both weapons and took hold of her face. 'You all right?'

She was staring wide-eyed at the men bleeding out at their feet. 'I... Yes.'

Of course she was trying to be brave, because he was asking it of her. But unfortunately, the worst part was still ahead of them. It was time to see just how much she trusted him. 'Do you remember the first time I saw you atop the wall?'

The sound of boots pounding the stone steps drifted

out to them from the turret. She looked over her shoulder.

'Don't worry about them,' Blackmane said. 'Focus on me.'

She turned back to him. 'Yes, I remember.'

'Where is she?'

She flinched at Hodge's voice in the distance.

'Your arms were outstretched like wings,' Blackmane continued, 'because you wanted so desperately to fly away from this place.'

Isabel sucked in a breath at the increasing noise behind her. 'I remember.'

He brought his face close to hers. 'Today, I need you to fly.'

'What?'

He pulled her over to the embrasure and lifted her onto it. 'Keep your body as straight as possible. Enter the water feet first.'

She clung to his arm. 'You want me to jump into the moat?'

'I'm going to jump with you.'

'But I cannot swim.'

Hodge emerged from the turret and frantically looked around, eyes landing on Isabel.

'Trust me,' Blackmane whispered.

Hodge took a tentative step in her direction. 'My beloved. Get down. I beg of you.'

She looked out at the pitch-black water below. Blackmane was worried she would climb back down, but then Margery appeared out of the dark, hovering in front of

Isabel for a moment, as though extending an invitation to join her on that side of the wall.

While Isabel was distracted by the eagle, Hodge made his move, rushing forwards to stop her. But he was not fast enough.

Isabel closed her eyes and leapt from the embrasure.

CHAPTER 38

The falling part felt eternal. Every time she thought she was going to hit the water, she fell a little farther. Actually hitting the water was even more terrifying. The cold, the lack of visibility, the roaring in her ears. The realisation that she was going to drown. She could not even tell which way was up, and she swallowed copious amounts of putrid water as she flailed about. Then an arm caught her waist, dragging her to the surface. She emerged with a gasp.

'You're all right,' Blackmane whispered as he swam her to the edge.

Tolly was there, waiting for them. He grabbed hold of Isabel the second she was within reach, lifting her out of the water. 'We need to go—now.'

Blackmane exited the moat and scooped her up, carrying her over to the waiting horses. They were galloping towards the trees a moment later.

Isabel was well aware that they were being pursued but could do nothing to help other than hang on. At one point, Tolly fell back and disappeared from sight. Just when she was starting to worry, he reappeared from the side, his horse falling into stride with theirs.

'How are you doing?' Blackmane asked over his shoulder.

The cold air whipping her wet body was unbearable. 'Good.' He had come for her and by some miracle gotten her out, so she did not dare complain.

Movement in her peripheral vision had Isabel turning her head. And there was Margery, flying alongside them. Isabel reached out a shaky hand, fingers stretching for her. The eagle glided closer until fingers met feathers.

'Did you see me fly?' Isabel asked the bird.

The eagle continued alongside them for another minute before lifting into the air again and disappearing amid the conifers.

The horses began to tire, so they were forced to slow down. Thankfully, they had lost the guards pursuing them.

Tolly removed his cloak and wrapped it around Isabel. She had not realised how cold she was until the wool enclosed her. Then the shivering began. Blackmane must have noticed, because he stopped the horse and moved her in front of him. It was surprising how much heat she got from those arms being around her. Defenders were also made of flesh and blood. If she was cold, there was a good chance he was too.

'I can still taste the water,' she said into his neck.

'Try not to think about it.'

Her eyes closed. 'I cannot believe what you just did for me.'

He did not reply.

'I have missed you,' she whispered.

Still no reply.

Tolly slowed his horse to ride alongside them. 'Patrol point ahead. Once we're through, we're in the clear.'

It would be the first time in her adult life that everyone she cared about was safe at the same time. Safe and *free*.

The wastelanders at the checkpoints were not standing in the middle of the road ready to ask questions. They came from the trees on either side, bows loaded and aimed at the men. Both Tolly and Blackmane had expected them, but that did not stop the defender from tensing when they appeared.

A few questions later, they were on their way once more.

The temperature continued to drop, and Isabel continued to shiver. It was fine, though. She was safe. She was safe with *him*.

By the time they reached Llanelieu, light was beginning to creep in, turning their surroundings an eerie grey. Isabel did not know what to expect when they arrived at Maddock House. Would he lower her to the ground and go on his way? Would he come inside? Maybe pretend he did not have to return to Chadora?

The separation was inevitable.

'Will you rest your horse a while?' she said against his stubbly skin.

He nodded. 'Yes.'

She was not prepared for how she would feel laying eyes on Maddock House again. She definitely was not prepared for the sight of her mother, her brother, and Ita standing together out front. There were a few people missing from this picture, but it was still more than she could have hoped for after such a long famine and period of unrest. It was a lot more than most people had.

Everard ran out to help Isabel down from the horse. She hugged him tightly. He had grown taller in the months that they had been separated.

'You smell so bad,' he told her.

She might have smiled had she not been so cold. The shivering had depleted her of any remaining energy.

Gwenore appeared beside them. Isabel assumed her mother would wait until she was clean before making any physical contact but was surprised by an embrace.

'Forgive me,' Gwenore whispered.

Isabel drew back to look at her. 'For what?'

Her mother's eyes shone with unshed tears. 'For all of it.'

It was a lot in Isabel's current state. She looked back at Blackmane, fearful that he would find the outpouring of emotion too much and ride away without so much as a goodbye.

Everard took the three horses off to the paddock.

'Shall we boil you until you're sanitary?' Ita asked, watching the scene from a few feet away.

Isabel managed a smile. 'Whatever warms me up the fastest.'

Gwenore put an arm around her daughter and guided her towards the house. 'You really do smell bad.'

Isabel looked over her shoulder, eyes meeting Blackmane's before she was whisked away inside.

~

Ita led Blackmane upstairs to a small room with nothing in it except a pail of steamy water, a towel, a small piece of soap, and a pile of clothes. 'We're a little light on furniture right now,' she said, glancing around the empty room. She gestured to the clothes. 'Compliments of Rabbit. He's roughly the same size.'

'Thanks.'

She met his eyes. 'You got her out.'

'We did.'

Ita tilted her head and smiled. 'She'll be fine, you know. You don't have to worry about her. She's tougher than she looks.'

'I know.'

Ita left him to wash, pulling the door closed behind her.

Blackmane stripped and used the entire piece of soap to clean himself. Once dressed, he wandered over to the small window and looked out at the vibrant pink sky framing the trees. He was about to step away and go look for Isabel when he spotted her standing in the garden watching the same pink sky. Her hair was out and still wet. A blue cotton dress peeked out from beneath the large woollen blanket wrapping her. She looked to her left suddenly, then up at the house, eyes meeting his through the open window. It reminded him of the first time they had locked eyes at Hampstead Keep and the world had stopped. His world, at least. That was the kind of power she held over him.

She pushed hair back from her face and smiled up at

him, but it faded quickly. He felt cold for the first time since leaving Hampstead Keep. Moving away from the window, he headed downstairs to speak with her.

Her eyes remained on the sky when he stepped up next to her. She drew a long breath and released it slowly. 'What do you think of the house?'

'It's great.' He looked over his shoulder. 'Though the roof might need a second go.'

She laughed through her nose. 'That seems to be a popular opinion around these parts. I should probably point out that it does not leak.'

'That is impressive.'

'The original house had a shingle roof, but those are in short supply right now, as you can probably imagine.'

He nodded. 'It doesn't need a shingle roof.'

'Rabbit's father was a carpenter, so we got lucky there.'

'Was?'

She glanced down at the ground. 'He died in the camp last year.'

They were silent a moment.

'What do you suppose his real name is?' Blackmane asked.

'Probably something bland like Thomas or David.'

His mouth turned up.

Isabel reached for his hand, warm fingers threading through his. The internal response to such a simple gesture surprised him. His feelings were supposed to have faded over time, not multiplied. He had done everything to weed her from his heart and mind, even visiting the tavern to spend time with other women. But he had always left alone at the end of the evening, chest hollow and gut heavy with guilt.

He looked around the newly constructed gardens, trying to picture himself in this setting. It was laughable, yet desirable.

'How long do we have?' Isabel asked.

'An hour, maybe.'

She turned her face away from him, pressing her fingers to her lips.

He hated seeing her upset. 'Please don't cry.'

'I am not crying.' She sniffed. 'It is the blossoms from the tree over there.' She gestured vaguely. 'They make my eyes water.'

He turned her to face him, reaching up to wipe the tears off her cheeks. 'Seeing you cry is bad enough, but being the cause of your tears is like a kick in the teeth.'

She searched his eyes. 'I have never been kicked in the teeth, but I imagine it hurts.'

He tugged gently on her hand until she fell against him, his fingers curling into her damp hair as he held her head to his chest. She smelled of lavender soap.

Minutes slipped by. Neither of them moved nor spoke.

More minutes passed.

The problem with stillness was that it made space for emptiness. He had always found it better to keep moving. The faster the better.

Next thing.

Next thing.

Next thing.

Yet there was nothing empty about this moment. It

was tranquil, restorative. It was exactly what they both needed.

'If things were different,' she said, breaking the silence. 'If you were here, or I was there, would this have worked?'

He blinked slowly. 'Yes.'

She drew back to look at him. 'I am cold.'

He searched her face, then guided both her hands beneath his shirt. 'Better?'

She shook her head.

'What do you need?'

'Your hands on me.'

He held her face, rubbing his thumbs on her wet cheeks. 'Is that better?'

She shook her head. 'My lips are cold.'

His gaze fell to them, and then he brought his mouth to hers, kissing her softly for a long time. He wanted to memorise the taste and feel of her lips. Only when he felt his control slipping did he break the kiss and drop his forehead to hers. They remained that way until their breathing returned to normal.

'I need to ask you something,' he said.

She drew back, waiting.

'If there was a way I could be here, would you want that?'

Her eyes moved between his. 'More than anything.'

'Good.' He nodded slowly, his mind working. 'I need to return to Chadora to settle some things, and then I'm coming back.'

She stared at him, visibly confused. 'Why?'

'Are you really asking me that?'

'For how long?'

'Until you tell me to leave.'

'What if I never tell you to leave?'

He looked in the direction of the house. 'Then I'll have plenty of time to fix that roof.'

She stepped back from him. 'If this is a joke, it is not funny.'

'It's not a joke.'

Clearly she was struggling to process what he was saying. 'You cannot leave Chadora. What about Tatum, Alveye, and Hadewaye?'

'They'll be fine without me.'

'And will you be fine without them?'

He sighed. 'If you don't want me to return—'

'Of course I want you to return, but I do not want you to regret it later. If all of this had not happened, you would not even be here. You would have continued to move forwards with your life and forgotten all about me.'

He waited for her to fall silent. 'Are you finished?'

'For now.'

Margery circled overhead. Isabel raised an arm so she could land. The eagle got comfortable, as though waiting to hear his response.

'There's no moving on from you,' Blackmane said. 'Trust me, I've tried.'

She studied him for the longest time before asking, 'Would you like to pet her?'

'The bird?'

'No, Ita.' She laughed. 'Yes, the bird.'

He reached out to stroke her feathers. She did not move away or attempt to slice his face open, so he took that as a good sign.

'She is an excellent judge of character,' Isabel said, looking up at him. 'Go do whatever you need to. We will be here waiting for you when you get back, defender.'

'Stay out of trouble until I get here.'

Her lips turned up. 'I make no promises.'

CHAPTER 39

*B*lackmane was on his way to see the warden when he was intercepted by three very unhappy defenders fresh from the training field. They were sweat-soaked with grass in their hair and matching scowls.

'Firstly,' Tatum said, 'what the hell were you thinking going to Hampstead Keep by yourself?'

Alveye shook his head like a disappointed parent. 'You could have been killed.'

'We've been worried sick,' Hadewaye added. 'Tatum has been running extra laps to manage the stress.'

'And you know he hates to run,' Alveye said.

Tatum held up two fingers. 'Secondly, what in God's name are you wearing?'

Blackmane looked down at his clothes.

'And thirdly,' Tatum said, drawing Blackmane's attention back to him, 'did you get Isabel?'

Blackmane's eyebrows lifted slightly. '*That's* the order of your questions?'

Tatum looked down at the peasant clothes again, then said to Alveye, 'Should the clothes question have been first?'

'I'm going to assume Isabel's safe,' Hadewaye said, 'or you wouldn't be here.'

Blackmane nodded. 'She's back at Maddock House. I'll answer your other questions after I've spoken to the warden.'

Alveye's eyes narrowed with suspicion. 'About what?'

'He needs to know I'm back, for a start.' Blackmane shifted his weight. 'And there's another matter I need to discuss with him.'

'What other matter?' Tatum asked.

The warden exited the armoury and looked around, expression hardening when he saw Blackmane. The defender immediately broke away from the group and headed towards him, but the others only followed him.

'Good to see you alive,' Shapur said, frowning down at his clothes. 'Where is your uniform?'

'I took an unplanned swim in the moat, sir.'

Shapur nodded. 'I gather Lady Isabel has been reunited with her family?'

'Yes.'

'And Hodge?'

'Alive and well.'

'Good.' He gave a curt nod. 'Go get yourself cleaned up.'

Blackmane glanced behind him to where the others were eavesdropping. 'There's a matter I wish to discuss.'

The warden sighed. 'Go on.'

'I'd like to return to Llanelieu.' He paused. 'To live.'

There was an exchange of colourful language behind him. Shapur glared in the direction of the other defenders until they fell silent.

'I suspected there were feelings involved,' the warden said, 'but clearly I underestimated the extent of them. Surely you of all people are not foolish enough to throw everything away for a woman you barely know.'

That was a reasonable response. 'I'd prefer not to throw anything away if I can help it. I have an idea I'd like to put forwards.'

Shapur crossed his arms. 'I am listening.'

'We're all listening,' Tatum said behind him, resulting in another warning glare from Shapur.

Blackmane cleared his throat. 'King Becket has expressed on several occasions that he's in support of Carmarthenshire's independence and wishes to build relations with them in order to reduce threats outside our walls, and in hope of improved trade opportun—'

'I am well aware of King Becket's reasons for supporting them,' Shapur said. 'Get to the point.'

Blackmane nodded. 'They need help setting up permanent and sustainable protection of the region. Those protecting them at present have no formal training and no income to support their families. There's no structure. No long-term plan. They're still living day to day because that's what they've done for years. It's all they know.'

Shapur was silent a moment. 'And you would like to help with what, exactly?'

'I could get their army into shape, help train the soldiers.'

'That is an impossible task for one man.'

'What about four men?' Tatum asked, stepping forwards.

Shapur looked at the other defenders. 'Suddenly you all wish to go to Llanelieu?'

'We're a team, sir,' Hadewaye said.

Alveye nodded in agreement. 'One goes, we all go.'

Blackmane's throat felt uncomfortably tight suddenly.

Shapur's gaze returned to him. 'And when the embers of this new love die out, am I to expect a transfer request back to Chadora?'

Tatum spoke up at that. 'I know this man better than anyone, sir. If he commits to building an army in the wastelands, then he'll stay there until the job's done.'

Shapur drew a long breath. 'I shall discuss the matter with King Becket, but I would not go packing up your belongings just yet. He is moving cautiously. I will send for you when I have an answer.' He went to walk away.

'Sir,' Blackmane said.

The warden stopped, waiting.

The next part was difficult to say. 'I want you to know that I'll be returning to Llanelieu regardless of the outcome of that conversation. I'd prefer to go with my team, and in uniform, but I'll go without those things if I have to.'

Shapur's jaw twitched. 'And I wish to remind you that your feelings will never come before what is in the best interests of this kingdom.'

Blackmane nodded. 'I understand.'

'Go get yourself cleaned up and into a uniform, defender.'

Blackmane saluted. 'Yes, sir.'

CHAPTER 40

*J*sabel admired the vegetables in her basket, freshly harvested from their gardens. It had been a long time since she had seen so much colour and variety. Her whole mood lifted at the sight, then crashed back down when she looked out at the empty road. It had only been a month since Blackmane had returned to Chadora, but it felt like a year. The not knowing was the difficult part. Not knowing his plans.

Not knowing if he had changed his mind.

Perhaps his friends had convinced him that leaving would be a mistake. And maybe they were right. She even started wondering if he had simply told her what she needed to hear in order to make the separation easier.

Would he write if he had changed his mind? Surely he would. He knew she was waiting for him. She pictured herself, twenty years into the future, still sitting in the same garden, staring at that same road.

The clapping of wooden swords pulled her from her thoughts. Everard and Rabbit were sparring on the lawn.

Her brother had been teaching him defence moves. The wastelander may have killed more people than Isabel cared to think about, but it was Everard who had all the formal training.

Isabel smiled at her brother as she passed him on the way to the house. As she neared the front door, Ita and her mother stepped through it, baskets in hand.

'Mushroom hunting?' Isabel asked. A few days of heavy rain meant optimal mushroom-picking conditions.

Her mother nodded. 'You should come with us.'

She rarely ventured far from the house anymore for fear of not being home when Blackmane arrived. 'I'll stay and make a start on dinner.'

Gwenore tilted her head. 'He will not turn around and go back to Chadora if he arrives to an empty house.'

Isabel swallowed. 'I know. I will come tomorrow, I promise.'

Ita gave her a knowing look as she passed. 'We'll be back before dark.'

Isabel went inside, washing and chopping the vegetables to be used in the cawl she was making. When everything was ready, she prepared the stove. She never lit it, but she was more than happy to do the work up until that point.

The light began to fade, and there was still no sign of her mother and Ita, so she went in search of her brother out front. He could light the fire for her, and she would return to cook once the flames had settled. While she was slowly getting more comfortable around fires, she had a way to go.

Outside, she looked around for Everard and Rabbit,

but they were nowhere to be seen. She listened for them, certain she had heard their swords clapping away only a few minutes earlier.

'Everard!' she called.

There was no reply.

She wandered down to the paddock to see if they were working on the half-built stables they had committed to finishing before winter came around again. They were not there either. The horses were pacing the fence line, ears pricked forwards and tails lifted. She paused to watch them a moment, then looked over at the trees on the other side, expecting Ita and her mother to emerge with their full baskets in hand.

But no one appeared.

Taking a final look around, she retreated to the house.

It was dark now, so she closed the door behind her and slid the lock into place. The others could knock and wait for her to open it when they finally decided to show up.

She headed for the kitchen but froze a few feet from the door. There was smoke and heat coming from it, and when she listened, she heard the distinct snap and crackle of burning debris. Someone had lit the stove while she had been out of the house.

'Everard?' she called.

Silence.

Slowly, she walked to the kitchen door and peered inside. The stove was not only lit but roaring. Her heart sped up at the sight, at the noise, at the realisation that her brother would never leave a fire in this state for her to walk into. He would never leave it unattended to begin with. She had not been the only one in the house the day it burned down. While he got out physically unscathed, the mental trauma still lingered to some degree for all of them.

It was difficult to breathe when the fire was consuming all the oxygen in the house. She turned, ready to flee, then stopped again when she saw the front door sitting wide open. She had definitely closed it behind her —and locked it.

The pounding in her ears competed with the noise coming from the stove.

Run.

But before she could make a dash for the open door, a voice reached her from the stairs.

'There is no need to be afraid, my beloved.'

Her gaze cut to the staircase, and there was Hodge seated comfortably on it, elbows resting on his knees, watching her.

He was in her house.

All words seemed to abandon her in that moment. She could barely think, let alone talk. And while running was still the smartest option for her at that point, her legs also seemed to be failing her.

'You really are surprised,' he said, rising and descending the few stairs to the bottom. His eyes swept the full length of her. 'I swear, you are the only woman I know who grows more beautiful with the passing of time.'

She swallowed a few times, testing to see if her tongue would cooperate in forming words. 'What are you doing here?' she managed to get out.

His face pinched with concern. 'Is that fear I hear in

your voice? Beloved, do not be afraid. You never have to fear a thing when I am around.'

He was the very thing she had to fear. Her mind was getting wild with worry now. *Where are the others?*

'Now,' he said, clapping his hands together, 'I know someone always lights the stove for you in the evenings, so I took it upon myself to do it in their absence.'

She did not want to think about how he knew that. 'Where is Everard? He was out front, and now I cannot find him.'

He took a few steps towards her, and she took a large step back.

He slowly raised his hands. 'It is all right.'

She pressed a hand to her stomach. 'Where are they?'

'Safe.'

'What does that mean? Safe where?'

'With my men.'

Her breath hitched. 'What is going on?'

He took another, much slower step towards her. 'I needed to talk to you alone.'

'No.' She shook her head. 'I do not want to talk to you. What are you doing here?' That last question came out strangled, her expression collapsing mid-sentence.

His face filled with pity but not remorse. 'Beloved. Must we do this again and again? You know why I am here. You know what I want. It is time for you to come home.'

She shook her head profusely this time, backing all the way up to the kitchen door. 'No. No. Never again. I would sooner die than go anywhere with you.'

'Now, that is hurtful.' He walked over to the front door

and pushed it closed, then locked it. 'It is getting rather breezy now that the sun has set.'

He headed for her then, and she backed up into the kitchen until she felt the wooden bench beneath the window press into her spine.

'You are like a frightened horse,' Hodge mused.

She gripped the bench behind her. 'Do not come any closer.'

Hodge drew a slow breath. 'Must there always be a scene with you?' He walked over to the stove and began stuffing it with sticks and small logs. Isabel watched in horror as the flames intensified.

'Soon it will be much too hot in here,' he said, 'and you will exit willingly at my side instead of being dragged out of here like a dog.'

Her eyes never left the fire. 'How did you get into Carmarthenshire?'

'It was not easy, let me assure you. It has taken weeks of planning to breach that little border of yours, but we found a way through eventually.' He continued to shove more wood into the fire despite it being so full that he was struggling to fit it. 'I was fearful of what I would find upon arriving here. I was plagued by imaginings of you and Blackmane playing house together. You can imagine my relief when I found you here and him nowhere in sight.'

She swallowed, her mouth growing increasingly dry. 'How long have you been here?'

'In Llanelieu? Six days.'

Six days?

'I have been observing and getting a feel of the place

and your life here. It is no Hampstead Keep, but I see how much you enjoy working outside in the gardens. Though they are not as impressive as the gardens back home.'

The thought of him watching her for six days made her feel physically ill. 'That is enough wood,' she said when an ember fell from the stove and flitted across the floor.

He went to stamp the ember out. The problem was the wood was popping all over the place, sending more things flying than he could put out.

Sweat gathered on her brow and trickled down her back, partly due to the heat but mostly due to the fear. She needed to get out of the kitchen, out of the house.

Releasing the bench, she dashed for the door, but Hodge blocked her exit at the last second, and her body slammed into his. He reached up to steady her. 'Where are you running off to? We leave together, remember? Calmly and willingly.'

She began to cry. 'I cannot breathe.'

'Shh.' He stroked her hair in an attempt to soothe her, but it had the opposite effect. She pulled out of his hold and backed up to the bench again.

'Why are you doing this?' The words came out on a sob.

He looked around the smoke-filled kitchen. 'It is better to face our fears together.'

The stove spat out a huge chunk of burning wood. It landed between Isabel and Hodge, and he made no effort to stamp it out this time. Isabel slid down to the ground, forced to watch it burn as she prayed the floor would not catch fire.

Hodge crouched down to her level, watching her like she was the most fascinating thing in the world. 'Do you wish to be rescued?'

Her gaze went to his sweat-soaked face. 'What?'

'Do you want me to pick you up off the floor and carry you out of here, like he did?'

She was completely lost for words. And he was completely insane.

Moments slipped by as they stared at one another. The noise in her ears quietened long enough for her to hear her own thoughts. And her heart slowed down, too, likely due to the heat. She shook her head. 'No.'

'No?'

'If my options are to leave in your arms, only to be trapped by you again, or to burn to death in this very spot, then my answer is no. You can leave without me.'

Hodge rose and marched over to the fire, pulling a burning log from it with his bare hands. 'I am not leaving Llanelieu without you. We leave together, or we burn together.'

The tears on her face were evaporating as quickly as they appeared. She lay down on the floor and drew up her knees. 'Then I hope you are ready to burn for all eternity.'

*K*ing Becket wanted to see the people of Carmarthenshire back on their feet as much as Blackmane did, but there were concerns that sending a unit of men to help train a rebel army would look a lot like they were preparing for war.

'Now is not the right time,' the warden had told Blackmane, sounding almost disappointed. 'King Edward has given them space and time, ensuring all the boundaries the wastelanders have put in place are respected. Unless something changes, it is best we stay out of military matters.'

It had been a hard thing to hear. It had been even harder to hand over his uniform and say goodbye to the people who had been his family for the past five years. He had tried to carry on with his old life and purpose, to find contentment, anything to fill the emptiness, but nothing had worked.

'We can't let you go alone,' Tatum had said. 'We'll come with you.'

But he could not let them do it, could not bear to see them hand their uniforms over too. So now he was on his way to Llanelieu, alone, where his other family waited for him.

He was a mile south of the village when Margery appeared overhead, circling low as she awaited an invitation to land. He obliged, extending an arm to her. She landed, talons digging into his flesh. Then the yelping started, the same unsettling noise she had made the day she came to find Ita in the forest.

'I really hope this fuss isn't about me coming to live with you.'

The bird took flight, shooting off in the direction of the village.

An uneasy feeling flourished in Blackmane's chest. Despite his mare being fatigued, he pushed her into a slow canter for the final mile.

Maddock House sat on a gentle hill outside the main village. A soft glow came from it, making it visible from the road.

He stopped halfway up the gravel path that led to the house, listening. At that distance, he should have been able to hear the hum of conversation and tinkle of plates, but he was met with complete silence. His eyes went to the horses pacing the nearby fence line, tails raised like flags.

Something was wrong.

Lifting one arm, he waited. A few moments later, Margery came to land on him, but this time she did not make a sound.

'Where is she?' Blackmane whispered.

The eagle twitched in the dark, then flew off over the house. He dismounted and moved off the gravel path onto the grass, leaving the horse behind so no one would hear him coming. The warden had let him take the mare under the pretence that it was the quickest way for him to exit. She was a gift from a man who had no idea how to give.

Blackmane continued slowly and silently all the way to the front door, finding it locked. He crept to the window and peered through the shutters. The glow coming from the kitchen was intense, and the house was full of smoke, the smell seeping out to greet him.

That marked the end of his subtle approach.

He returned to the door and kicked it open, entering the house with a ready arrow. The smoke grew thicker as he neared the kitchen. When he reached it, he could barely see a thing, and the air was stifling hot. He fired an arrow at the window shutter, knocking it open. The smoke was sucked through it.

'Unbelievable' came Hodge's voice through the smoke. 'It seems I am not the only person watching you from afar, my beloved.'

Blackmane gauged the scene before him. He could now make out Hodge standing on the far side of the kitchen, a sword in one hand and a piece of burning wood in the other. It took Blackmane a moment to notice the body curled in a ball on the floor at the earl's feet.

Belle.

'Shoot me and this will land directly on top of her,' Hodge said, holding the burning wood above her head.

Blackmane was still trying to figure out what was

going on. 'Belle,' he called to her, trying to figure out if she was conscious.

Isabel opened her eyes and looked straight at him. The muscles in his chest relaxed.

'Oh,' Hodge said. 'It is *Belle* now. How intimate.'

Blackmane glared in his direction. 'What the hell have you done to her?'

Hodge wiped sweat from his brow. 'Actually, I am being very patient given how dramatic she is being.'

Blackmane wondered if he could shoot the wood out of his hand without burning her in the process. He did not think so.

A soft laugh came from Hodge. 'Look at you scrambling to figure all this out. What are you going to do, defender? We both know you will not risk her getting hurt. But that is not the only reason you hesitate, is it?' His lips curled into a snarl-like grin. 'You cannot harm me, can you? Even though your heart is bursting with hate for me.'

Blackmane did not respond.

'I know this because you came into my home and killed many men.' He paused. 'Except the only man you wanted dead.' He broke off in a cough. 'You really are exceptionally loyal. A fine example of a soldier.' He coughed again. 'That is the difference between you and me. I would kill you in a heartbeat.'

Blackmane looked down at Isabel, and she slid her hand a few inches towards him.

'Shall we test that loyalty?' Hodge asked, eyes watering profusely. 'Shall I drop this burning wood and see if I live to tell the tale?'

'If you drop it, you'll hurt her, and I know you don't want that.' He took a small step into the room, pushing against the heat repelling him. 'How about you put that piece of wood into the stove, and then I move aside and let you leave?'

Hodge shook his head. 'No, defender. We will not be playing by your rules this time.'

Blackmane saw something flash past the open window. A moment later, Margery flew through it, wings beating and talons reaching. She snatched the burning wood from Hodge's hand and dropped it at Blackmane's feet on her way out of the kitchen. He stomped on the wood until the flames died out, then looked at Hodge, who was staring wide-eyed at his empty hand.

'You're right,' Blackmane said. 'I'm exceptionally loyal.' The string of his bow tightened. 'And sometimes loyalties shift.' With that, he released the arrow.

It struck Hodge in the stomach. He doubled over, clutching at the wound and staring down at the protruding arrow with disbelief.

'That's for every person you imprisoned and killed in cold blood,' Blackmane said.

Hodge lifted his gaze, eyes wild with fear.

'And this one's for Belle.' He released the next arrow straight into his eye.

Hodge collapsed on the ground, all air expelling from his lungs as he landed. Blood pooled around him.

Blackmane rushed over to Isabel, slinging his bow over one shoulder before scooping her up and carrying her out of the house. He took her far away from the smoke before setting her down on the ground.

'Are you hurt?' he asked, checking her for injury.

She coughed and shook her head, looking frantically around. 'Where are they?'

'I didn't see anyone when I arrived.'

'Belle!' someone shouted, prompting Blackmane to reach for his sword. He relaxed when Everard ran into sight, heading straight for his sister.

'Where is he?' the boy demanded. 'What did that bastard do to you?'

Isabel reached up to touch his face. 'It is all right. It is over. He is dead.'

Everard looked around, breathing hard. 'I will kill him myself if he is not.'

Isabel attempted to soothe him while coughing into her hand.

'Where are the others?' Blackmane asked.

'With Tolly.' His face was pinched with anger. 'These men just appeared out of nowhere, knocking Rabbit unconscious and me to the ground. All we had to defend ourselves with was wooden swords.'

'Is she all right?' Ita called through the dark.

'She's over here,' Everard shouted back.

Ita and Gwenore appeared through the dark, rushing over to Isabel.

'Thank God,' Ita said. 'Where is he? I'm going to kill him with my bare hands.'

Everard looked in the direction of the house. 'Apparently we're too late.'

Gwenore wrapped her arms around Isabel. 'Oh, darling girl. You reek of smoke. What happened?'

That had Everard marching off towards the house. 'I

am going to make sure he is properly dead.'

'He's definitely dead,' Blackmane said, only to be ignored. 'But throw some water on the stove, would you?'

'I'll go with him,' Ita said, following the boy.

Gwenore smoothed Isabel's hair back from her face. 'I am so sorry. These men appeared in the forest, pointing weapons at us.' She pressed her lips together. 'Did he hurt you?'

Isabel shook her head. 'No, I am just a little dizzy from all the smoke.'

Blackmane stood back and let her mother fuss over her while he calculated the mental damage done by the dead lord inside. 'How did you all get away?'

Gwenore looked up at him. 'Tolly showed up with some of his men. He is on his way with the Rabbit.'

'It is just Rabbit, Mother,' Isabel said, 'not *the* Rabbit.'

'How am I to know the correct format for such a nonsense name?'

Blackmane went to collect his horse, spotting Tolly in the distance as he did so. His brother emerged from the trees on foot, Rabbit sitting atop his horse with a blood-streaked face. Blackmane headed towards them.

'You're upright, so that's a good sign,' he said to Rabbit.

Rabbit muttered a string of curse words as he dismounted the gelding.

Tolly nodded in Isabel's direction. 'A well-timed arrival by you, I see.'

'Likewise.' The gratitude Blackmane felt for his hero of a brother was overwhelming.

'Where is he?' Tolly asked.

Blackmane did not have to ask who he was talking about. 'The kitchen.'

'Dead?'

A nod.

'I'll take care of it.' He walked over to Rabbit and dragged his arm around his shoulders. 'Let's go get you cleaned up.'

Blackmane took the two horses down to the paddock and removed their tack, then headed back to Isabel.

Gwenore squeezed her daughter's hand, then rose. 'Stay here and catch your breath,' she said. 'I will see you inside when you are ready.' Then she walked off towards the house.

Isabel drew her legs up and dropped her forehead to her knees. Blackmane sat beside her, saying nothing. After a few minutes, she turned her head and looked at him.

'Are you going to get in trouble?' she asked.

'For what?'

'For killing him.'

He shook his head. 'I handed in my uniform before I came. Bad timing for him.'

She exhaled. 'I am sorry.'

'What for?'

'That there was not another way.'

He pulled her closer to him.

She kissed his cheek before resting her head on his shoulder. 'I do not know what I did to deserve you, Ryder Blackmane, but I love you. I understand that the timing of this confession is far from ideal, but I am worried if I do not tell you now, then something else will happen, and I might not get the chance.'

They sat in silence for a minute.

'Have I made you uncomfortable?' she asked quietly.

He pressed his lips to her smoky hair. 'Not at all. I was just trying to remember when I fell in love with you. It was fast, I know that much. Maybe too fast.'

'Try to remember when,' she murmured.

He thought for a moment. 'It might have been the day we arrived and you were atop the wall. You looked straight at me, and something broken in you clicked with something broken in me. I didn't really understand it at the time.' He rubbed his cheek against her hair, eyes closing. 'I should have killed him in the forest the first time he grabbed you. I'm sorry I didn't.'

'You are not allowed to look back on that time with anything other than pride.' She reached for his hand. 'You are one of the most honourable men I have ever met. That was my mess to clean up, and I am filled with shame at my failure to do it sooner.'

'Don't.' Blackmane's arm tightened around her. 'Don't pretend like you had choices back then. You needed help.'

'And along you came. My weapon of choice.' She coughed into her hand, then settled against him again. 'Ita has been teaching me to use a bow and arrow.'

'And how's it going?'

'She says I have the worst aim she has ever seen.'

Blackmane chuckled. 'Then you'll be most improved by the time I'm done with you.'

She looked up at him. 'I hope you brought your patience with you to Llanelieu. She is not exaggerating.'

He lowered his lips to hers. She tasted of smoke and salt. 'The world has enough killers. What it doesn't have is enough light. You were never supposed to hold a bow in your hands. You were put on this earth to illuminate the darkness.'

She swallowed, eyes welling up. 'What if he took all the light from me?'

'Impossible. No mortal can steal from the sun.'

She buried her face in his shoulder and cried silently. He let her cry, knowing first-hand what holding trauma inside did to a person. He did not want that for her.

Margery dropped down onto the ground in front of them, tucking in her wings and walking over to Isabel with what Blackmane imagined to be a worried expression.

'I'll never judge your choice of pet again,' he said.

Isabel reached for the eagle and placed her on her lap, kissing her feathery back. 'Thank you,' she whispered. 'He will never lock either of us up ever again.'

Blackmane watched them comfort each other while Hodge's corpse was carried out of the house behind them.

'If my purpose is to illuminate the darkness,' Isabel said, 'then what is your purpose?'

He leaned forwards and kissed her shoulder. 'To guard your light.' When he noticed Margery looking at him, he reached out and ran a finger down her beak. 'It's all right. We'll do it together.'

EPILOGUE

*I*sabel took aim at the hare, staring at it down her arrow. The moment it stilled, she released and watched it sail through the air—landing ten feet from her target. The hare paused, eating momentarily, looking around before resuming.

'How are you getting worse?' Ita asked from her viewing spot.

'I am not getting worse.' Isabel looked to Blackmane, who was beside her. 'Am I?'

He pinched the bridge of his nose. 'The important thing is you're practicing.'

Her shoulders fell. 'Oh. I see.'

He stepped up and took the bow from her, kissing her as he did so.

'You did say my hands were never meant to hold a bow,' she said brightly.

'Or a sword, apparently,' Ita said. 'Or a knife, or an axe—'

'Yes, all right,' Isabel said. 'Thank you for your input.'

Her eyes remained on a smirking Blackmane. 'Same time tomorrow?'

He returned to kiss her again. 'I have work, remember?' He had been put in charge of training the younger recruits as well as running weekly sessions for experienced soldiers wanting to sharpen their skills.

Isabel looked expectantly at Ita.

'I'm attending the session too' was her reply.

Isabel exhaled. 'Then can I attend?'

'No,' Blackmane and Ita replied at the same time.

Ita walked over and threaded her arm through Isabel's. 'You should work on the new garden. There is not a person in Llanelieu who matches your skills there.'

'Or maybe I will practice on my own.'

Blackmane glanced in her direction. 'Just make sure your mother and brother are safely inside first.'

Ita laughed.

Everard came out of the house and looked around. Spotting them, he cupped his mouth and shouted, 'Defenders approaching!'

The three of them exchanged a questioning look, then headed around to the front of the house. Trotting along the road towards them were Tatum, Alveye, and Hadewaye. A smile flickered on Blackmane's face before being replaced by a serious frown. He walked out to meet them, and Isabel followed.

It had been two months since Blackmane left Chadora, and while he seemed happy in his new life and role here, Isabel knew he missed his friends. It was evident in the topic change whenever she brought them up in conversation.

'There he is,' Tatum said, pulling up his horse and dismounting. 'Unshaven and dressed like a ruffian.'

Isabel's brow pinched. 'I made those clothes.'

'I can tell by the excellent fit and fine needlework,' Tatum said awkwardly. He pulled Blackmane in for a brief hug, clapping him loudly on the back. 'You've lost muscle.'

'I'm exactly the same size as when I left.'

Tatum stepped back and looked him up and down. 'We'll see.' He came to greet a grinning Isabel, kissing her on the cheek. 'I'm sorry we missed the wedding. The warden isn't much of a romantic.'

'Do not apologise. It was small, simple, and perfect. It turns out Ryder is not one for public declarations of love. Who knew?'

'Definitely not us,' Alveye said, coming to kiss her.

Isabel looked over to where Hadewaye was holding on to her husband while he stood stiff as a board.

'This is the longest we've ever been separated,' Hadewaye said when he finally let go.

Alveye rolled his eyes. 'It's only been a few months.'

'A long few months,' Hadewaye added.

Blackmane was quiet amid the noise of their arrival, but Isabel could see the lift in his demeanour. He was happy.

'So,' she said, looking between the defenders. 'What brings you to Maddock House?'

Alveye and Hadewaye exchanged a mischievous look.

'What are you all up to?' Blackmane asked.

Tatum reached out to squeeze his shoulder. 'You may recall when you left that King Becket told you he would not be sending a unit to Carmarthenshire because England was being respectful of the borders, Chadora wished to remain neutral, etc.'

Blackmane lowered his brows. 'I remember.'

'But then a certain lord went against his king, putting a further divide between England and Wales and getting himself killed in the process.'

Isabel stepped closer to Blackmane and slipped her hand into his. 'We definitely remember that part.'

Blackmane's hand tightened around hers.

'King Becket has since decided that he'll support Carmarthenshire through their recovery to ensure they're able to better defend themselves in the future,' Hadewaye said.

Blackmane looked between the men. 'What are you saying?'

'We're the support,' Tatum said. 'We've been posted here for twelve months to assist in any way we can, with the aim of building relations between the two kingdoms.'

Isabel's smile widened. 'Really? You are to remain here for a whole year?'

'There's more,' Hadewaye said, walking over to his horse. He pulled out a parcel wrapped in cloth and carried it over to Blackmane.

Blackmane let go of Isabel's hand. 'What's this?'

'That's your uniform,' Alveye said. 'The warden asked us to give it to you.'

Blackmane stared down at it for the longest time before asking, 'What's the catch?'

Tatum frowned. 'Well, you'll have to work, for a start.'

'I already work.'

Isabel reached up and touched his arm. 'The man is gifting you a year.' She gave him an encouraging smile. 'Take it.'

Blackmane searched her eyes, then looked back at the others. 'Who will be in command?'

'Me, of course,' Tatum replied.

Blackmane pretended to hand the uniform back to Hadewaye, and they all laughed. Isabel had trouble looking away from her husband on those rare occasions. His laughter felt as good as her own.

'Shall I get some food cooking?' Ita called from the front door.

Isabel looked back at her. 'Yes. Coming.' She turned to Blackmane and pushed up onto her toes to kiss him. 'I will leave you to get the horses settled.'

'We won't be long.'

She walked off towards the house, her feet and heart light.

'He looks happy,' Ita said when Isabel reached the front door.

Isabel looked back at the four of them. Their banter carried on the breeze. 'He really does.'

She glanced up at the sky where Margery was circling overhead, spying on the new arrivals, then headed inside.

The next morning, Blackmane changed into his uniform and paused at the mirrored glass on his way out of their bedroom. The sight warmed him. It was not the uniform he had missed but everything it represented. Putting it on felt a lot like home.

The smell of fried eggs and fresh bread had him heading for the kitchen, which was alive with conversation and laughter. Everyone was squashed around one table, listening to Tatum tell the story about the time Alveye woke up with a piglet in his bed with no recollection of how it got there.

'The most likely answer is one of these three men put it there,' Ita said as she set a plate of eggs in front of the defender.

Alveye waved his fork in Tatum's direction. 'That's exactly what I said.'

Blackmane looked around for Isabel, then realised she was not among them.

'She is out back,' Gwenore said, reading his concerned expression.

He nodded and went outside, finding her racing along the tree line at the back of the property, Margery dashing on either side of her. According to Ita, that was how Isabel had taught her to fly when they were young. Given that golden eagles could glide up to 120 miles per hour, it was not much of a race, but Isabel ran her heart out anyway.

While tempted to call her in for breakfast, the sight of her running free without a wall in sight kept Blackmane silent. He wandered down to the woodpile and leaned against it, watching her run until she could no longer breathe.

'You win.' Isabel laughed, raising her arm so the eagle could land. She spotted Blackmane then, and a smile spread across her face. He watched her as she made her way over to him, soaking up the light coming from her.

'Good morning,' she said, kissing him.

He caught her around the waist, pulling her close for a second kiss, then tapped Margery's beak affectionately. 'You're up early.'

She stepped back and drew a big breath. 'I was too worked up to sleep.'

His eyes narrowed. 'About what?'

'I learned some rather big news last night, but I did not wish to distract from your reunion, which was so heart-warming to witness.'

Blackmane straightened. 'What news is that?'

'When Margery did not come home for dinner last night, we got worried and went looking for her. We ended up about a mile north of here.' She looked around. 'No, it must have been west, because I remember the sun was setting in front of us.' She paused again, bringing a finger to her mouth as she thought. 'No, sorry, it was south. The sun was definitely setting to my right. It was cloudy, as you probably remember, but the sun was still breaking through.'

He rubbed his forehead. 'I love you, more than anything, but could you please get to the news part of the story?'

'Yes, yes, sorry. It was definitely south.' She kissed Margery on the beak before continuing. 'So I am calling for her, over and over.'

His hand fell away. 'You're killing me.'

'And finally, she calls to me from up high in this tree.' She was almost combusting with excitement at this point.

'I see there are *two* eagles up there.' She paused. 'And they are sitting in a *nest*.'

Blackmane blinked. 'Right. So the big news is the nest?'

'Are you not excited?' Isabel asked, taking hold of both his hands.

'That depends. Does the nest mean Margery will no longer be sleeping in our bed?'

Isabel's face fell. 'I had not thought about that part.' Her expression turned stoic. 'No, it is definitely time. I raised her to be independent, taught her to fly and to hunt.' She squeezed Blackmane's hands. 'And now *we* taught her how to find love.'

Reaching up, he brushed his thumb down her cheek. He could not have loved her more if he tried. 'Let's hope her journey there was a little less turbulent than ours.' His hand fell away. 'Come inside and eat.'

Isabel looked at Margery. 'Are you hungry?'

The eagle flew off towards the house, entering via the kitchen window. Blackmane took Isabel's hand, and they slowly walked that way.

'Can you hear that?' Isabel asked, eyes bright and teeth on display.

He knew exactly what she was referring to. It was the sound of everyday life. 'I hear it.'

Tolly emerged from the house then. They had not even heard him arrive.

'Full house, I see,' he said.

Blackmane nodded. 'A bit more crowded than usual.'

'Have you eaten?' Isabel asked. 'We have enough eggs to feed a... well, an army.'

'Ita's fetching me a plate as we speak.' He leaned against the doorframe. 'I hear we're going to have some extra help to get our army in order.'

'Certainly looks that way,' Blackmane replied.

Laughter erupted from the open window, making them all look in that direction. Tolly straightened and headed back inside.

'Now the whole family is here,' Isabel said quietly.

Blackmane ignored the tightening in his throat and gestured for her to go ahead of him. When he reached the door, he paused and looked back, gaze sweeping the tree line.

'You coming?' Isabel called.

He remained there a few seconds longer, then followed her inside.

ACKNOWLEDGMENTS

I would like to express my gratitude to the many people who contributed to this book. My biggest thanks goes to my readers. Without you guys, I wouldn't get to do what I love. Next, a huge thank you to my hubby who supports and encourages me even though my writing takes time away from the family. I love you to bits. A big thank you to McKinley, Kristin and the team at Hot Tree Editing for polishing the manuscript into something beautiful. A shout out to my proofreader, Rebecca, for catching everything I missed. A round of applause for my cover designer, Stuart Bache (Books Covered), for this gorgeous cover. And finally, a huge thank you to my Launch Team for your encouragement, honest reviews, and being the final set of eyes on my work. You guys are amazing.

ALSO BY TANYA BIRD

You can find a complete list of published works at
tanyabird.com/books